Alana's Tale

Book 2 of Corwin's Chronicle

by T F Gray

The characters and events in this book are fictitious. Any similarity to real persons, living or dead, is coincidental and not intended by the author.

CIP information available upon request.

The views, thoughts, and opinions expressed belong solely to the author.

Printed in the United States of America

Chapter 1

The old man shifted the heavy leather bag from his right shoulder to his left. The sun slanted west toward Cornwall and the sea, but the brilliant summer day still burned. He wiped his brow with his worn brown sleeve. To his right, a wain loaded with sheaves of wheat, the last of the season's harvest, rumbled toward him. He hastened his pace to meet it.

"Ho there!" he hailed the driver. "Might you have room for one old man in that cart?"

The young man pulled up on the lines, and the ox stopped. "Who might you be?"

The old man bowed, a courtly gesture, so out of place in the middle of the stubble. "My name is Corwin, and I am a teller of tales."

His words had their intended effect. "A storyteller! Let me give you a hand up!"

Once Corwin had settled, a flick of the reins sent the ox into motion, and the cart lumbered up the path. The castle they approached was not much to speak of, a lonely tower guarding a ridge no one had tried to attack in centuries, surrounded by stone walls and two score peasant huts. Once, in those far off, disorderly days, it might have been a stronghold of some minor prince; now it would hold no better than a knight and his family.

A young guard lounged in the shade of the gate, whetting his knife on a stone. "John," called the driver, "tell Lady Columba a storyteller is here." The guard looked up at the word *storyteller*, in his eyes a Christmas that had never yet come, jumped to his feet and ran off. He returned minutes later and escorted Corwin into the castle, to a tiny chamber barely big enough for the straw pallet it held.

Corwin was touched by this honor they had shown him. He'd spent many a night in a hall filled with sweating guardsmen, or on an ash-strewn kitchen hearth in far grander places, listening to the

3

scurrying of rats. This chamber had a door, and a tiny slit window that brought the scent of herbs from the garden below. Fresh rushes were strewn on the narrow bit of floor, mixed with meadowsweet. He lay on the straw pallet, resting his aching bones.

* * *

At dinner he stood and bowed and asked what tale might pleasure his hosts.

"Sit," said his host, Sir Dalbert, "and eat. I'll not have a man work on an empty stomach. There will be a bonfire tonight, in honor of the harvest, and you will tell your tale to all my folk."

"You are a kind man, sir, and I thank you. And I thank you, milady, for the comfortable chamber."

Corwin swept a courtly bow, and the Lady Columba smiled shyly. It seemed to him that she had received little thanks in the course of her life. She had been a beauty, he could tell, with pale skin, faint freckles, and startling green eyes. To the right of the knight sat his sons, four of them, all half-grown or better. To the left of the lady sat their three daughters, all of them seemingly of marriageable age, yet still living at home.

There was little talk at dinner, and Corwin watched, trying to decide which of his tales might suit this audience. Whatever fire had once burned between the knight and his lady had turned to ashes some time ago, he could tell. They shared a trencher, but might as well have been a thousand miles distant. No smiles passed between them. Their youngest child, a son, could not be less then twelve years. His brothers and sisters had all inherited their father's look and bulk, but he was slight of build, his mother's son. All of the children had their father's dark locks, save one, the youngest daughter, her head crowned with a flaming sunset of ringlets that cascaded down her back in two thick braids.

The meal done, the family moved outdoors to where the peasants filled the courtyard. The narrow yard was packed, young boys venturing out to sit on the roofs of the sheds. Guardsmen lined the walls and the maids clustered near the kitchen, with the sharp-eyed seneschal watching to see which maid was making sheep's eyes at which guard.

4

Servants brought chairs for the knight and lady and a bench for their daughters, who dutifully sat, baskets of clothing to be mended between them. The sons lounged on the ground with the dogs. A small stool was set up for Corwin, with a goblet and pitcher of watered wine on it.

Lady, he prayed silently, *what tale should I tell?*

Make a tale of my children the faer, as they were in the Far Days. Tell a tale for the red-headed daughter, answered the Lady, goddess of the faer.

Lady, what can I do? How can I convey the truth of the faer without lying about them?

Mouse King, replied the Lady. *The essence is what matters.*

But Lady, I have not found a way to convey to my listeners that they communicate without speaking.

You must tell the tale to my quetan *children in a way they will understand.*

But vaira *and* ksh? *How can I possibly . . . ?*

Mouse King, the Lady told him, patient and soothing as always. *You will find a way for them to understand.*

He began.

Alana's Tale

The sentry squinted through the swirling mists at the dark figure approaching the outer gate. There was no need to call out a challenge. The somber clothing, the rolling gait, and the hour of his appearance all marked the man as Murdoch. The sky lightened as the sun crept over the horizon to confront the nighttime chill. The faint scent of breakfast fires floated past on the breeze. The sentry waited until he could see the three silver disks shining on Murdoch's sword belt before calling below for the others to open the gate.

The gate opened into a narrow, dark passage, framed by the thickness of the outer wall. Murdoch stopped, and spoke softly to the saluting guardsman. "Who is sentry?"

"Jonas, sir."

"Bring him here."

He waited in the darkness, shaking the dew from his cloak, wiping the clammy drops from his grizzled beard and flinging them to the paving stones. The pair returned and saluted.

"You did not challenge me.," Murdoch said.

"No, sir."

"Your duty is to challenge all comers."

"It was you. I didn't think—"

"And how did you know?"

"Well, sir, I could see your sword belt."

Murdoch sighed. "You have your duty, Jonas, and it is not to open the gate to every man with three buttons on his belt. One more lapse and you will be carrying slops for the chambermaids."

Jonas nodded nervously. His companion grinned, then sobered as Murdoch's stern eye swept across him.

Murdoch was not a learned man; a few letters were all he knew: *M* to sign his name, and a smattering of the others. Still, at times, deep in the night, he would wonder at the way his life was bound by one of them, the letter *D*: the Devil, his duties, his daughter, and the Dance. He stalked the shop-lined street that led uphill from the wall to the market square.

Oath-breaker, blacksmith in warrior's plumage, all this for her love. For Joy. For her, he had set aside his oath, sworn upon his mother's soul, to neither touch a sword nor raise his hand against another. Instead, he had wielded a sword in her defense and then again to protect the kingdom. Murdoch passed through the crowd, creating a ripple like a ship plying quiet waters. Men bowed, women curtsied, girls shyly peeked from behind their mothers' skirts, and a flock of urchins followed in his wake, trying to copy his stride. God, he realized now, had no use for those who broke troth with Him. Murdoch had become the plaything of the Devil, who had exacted his due with fine-wrought skill.

Murdoch, king's champion, had protected the kingdom for fifteen years. Once, he had averted war, and countless times he had ridden to stop the depredations of raiders or bandits, but he could not protect Joy from himself. She lay in her grave: her blood, her strength, her life itself spent in the agony of childbirth, bearing a son, his son, who had not lived an hour.

A wall, invisible, but as broad and solid as those that surrounded the city, lay between him and the others. His eyes opened onto a land as barren as the Erg of Tuneed in the deserts of the legendary south.

His life continued, unchanged in all appearances save one. He would wake, alone, in the depths of each night, slip out the postern gate, and walk through the blackness, biding his time until the rising sun would bring him duties to distract him from his pain.

He entered the castle grounds. Despite the early hour, servants were bustling. Today marked the celebration of King Galeschin's birthday. Most of the nobles had arrived the night before with their families. The masters would come to the feast as well, each bearing tribute from his guild.

"Leave off, Lady Matilda, please!" Princess Alana's voice rang out from her chamber window.

Murdoch looked up. Joy had been Alana's governess for those few happy years. After Joy's death, Matilda Nursemaid had taken back the reins. *So many of us were hurt by Joy's death. And it was me, my desire for her, that caused it all.*

* * *

"A lady is judged by the height of her brow, my little princess," said Matilda, holding tweezers in her right hand and reaching for Alana's arm with her left.

"Is not a lady judged by the fullness of her hair?" Alana responded, backing away and keeping her scarlet locks out of the crone's reach. The word hardly did justice to the fire of Alana's crowning glory. There was no lack of redheads in Gwalhafed, but even there, Alana's hair stood out. It was a dark red, almost crimson, with lighter strands mixed in, like the flames of a raging fire.

"Just let me pluck a little, half an inch or so. It will enhance your features."

"Is there nothing a lady is not judged by?" asked Alana, edging toward the doorway. She kept her voice in a pleasant tone. It made everything so much easier with Matilda.

The elderly woman thought for a moment. "Why, no, not that I can think of. Come here, my little princess."

"But, Lady Matilda," said Alana sweetly, still moving toward the chamber door, "it's so close to the feast. My brow would be red, and surely I would be judged for that, would I not?"

"A little powder will cover that, Highness. You'll need it for your freckles, at any rate. A little more won't be noticed. Come here!"

But instead, Alana slipped through the door and raced down the hall, as quickly as her bulky kirtle would allow. It was her best dress, the one she had to wear on state occasions: heavy, dark green wool with the gold of Gwalhafed embroidered on it.

"Decorum!" echoed Matilda's voice down the hall.

Alana scurried around the turning and into tall Lord Mallow and his son Richard, dark-haired, blue-eyed, the two of them like older and younger versions of the same man.

"You escaped, I see," said Richard, smiling. He went down on one knee. "Fear not, fair lady, for I will rescue you, as soon as I have become a knight and we may marry."

This agreement between their families had stood since Richard was two and Alana a newborn, eighteen years before. In the tiny kingdom of Gwalhafed, with its limited supply of noble blood, there were few alternatives to Richard as a spouse. *My father chose well*, Alana thought. Richard's face was so close to hers, only a little bit lower, with him on his knees. She wanted to kiss him, and wondered what that would be like. She leaned closer.

"Alana!" Matilda's voice rang from the hallway behind them.

"Quickly!" said Richard. He leaped to his feet and grasped her hand. They ran to the nearest stairs, he with his longer legs half dragging her. They ducked into the nearest of the corkscrewing stairwells and climbed to the next landing, just far enough to be out of sight from the hallway.

"Oh! Lord Mallow!"

There was a pause. Matilda, ever perfectly adhering to the forms, would curtsy, and require Lord Mallow's assistance to rise, and then a moment to catch her breath. "Have you seen the princess?"

Alana and Richard crouched on the stair, hardly daring to breathe.

"Oh," his father said, "she went to the king's chamber."

Matilda thanked him, and the pair waited, stifling giggles. Richard dropped an exaggerated curtsy, as they knew Matilda would do. Alana grasped his arm and pulled him to his feet, as she knew Lord Mallow was doing. He stood. Her hand was still on his arm. She looked into his eyes, so blue, like the sky above. He leaned closer.

"Ahem," Lord Mallow stood on the step below them. "You're not married yet."

* * *

Murdoch stood at the side of the king and watched as the gifting began. First came the nobles, bearing wines and furs, sheaves of wheat and gold trinkets, tokens of the tithes that their lands paid in earnest. Behind them, lined up patiently in their Sunday best, stood the chief of each of Gwalhafed's guilds: the shepherds, wool weavers, spinners, and dyers taking pride of place. Murdoch stood near the wall, below the dais, watching Galeschin—the care with which he greeted each guest, the gratitude he displayed for each gift—and was overwhelmed at the strength of the love he bore for his king, and lulled, he thought later, by the ample feast and bountiful wine.

The end of the line had reached the middle of the room. A stranger stood at the end of it. Murdoch beckoned a guardsman. "Sams, ask the gate ward who that man is."

He studied the man as he waited for a reply. The man was young, of middling size, with the straight shoulders and far-seeing eyes of a horseman, his clothing well-made, but spattered with mud from his recent journey. The inner side of his boot was scuffed, particularly across the instep, where a stirrup would rub. He was unarmed and held a box, on top of which lay a sealed scroll. His face was impassive, with none of the affection that shone in the faces of the others.

Samson returned. "A messenger with a gift for the king" was all the answer he brought. It told Murdoch nothing he had not already learned. As the man moved up through the hall, Murdoch moved closer to Galeschin and stood, arms crossed, seemingly at ease, but with his hand resting lightly on his sword.

At last, the messenger knelt at Galeschin's feet. He took the scroll and presented it to the king. Galeschin unrolled it and as he read, his eyebrows rose. "It's from Rolf."

Murdoch's fingers closed on his sword hilt. He could hear the gasps and grumbling of the guests.

"His Highness the Prince Uncle Rolf?" Alana said, using the title she had given him when she was a tiny child and Rolf her only, but even then not favorite, uncle. "After all these years? What could he possibly want of us?"

In reply, Galeschin read the letter aloud:

> Dearest Brother,
> Little did I know, in the days of my rash youth, of the strength of the ties binding kin, or the deep remorse that would haunt me. I grieve at our long parting. Accept this gift, I pray you, as a token of my regret for my ill-mannered behavior and allow me to return to the bosom of my family.

The messenger presented the wooden box to the king. Galeschin opened it and gasped in surprise. He took the gift from the box. The fabric unfolded, the color of twilight glimmering in the light of the hundred candles in the chandelier and the fire flickering in the immense fireplace. It was a cloak of Arte di Callimala wool, from the renowned Florentine dyers' guild, a length of which commanded a price as high as three years of a skilled stonemason's services. Galeschin stroked its softness lovingly, put the cloak on his shoulders, and fastened the golden clasp.

"In token of my joy at my brother's return, I will wear this cloak until he arrives," he said.

Some in the crowd grumbled. Even after fifteen years, Rolf's attempt to take the throne had not been forgotten. But others applauded. Murdoch noted that several of the nobles—among them Lord Valan, Rolf's former squire—seemed particularly pleased.

Galeschin turned to the messenger. "Go to the kitchen and eat your fill. We will give you a fresh horse so you may return to my brother with all possible speed and tell him to hasten."

The messenger bowed and left.

The king turned to his daughter. "Has your uncle finally come to his senses? He certainly seems to have made his fortune." His fingers stroked the finely woven fabric and he sighed as he said, more to himself than to her, "Perhaps it has set his soul at ease."

Chapter 2
Charity

"Here you go, Sire," trilled Sarah. "Sausage, pasty, scones, porridge, raspberries, cream, and hazelnut cream." She placed the tray on the sideboard. The morning sun twinkled through the leaded panes of the solar.

"Just a little of that porridge, if you will," King Galeschin replied.

Sarah's eyebrows rose.

Alana could see what she was thinking: *Is there something wrong with the food?*

"I'll have one of those lovely scones and a slice of that beautiful pasty," Alana said. Sarah smiled again and served them.

Rolf is returning. That would be enough to take anyone's appetite, Alana thought. *It has certainly taken mine.*

When Sarah left the room, Alana fed her pasty to the nearest dog.

"What say you, Hounshel?" the king asked his father-in-law, his chief advisor.

Hounshel shook his head. "All we can do is watch him and wait. I've given orders that his correspondence be shown to me before it leaves the castle. What else can we do?" Their discussion had gone on for a week, since the feast.

"No word from your men in Velendruch?"

"Only that there seems to be no sign of any intent to invade us."

"Which narrows it to two possibilities: Rolf's repentance is genuine, or he's hatching this plot all by himself." Galeschin scooped up a spoonful of porridge, looked at it, and put the spoon back in the bowl.

"Not entirely. Did you note how cheerful Valan looked at the news of his return?"

"Yes, and Fyan, Fynn, and Rossley as well. Perhaps this is a blessing," Galeschin mused. "It would be better to have him here, where I can keep an eye on him, than in Velendruch, conspiring with God knows whom."

"But how will you tell if his repentance is real?" asked Alana.

"Give me five minutes with him, and I will know."

"I would give him a room in the dungeon," she said.

"It would be such a happy world, if all men were perfect, Alana, but alas, that is not the case. A ruler must work with what he is given. Think of Rolf's gifts! As rude as some of his comments were, there was truth to them. He is taller than me, and better at sword. Rolf always spoke of the lack of a university in Gwalhafed. I'll see to it that he devotes himself to bringing men of learning here and spending that fortune he has amassed on founding a university, rather than on plots to unseat me. Even if he means ill, perhaps some good can be salvaged from it."

Hounshel nodded. "But do you still want to go today? Do you think it wise?"

"I have promised to bring aid to Eisen Valley. A king does not forswear."

* * *

"Are you ill, Father?" asked Alana, as they mounted their horses in the castle courtyard. "You hardly touched your breakfast."

"I'm fine," he said. "Just a little headache on a gray day. The ride will do me good."

He ran his finger along the neck of his blue cloak, where it had begun to bind him. He had held to his vow in the week since his birthday, removing his brother's gift only to bathe and sleep.

"And besides," he said, as he swept his hand back to indicate the line of loaded carts, "we have all these gifts to give."

The lands of Lord Valan, high up in the Eisen Valley, had been devastated by flooding that autumn, and the king had resolved to come to the aid of the beleaguered people.

"You sent aid last month."

"Food, yes, but their need is great. Many of them lost everything, and they still have the winter to get through."

Alana frowned. "Still, to benefit Valan? He may be your vassal, but he is not your friend."

"True," said her father, "and all the more reason to go to his lands and show generosity to his folk, to remind them that loyalty to their king is rewarded."

"I suppose," she said.

"Let us go," said the king. The gates swung back and the procession emerged, a dozen mounted knights followed by the king on Aeneas, his fine black horse, and the princess on Meadowsweet, her white palfrey. A line of twenty carts came behind them, full of food from the royal stores: sacks of barley and wheat, bushels of apples, piles of cabbages. Four more carts waited outside the castle walls, holding everything from bolts of linen and woolen fabric, needles, thread, and buttons, to cook pots, hammers, and saws—everything that might be needed to rebuild the lives that had been swept away. Another cart brought up the rear, filled with great, round barrels of ale from the Cock and Bull, courtesy of Saul, the innkeep.

They wound down the castle hill to the road at the bottom. There, they took the eastward turning; in an hour's time they reached the Eisen and turned northward onto the road along its bank. There were signs here of the flood, just two months past. Valan's folk had scraped a narrow path in the thick mud overlaying the road as they waited for the land to drain for planting. The road climbed, growing steeper, and the horses and oxen strained to pull the carts.

They entered the narrow canyon carved by the Eisen. Here, the road, carved from the buff-colored cliffs, ran along the edge of the river that surged fifty feet below. The day was pleasant, not terribly warm, but the horses' flanks were lathered from the effort.

Alana threw back her hood, and her fiery hair blazed in the sunlight. She glanced at Galeschin. "Father? You *are* ill."

She reined in her horse and the procession stopped. The carters and their escort removed their cloaks and drank from skins of water. "I beg you, take half the escort and go back."

He shook his head. He loosened the fastening of the cloak where it chafed his neck, but did not take off the hood. "No, we are expected. It wouldn't do."

"But you went there the week after the flooding, with the first shipment of food."

"They've worked hard for the past month, rebuilding their homes. It is important that they know that I care for them, that I am proud of their hard work, and besides, we have all these

14

things to give them. I'd miss the best part." He swept his open hand toward the carts. Alana noticed that it trembled.

"The blankets will keep them just as warm, whether you give a speech or not."

Galeschin smiled. "True, but I am king, Alana, and the people rely upon me for more than blankets. I said I would come, and so I must. A king, or a queen, as you will be one day, has a covenant with the people. One cannot allow one's frailties to interfere, nor personal whims to cloud one's judgment." He paused, then added mischievously, "I would hope this is not new to you."

"No, Father." *How could it be? I've heard it every day of my life.* "But still, Papa, shouldn't you take care of your covenanted self?"

"Am I getting that pompous?"

"Never. But you look dreadful."

"It's not far now. I can rest when we reach the castle."

* * *

As the sun reached its zenith, they came to the gate of Eisenburg, Valan's seat. The castle was itself carved out of a great cliff, with a narrow waterfall cascading down nearby. Legend said that the entire land had once been a lake, but that the mountains ringing it had been broken—by a dragon, said some, by a hero, said others—and the water drained, leaving a bowl-shaped valley filled with rich, deep loam.

Lord Valan stood, as a proper vassal should, beside his horse outside the gate, waiting for his king. He wore pale blue, as always, his flaxen hair glinting in the sunlight. Behind him, the road writhed up the cliff, twisting itself to find foothold, each eastern bend drenched in the spray from the waterfall that carried the Eisen down from its mountain valley. At last, the road reached the castle's upper gate, which looked, from the valley floor, no bigger than a mouse hole.

As they approached, Valan bowed, his blue eyes wary in his sharp-featured face. "A good day to Your Majesty," he said, "and greetings to you, Highness."

Nothing in his words was amiss, but Alana felt a chill from him as palpable as a block of ice. She nodded in response, thanking God that her father had seen fit to betroth her to Richard, and not him.

Valan took his place beside the king, yet, Alana noticed, at some distance, and prattled on about the feast he had planned. "There's a boar, with some of the burgundy my father laid down, and a pair of fine fat does—we've some of our own vintage for that . . ."

"That would be nice," said Galeschin.

The gate closed with an echoing thud. *This castle, so well designed to keep invaders out, can keep prisoners in just as well,* thought Alana.

The crowd of peasants cheered as the king passed. If they expected a speech, they were disappointed. The entourage reached the castle steps and dismounted. A little girl curtsied and presented the king with a bouquet. Alana noticed that his hand was shaking as he took it. He waved to the crowd, passed the bouquet to Alana, and slowly climbed the steps to the great hall. He was sweating when he reached the top.

They entered the hall and sat, taking the place of honor at the high table. Valan nodded to the major domo and a seemingly endless procession of servants began to serve a truly royal feast.

Galeschin barely touched it. He nibbled at his fish, took a bite of one of the marvelously tasty marinated vegetables, and drank the Rhenish in small sips, but tasted neither the meat courses nor the stronger wines. Alana herself ate little and watched her father warily. *Valan seems not to notice anything amiss. Indeed, he presses delicacies upon Papa. The perfect host. Look at him.*

"And, Sire, you really must try these little meat pies, yes, with —here, if I may—one of these cornichons, just the right touch for such a savory treat. Oh, yes, you there, bring His Majesty a goblet of the, let's see, yes, I think the ale goes best with these. And for Her Highness, as well." He smiled at Alana. "My lady, here, you must try this and tell me if you don't find it the best pastry you have ever eaten."

"It melts in my mouth, as light and delicate as Cook's own." *But dear God, what is wrong with Papa?*

"And here, Sire, eat the garnish! Delightful stuff."

No one could be that obtuse. Even the courtiers were muttering among themselves and staring at Galeschin. "Papa, would you like to rest now?"

16

"That would be nice," Galeschin whispered.

"Highness, this is hardly the time. We've not served the dessert yet. I know his majesty wouldn't want to miss that, would you, Sire?"

Mother of God, he is like a cat toying with a mouse. "I must insist, Valan." Alana stood. and everyone in the hall rose with her; one did not sit if royalty stood.

Valan stood, too, but he stared down at her with ill-disguised contempt. Alana did not come up to his shoulder. "As you wish, milady."

They were shown to a drafty north-facing chamber, where Galeschin lay on the bed sweating and shivering, covering his eyes against the weak light from the window. Alana sat, her attention alternating between her father and the view. Valan's lands stretched below, the river winding through fields newly green with sprouting winter wheat, the hills surrounding them barren now, cut with ravines carved by the autumn rains. She remembered woodlands there on her last visit, years past. Beyond the hills rose the mountains that formed Gwalhafed's northern boundary: steep, unconquerable. They were said to be haunted, a land of forest faeries. None of the few who had ever gone into them had returned.

After an hour, she shook her father's shoulder gently. "Do you wish to stay the night, Papa? If not, we must leave, to get home before dark."

His face was red and swollen. "Let us go," he whispered.

When they got to the courtyard, he stared at Aeneas, saddled and ready for him. "Let me ride in a cart," he said. "I am too tired to mount."

* * *

When the last of the carts left his gate, Valan summoned a messenger. "Follow the king's procession, but do not let them see you. Then ride quickly to Velendruch. Take word to my lord Rolf: 'I fear for your brother's health. Come now to Gwalhafed.'"

Then he went off whistling to give the order for the furnishings of the north-facing room to be burned.

Chapter 3
Plague

Alana moaned in her sleep. In her dream, she ran, half-dragged by the enormous red-haired woman. "Lady Joy, let's stop. My legs are tired," she whimpered.

"Quiet, Highness ." Joy stopped at the joining of the corridors and listened. She pulled Alana into the right-hand turning. Alana felt her legs sag. "You must give me your book," Joy whispered earnestly. "I promise you will get it back." She snatched the red leather-bound volume from Alana's reluctant grasp and tossed it to the floor of the left-hand turning.

Alana wailed in dismay. "My book!"

"Silence!" Joy hissed, with terrifying intensity. Tears welled in Alana's eyes.

At the sound of running footsteps, Joy startled, her eyes wide as a doe's. Picking up Alana and clamping her hand across her mouth, she ran.

Rolf was searching for them. Alana could hear the pounding as he opened doors, searched rooms, and then slammed doors shut along the corridor, coming closer, closer. Then she heard him at the garderobe door as she cowered beneath the form holding her mother's dress, her eyes closed tight.

She woke with a start.

The afternoon sun slanted through the casement, and the turtledoves cooed outside. She was in her own antechamber, and had fallen asleep sitting on the bench. The pounding in her dream was a polite knock at her chamber door. John the page entered and stood wide-eyed and solemn.

"Highness, your father has asked to see you."

She had waited all that long night and through the morning in his antechamber, while the doctors tended him. At noon, she had refused lunch and gone to her own room.

18

Alana stepped into the hall. John led the way, a small, thin boy, Lord Cirgan's youngest son, with his father's mop of curls. He was her father's favorite of the flock of pages who roamed the castle. John's small shoulders slumped and his step dragged. The slouch of his shoulders brought her sadness, at last, into focus. It had seemed unreal, that Galeschin could die, that the sickness rampant elsewhere could stretch its skeleton finger into Gwalhafed and touch only one person, its king.

"John," she said, and the boy turned.

"My lady?"

She held out her hand to him and he slid his into her grasp. They said nothing, walking slowly down the stone flags of the hallway, but the warmth of their hands, each upon the other's, spoke for them. Yes, Galeschin lay dying. No, they would not be left alone.

They reached the door to the king's antechamber. She squeezed John's hand and then let go. He looked up at her, his lower lip quivering. She straightened her shoulders and he held the door open.

The room was muffled with dark curtains and dizzyingly hot from the fire that provided light. Two doctors in velvet robes and ridiculous hats stood in a murmuring conference with Richard. A village wise woman, brought in by the doctors in their desperation, tended a pot on the fire, her bundles of herbs spread about her on the floor.

"How is my father?" Alana asked.

The doctors bowed deeply and spoke in solemn tones. "We have bled him as much as we dared and administered tinctures of *mercurius* and *plumbum*," said the first, a tall man with deep-set eyes.

"He is in God's hands now," said the second. They bowed again and turned to leave.

Alana heard a rustling at the door. Matilda Nursemaid came in with wreaths of garlic and herbs hung on one arm and swaths of dingy cheesecloth garlanding the other.

"Here they are, as you requested," she said to the wise woman. "Fifty garlic bulbs, rosemary, rue, wormwood, lavender, and sage woven into wreaths. And the cloth has been soaked and dried as you directed." Her plain face made it clear that she found the results entirely distasteful.

"What's this?" asked Alana.

The woman looked up from her cauldron. "Those who tend the king must be protected from the sickness," she said.

"I see," said Alana, wrinkling her nose. "I want to see my father now."

"Of course, Highness, as soon as you are properly protected."

"Must you?" said Alana, horrified, as the woman placed the first wreath about her neck.

"Highness, your royal father has asked for you. He may well die. What would happen to the kingdom if you were to die as well?" Another wreath of wilting herbs followed.

"What is the point of all this?" asked Alana. She poked at the wreath that scratched her neck. "I smell like a *bouquet garni*."

"Highness, these herbs will ward off the sickness."

"But the garlic!" Alana tried to ward off the garlic wreath as the wise woman put it over her head.

"For the evil eye."

She turned to her old governess. "Lady Matilda!"

"Highness, this woman says that these things will protect you. I would rather be stolen by forest faeries than let anything happen to you. We must take every precaution."

Matilda and the herbalist draped the first of the three layers of cheesecloth, which had been soaked in a tisane of lavender, rue, and sage and dried to a dismal green, over Alana's head.

"Now, my little highness," said Matilda, "go to your father. Your ladies and I will go to the chapel, to light candles to the Virgin to protect you."

"I'll frighten him to death. He'll think me a ghost," Alana protested, but she obediently turned and went through the door to the inner chamber.

The room was entirely dark, lit only by cracks of light from the edges of the window draperies. She found Galeschin by his labored breath. "Papa?"

"Alana," he whispered, through cracked, parched lips. "Has Rolf arrived?"

"Not yet, Papa."

"Take care to see him as he is. Remember . . . all I have taught you."

She bit her lip in a vain attempt to keep her voice level, to stop the tears that spilled from her eyes. A whispered "Yes, Father" was all she could manage.

"Water. I thirst . . ."

Alana held the cup to his lips. He drank greedily and fell back exhausted. "Marry Richard and get you a man child as quick as you can. Remember to encourage them, the people, in art, in learning. Build roads and schools. Remember . . . all the kingdom. . . reach out to all . . . justice . . . encourage them. . . ."

He stopped, the short speech leaving him gasping. Alana stroked his forehead. It burned to the touch and was drenched with sweat.

"Learning . . . invention . . . be kind to them all ." The words were a soundless whisper.

Alana wadded up a handful of cheesecloth and mopped his brow.

"Rolf . . . has he . . . ? I must see . . . him. . . ." Galeschin struggled to sit, but could barely raise his head. "Remember . . . all. . . ." He fell into a fitful doze.

"Papa? *Papa?*" Alana felt the fear rise within her. Light flashed into the room as the door opened, then shut, and for an instant she saw her father's face, grotesquely swollen. She heard the soft rustle of skirts and of dried herbs and turned to see the ghostly form of the wise woman, wreathed and covered with cloth, like death, she thought, like death come to gather her father in.

"*Papa?* This must stop. Rise up father. Rise up and laugh. This jest has gone too far."

She grasped at him, clutching the blue cloak, his brother's gift, that he wore still, true to his word. She felt the woman's hand on her shoulder, restraining her.

"Highness. Please. You must not touch him, lest you become ill, as well. Highness, please, you must leave him now. He must rest and I must tend him."

"You *will* make him well," said Alana. It came out neither quite command nor question.

"I will do what I can. Please. It is not wise to stay. You must live, in case . . . in case. . . . Please."

The woman led Alana from the room. She stood staring at the antechamber fire as the wise woman lifted the veils from her.

"Had they called me sooner, there were more I could do," she said, taking up a goblet of dark liquid. "I will do what I can. Go to your chambers. You must change your clothing and hang it to air in the garderobe. You must anoint yourself with this." She pressed a vial of green-tinged oil into Alana's hand. "You must rest and gain strength for what is to come."

Alana nodded, aware of her sleepwalking state, but powerless to change it. She turned and left.

Murdoch stood outside the door. *He looks like a lost sheep,* Alana thought. "My father still lives," she told him. "You have been in the town?"

"Yes, Highness. The townsfolk are frightened, the taverns full of drunkards, the rest in church. A mob has burned the home of Maimonides the Usurer, blaming him for the plague."

"Were any injured?"

"A few cracked heads, when the guard stopped them. The ringleaders are in the dungeon. No one was burned, but the family lost all."

"Offer them refuge here."

Murdoch hesitated before replying. "I did. They refused for fear of the sickness."

Alana nodded. "Have any taken ill in the town?"

"Not from fever, Highness, but many from too much beer."

Alana wrinkled her freckled nose in disgust. "Has Prince Rolf arrived?"

Murdoch scowled. "No, Highness. I have posted sentries as far east as Hirday."

"Notify me as soon as he is seen," she said.

Alana rubbed her eyes. *I must rest now. I am uncommonly tired. Dear God, am I ill, too?* She clutched the vial the woman had given her.

"Highness?" said Murdoch. "Are you ill?"

She looked up at him. He, too had aged in just these few days.

"No, I don't think so." *I must stay calm. I am a princess. I must not show weakness.* "The wise woman has given me an ointment to protect me."

Her thoughts swam in her head. *Dear God. Father could tell. How will I read my uncle's intentions?* Her memories of Rolf were few and distant, but not one of them pleasant. *What if he is changed? How are we to know? What if he hasn't? What are we to do? Am I ill? Oh, Papa. I cannot think.* She straightened her shoulders.

"Please send for my ladies. They are in the chapel." She turned and walked away. Murdoch stood watching as her tiny form disappeared in the darkness at the far end of the corridor.

"Do not trust your uncle," Murdoch whispered.

Chapter 4
Rolf

As Rolf rode up to the gates of Gwalhafed Castle, the bells began to toll. The dank, chill November breeze tugged at his cloak. It seemed that even Dame Nature was in mourning, dressing the world in dull grays, festooning the rooftops with acrid wreaths of woodsmoke.

One could see the resemblance between the brothers, but Rolf was a darker man, his hair severely short and his beard precisely trimmed, and narrower in every way: his shoulders, his brow, and the breadth of his understanding. His pale blue eyes, so surprising in contrast to his black hair, missed no detail of the scene before him. The roads were thronged with crowds of Galeschin's subjects: weeping peasants wearing their best clothing, guardsmen and gentry in somber colors, all drawn as by a lodestone to honor the passing of their king.

The plague had taken him from them, the plague that had devastated Amytans and Velendruch, Caeland, and even as far as Gondaron. In Gwalhafed, it had claimed one victim only. Each in that crowd knew the reason. Galeschin, the king who had so loved them, had made a bargain with death. To save them, he had died, leaving them all his orphans.

Rolf remembered Alana as a tiny, precocious spark of a child, who flitted through the castle like some exotic, crimson bird and would show up, silently, at the most unexpected moments, wide blue eyes above her freckled nose, taking in everything and seeming to understand an appalling amount of it. He saw her again for the first time in fifteen years as he entered the castle courtyard.

Alana descended the steps leading from the great hall, dressed in an unadorned black gown, the white of her underdress showing in a thin line around the neckline, a dark gray cloak hanging from her shoulders. Her red hair blazed, but the fire of her slate blue eyes was extinguished. Eight strong men, Murdoch among them, preceded her down the steps, dressed in black, bearing the coffin containing her father's corpse. Her maternal grandfather, old Lord Hounshel, escorted her, his long, white locks contrasting with his mourning clothes, but it was he who leaned on her arm for support. The remainder of the council of nobles, all men, most of middle to advanced years, dressed in deep mourning, followed her through the corridor of dark-clad, stern-visaged soldiers who lined and protected the path to the burial place from the crowds of grief-stricken subjects. Surrounded by the men, she seemed no bigger than a child.

Rolf reined in his horse, his eyes drawn to Alana's hair, the only spot of color in the gray November chill. *Like a rose among cinders,* he reflected, with satisfaction. At that moment she raised her downcast eyes and looked directly at him. He quickly molded his face into a sorrowful expression.

* * *

At first, Rolf's was one of a sea of faces pressed against the glass dome of grief that surrounded Alana. Her attention was drawn to his face, its expression out of place among the mourners, but before she could note just what had caught her eye, his expression reflected the sorrow of the others. Looking at him, one could see that this was a man of ambition, ability, and high intelligence. Finally, her faint memories from her childhood revealed him to be her uncle, Rolf.

* * *

That evening, Lord Hounshel sat with Alana in her chamber. In the past week, she noted, his back had grown more bent and his eyes, once so loving and keen, now frequently seemed to gaze into a land that no one else could see.

"I have spoken with them all, and it stands in this manner." He cleared his throat, as if beginning a speech. "Count Valan stands with Rolf."

"As ever," she sighed, recalling their inseparability from the dimmest recesses of her childhood.

"Four others—Wembers, Fyan, Fynn, and Drent—will not swear fealty to a woman. They wish the nearest male heir—that is, your uncle—on the throne because there is no precedent for a queen."

"A problem to be solved by my marriage," she said .

"Drent says it's because a woman is not capable of ruling a kingdom." Hounshel pursed his lips thoughtfully and looked at her.

"Drent hasn't said a civil word to me since I beat him at chess when I was twelve."

"Desney, Strenholm, and Burrk present a possibility, however. Their reluctance to your rule is simply because neither you nor Richard is yet twenty-one years of age. They respect you and your ability, but point out that the kingdom has never been ruled by one who had not attained majority. Myself and the rest, of course, support your immediate accession." He folded his hands in his lap and regarded her.

"I do not trust my uncle," she began. "My clearest memory is of him and Valan pulling off flies' wings when they were both old enough to know better. It is an evil omen for him to arrive on the heels of my father's death. If it were only my wishes that counted, I would have him thrown into a dungeon or shipped back to Velendruch in a cage."

Hounshel shifted uneasily in his seat and seemed about to speak.

"However," Alana continued, "my father educated me too thoroughly for that. I must do what is best for Gwalhafed. If I treated Rolf that way, I would offend five of my most powerful vassals, who might well take up arms against me."

She sat in thought for a long moment. "A compromise is possible," she said at last. "If the council appoints you regent until my twenty-first birthday, I would agree to it."

Hounshel smiled with relief. "You are your father's daughter." He took her hand and kissed it.

Chapter 5
The Regent

The bier that had supported Galeschin's coffin had been removed and a long table stood in its place, its dark wood gleaming. Sixteen chairs: The king's armchair and one each for Alana and the fourteen nobles were set at perfectly regular intervals, with a bench behind the king's chair for the scribe. A silver goblet of water waited at each place, and two serving men with carafes stood at attention among the guards. The nobles entered two by two, Alana and Hounshel leading. When each had reached his place, with Alana and Hounshel flanking the king's chair, they all sat.

Fourteen nobles supported the throne of Gwalhafed with their tithes, with their loyalty, and with their lives, if needs be. In return for this, hallowed custom granted them some voice in the naming of their king. They lined the long sides of the table, clad in furs and silks, jewels glinting at their necks and on their hands, solemn now, as the occasion warranted.

Mallow—tall, broad-shouldered, and dark-haired—sat beside Lord Hounshel. Next sat Burrk, the eldest, like an unfledged bird: tiny, withered and bald. Past him were Shends, as lean and gray as a wolf, and the corpulent Abbersley, richly robed in velvet. Next came Cirgan, a solidly built man with a mop of curls beginning to go gray. Last on that side, sat Drent, a pale wisp of a man, with a self-satisfied face. Valan sat at the foot. Fyan was next, silver-haired, toying with his thin, gray beard, and then Fynn—short, ruddy, bear-like, his mustache draggling over his lips. Rossley sat next to him, fingers tapping the stem of his goblet. Wembers, next to him, was young, scarcely past his knighting, and looked around the table eagerly. It was the first time he had ever been called to council. Strenholm, as solemn and dignified as a tombstone, sat between Wembers and Desney, a small man with the quick motions of a fox. The last of them, Wickerts, sat next to Alana, his large brown eyes alert in his bearded face.

"It is customary," began Lord Hounshel, "that at this time the nobles reaffirm their loyalty to the House of Mann by swearing fealty to the king's heir." There was a rustle and murmur as he paused. "We are, however, presented with a situation unique in the history of our realm. Before we proceed, Princess Alana will speak to this issue."

The nobles whispered among themselves as he sat. Alana compelled their attention with her eyes before she stood.

"My lords," she began in her low-pitched voice. "I am aware of your feelings on this matter. It was, as you all know, my father's wish that I succeed him and to this end he educated me in state-craft. I have worked hard all my life to be worthy of his charge. However, I am aware that to have a ruling queen is unique and unforeseen in the traditions of our realm.

"It was my father's wish that Richard and I marry as soon as may be, and to that end, we have arranged to be wed at Yule. We understand that we are still young, by the standards of rulership, and that it is of concern to some of you." She nodded at Burrk, then toward Strenholm and Desney.

"Under my father's peaceful rule, our kingdom prospered. I would not see that destroyed by strife, and so I would present a proposal for your consideration." She paused, waiting for silence. "I propose that you name my grandfather, Lord Hounshel, regent until my twenty-first birthday."

She took her seat. Count Valan stood, the light of the hundred candles hanging above them gleaming on his perfectly straight flaxen hair and making the velvet of his dark blue surcoat glow softly.

He smiled at her, and she felt the chill of his look travel down her spine. "In this you are a true child of our beloved monarch," he intoned. "I find this proposal admirable."

Alana and Hounshel exchanged glances. One by one, the nobles spoke and gave assent to the plan, even Drent, who did so cheerfully, which only increased Alana's alarm. Alana looked at the men seated at the table. Some looked to her, or to her grandfather, while others exchanged comments with their neighbors in subdued voices. She sensed that she and Hounshel were no longer in control of the meeting, but she could not tell who was. Valan looked directly at her with a gaze that would have been unreadable to most, but she saw the victory in his eyes. She glanced around the table again and could tell that no one looked to him. The man who controlled the meeting was not present. But all of the men agreed. What further scheme could they have?

"It is done, then," said Alana.

"One moment, please, Highness," Valan's voice rang out from the other end of the table. "I speak today for tradition, and the noble lineage of the House of Mann. Under the rule of this house, our kingdom has ever prospered. I would be loath to see the control of the kingdom leave its capable hands, even to one so closely allied as our esteemed Lord Hounshel of Hirday. It is most fortuitous that we have, at this moment, a member of the royal house newly returned and capable of service. I nominate Prince Rolf, the brother of our late monarch."

The meeting dissolved into a babble of voices and Lord Hounshel pounded on the table with his fist to restore order.

"Surely," said Mallow, "you recall the unpleasantness of his departure?"

"Fifteen years ago, my lord, and water over the dam. A man may—nay, must—change in that span of time, and we have his recent letter to his brother to prove it."

Blessed Mother of God, thought Alana. *They should be shipped to Velendruch in the same box.* But her words, when she spoke, were sweetly reasonable.

"Lord Valan," said the princess. "My uncle has long been absent from our realm. He is a stranger to me and to all of us. Might it not be wiser to have someone more conversant with the affairs of the kingdom in the position of regent?"

"Blood will tell, Princess. His abilities come to him through inheritance . . . as do yours," he said pointedly.

"Let him try," whispered Hounshel. "He has only five to support him. The rest are your men." Alana nodded.

"We have two candidates for regent," Lord Hounshel announced, pounding the table again to silence the hubbub. "Are there others?"

Silence greeted his question. He turned to Mallow, seated next to him. "What is your will?"

"You, my lord."

The polling proceeded around the table. "Lord Hounshel," said Burrk, without waiting to be asked.

"Lord Shends?" asked Hounshel.

"Prince Rolf," he replied, staring at the table. Alana's stomach sank.

"I, too support His Highness," said Abbersley, smiling.

That will make seven for my uncle, Alana thought. *with me to break the tie.*

"I stand with Lord Hounshel," said Cirgan. "As any true man would."

"I support the House of Mann," replied Valan. "And so, of course, I stand with Prince Rolf."

Drent, Fynn, Fyan, Rossley, and Wembers all voted, as expected, for Rolf.

"Lord Strenholm?"

"You, my Lord Hounshel, of course," he said in his ponderous way, and smiled at Alana. *Only two left,* she thought, *and they are mine.*

"Lord Desney?

"I stand with Prince Rolf," he said.

Alana gasped.

"Highness," he said, "I do so out of concern for your grandfather's health. There will only be three years of regency. What harm could come in such a short time?"

That the last of the nobles, Wickerts, stood with Hounshel gave Alana little consolation.

Rolf was summoned. At Hounshel's request, the king's chair was removed from the table and one like those of the other nobles put in its place. Rolf stood between Alana and Hounshel, his head modestly bowed. As the murmurs subsided to silence, he raised his head and regarded them with his pale blue eyes.

"My lords, and lady," he said. "I am overcome by grief and by this honor. I will endeavor at all times to be worthy of this task."

When the council had ended, and the others left, he turned to Alana. "I had hoped we would meet on a happier occasion. I came as quickly as I could. Did he suffer?"

"Once the sickness showed itself, he died quickly, Your Highness," she replied.

30

"Please, Alana. I am your uncle. Let us not be formal with each other. Did he . . . speak of me?"

"Often. He asked constantly if you had arrived. He spoke of his love for you and his hope that your return would be a cause for rejoicing."

"It is not for some?"

"People remember, Uncle."

"I expected that. Please learn from my example, Alana. Action is quick, and regret slow and enduring. There is a long overdue task I must complete. Will you help me?"

"In what way?"

"I must make amends to those I offended. Since I have arrived too late to beg forgiveness of my brother, the first one I must speak to is Murdoch. I must admit, I am daunted. Will you come with me?"

"I will send a page to summon him."

"No, please. I feel that it is I who must go to him. Will you come with me and lend me courage?"

They made their way from the great hall through a warren of passages, silencing the clatter of the kitchen with their unexpected appearance, leaving whispers in their wake. They followed the hallways connecting the barracks, where astounded guardsmen bowed and stood gawking.

At last, they reached the room over the armory where the king's champion lived. Murdoch himself answered Rolf's knock. The warrior stood, unsmiling.

Rolf took a deep breath. "I have come to beg your forgiveness. For my treatment of your lady wife. And to offer my belated condolences on her death."

Murdoch gave no answer.

"I offer my hand in friendship," Rolf continued, matching his gesture to his words. Murdoch looked at the proffered hand, then at the princess.

Here stood two men, both sworn to her service: the regent and her champion. It would not bode well for them to be at each other's throats. Alana nodded, almost invisibly. With no change of expression, Murdoch clasped Rolf's hand, shook it once, and released it. Then he shut the door.

"I hope I need never do anything harder in my life," said Rolf. His face looked pale in the torchlight and his hand trembled as he took Alana's arm to escort her back the way they had come. The knot of guardsmen who had loitered in the hallway to witness Rolf's encounter with Murdoch dissolved before them.

Yes, Rolf had returned. If any in Gwalhafed did not know it now, they would soon, as gossip, with the speed of lightning, flew through the castle and into the town. Yes, Rolf had returned, a re-formed man.

Chapter 6
The Wedding

Yule dawned clear and chill across the marshland surrounding Lord Mallow's castle. It was the first day of the wedding, the one on which the blessing of the Holy Virgin would be invoked.

"Highly improper," huffed Matilda, as she fidgeted with the stubborn curls of Alana's flame-red hair, taming them into braids. "The Gifting of the Lady should be done at her demesne, not the groom's."

"Lady Matilda," replied Alana, "the hunting is better here."

"Still, to have to storm his own castle? Ridiculous."

The morning sun, slanting through the casement, glittered in Olwen's pale hair. As pale and slender as a wood sprite, Richard's younger sister had just turned twelve that spring. "Little Lord Emil sent me another poem."

"He's still writing poetry about you?" asked Alana.

"One arrived by messenger just yesterday. 'I pine for you. My face is blue.'"

"A pitiful verse," said Matilda.

"The rest is worse," answered Olwen, grinning. She peered out the casement. "I see them! They've just come out of the wood!"

Far across the field, the brilliant company emerged from the gray of the winter woods. Richard, as easy to distinguish for his great size as for his wedding finery, rode at the head of the troupe.

"What horse is that?" asked Lady Gwen, his mother. "I don't remember him riding that one before."

"A wedding gift from my uncle," said Alana. "From the stables of the royal house of Amytans."

"Magnificent," Lady Gwen said. The horse's chestnut flanks glistened in the wintry sun as he raced toward them. "A princely gift."

"Richard's magnificent," sighed Alana. There was no better word for her strapping bridegroom, clad in red, riding with the ease of one born to the saddle. His groomsmen came behind: Fyan's son Robert and two more Richards, followed by a cohort of cousins and retainers. "See how far ahead of the others he's gotten."

Soon the men arrived at the castle gate. Lord Mallow and his men engaged them in mock battle, a contest of riddles, most not fit for ladies' ears, a custom grown from the faint memories of the days when brides were won in earnest, as prizes in combat. Beaming, Lord Mallow ordered the gate opened. Richard and his companions, whooping with delight, stormed the castle. Laughing guests and servants bearing oak twigs, the symbol of Mallow's house, lined the stairway and struck them in mock defense. They raced up the stairs to Alana's chamber door and then courtesy prevailed again. After all the tumult, the bridegroom knocked politely: three sharp raps for Father, Son, and Holy Spirit, although the country folk still said the act called upon Maiden, Mother, and Crone to grant fruitfulness to the union.

Olwen, as the Maiden, opened the door. She seemed to grow larger as she majestically swung back the chamber door and stood, blocking it. "Who disturbs my lady's peace?"

Richard swept the plumed cap from his head and bowed deeply. "I, Richard," he began boldly, and then his eye was drawn past his sister, quite over her head, to where his radiant bride stood among the other women. He stopped, as if stunned, and stood, towering over Olwen and looking much like an oversized page who'd forgotten his etiquette and wasn't quite sure what form of address to use.

Olwen cleared her throat, raising a storm of laughter among the groomsmen lining the stairs. "Who disturbs my lady's peace?" she asked again.

"Ah, er, Richard," he replied, still looking over her head at Alana.

Alana's eyes appealed to Robert, who nudged Richard. "Come to claim ..." he prompted.

Richard awoke from his trance. "Come to claim what has been promised me," he said. He held out his hand.

Lady Gwen, as the Mother, stepped forth, leading Alana.

"Hold!" said Matilda, reveling in her role as Crone. "Will you honor this woman?"

"With all my life," replied Richard.

"Will you protect this woman?" she demanded.

"With all my strength," he said.

"Will you love this woman?" She stood a hand span in front of him, hands on her hips, her nose pointed up at his chin.

For a moment he seemed a child again, trying to think of a story to account for the missing tarts. But he looked over her head to his smiling bride. "With all my heart," he whispered.

Matilda curtsied stiffly and stepped aside.

"Are you full willing?" Olwen asked Alana.

"Yes," answered Alana, her eyes on Richard, "with all my heart."

Lady Gwen, weeping, placed Alana's hand in Richard's.

"Then go you in joy and may Our Holy Lady, Mother of us all, bless you."

Arm in arm, they descended the stairs to where the first of the wedding feasts awaited.

* * *

After the feasting, servants removed the tables and benches and prepared the great hall for dancing. Musicians puttered in the corner, tuning instruments, arranging themselves on their bench, waiting for the signal to begin their long evening's work, for today was Christmas Eve and the dancing would begin at sunset and last until the hullabaloo at midnight.

"Are we ready then?" asked Lord Mallow. He stood at the doorway, Lady Gwen's hand upon his arm. Rolf and his partner, behind them, nodded. Olwen and her dancing partner, Robert, came behind, with the bride and bridegroom, eyes still locked on each other, last.

"I suppose we'll have to put them on a leash to get them through the figures," whispered Robert to Olwen. "Richard. Richard! Time to dance."

Mallow signaled the door wards, who swung the doors back. At that, the music commenced. They stepped forward into the great room. Fire blazed in the enormous hearth and twinkled from the candles in their sconces. The great Yule candle gleamed from its wreath on the high table on the dais. The plain stone walls were garlanded with holly and ropes of fragrant pine. The other guests stood waiting, already formed into figures for the dance. Alana's group took its place at the center of the room and waited for the measure to come round again.

Gently, they stepped and promenaded, the women's gaily colored dresses swirling as gracefully as willows in the wind. Again they turned the figure while the other guests watched. At the third round, the other couples joined the dance. Around, around, and round again the dancers turned, a great spinning panoply of bold colors in motion.

* * *

When the musicians stopped and left to rest their weary fingers, the guests turned their attention to the great cauldrons of syllabub and spiced cider. Mallow handed Alana a cup.

"My lady," he said. "Drink with me to happiness."

"To happiness," she answered, "and to love."

Lord Shends came up to them and stood, his eyes worried beneath grizzled brows.

"A toast, my lord," said Mallow, his broad smile making creases at the corners of his eyes.

"A toast, yes, a toast," Shends stammered, looking at Alana. Then he seemed to remember himself. "To loyalty," he said, and drank. Again, he looked at Alana, and seemed on the verge of speaking.

Valan, already the worse for drink, stumbled up to them. "Shends, good cousin," he said. "I've promised Rossley's daughter to find her a dancing partner and I've promised her father to keep her away from the young bloods. You'll do nicely." He grasped Shends' arm and pulled him to where a figure was forming.

Alana and Mallow looked at each other. "An odd toast for a wedding," Mallow said.

"My lady," Rolf stood bowing before her. "Will you honor me with the next dance?" He took her arm and led her to the nearest figure. Again the music started, and they turned the figures. Alana could not see Shends, and the complexity of the steps soon drove any thought of him to the back of her mind.

Alana had learned the steps under Matilda Nursemaid's stern eye and come to regard the exercise as one more royal duty on an already lengthy list. She found that she was enjoying herself immensely, and soon realized that her uncle's skill at dancing played a part in it. That figure ended, she danced again, this time with Lord Drent, who, as she expected, had little grace; with Cirgan, who danced well; with Mallow, who danced better; and again with her bridegroom, who danced the best of all, surprising in one so large.

Finally, the musicians rested, and the company returned to the refreshments. The syllabub and cider had been replaced by Lamb's Wool and a posset.

Abbersley had planted his bulk in front of the posset and was holding forth to Drent. "A beautiful girl," he said, watching Olwen try to escape the attentions of Lord Emil. "Fine young filly. Were I thirty years younger. . . ."

Drent, to her amazement, did not laugh. "What a toady Drent is," she whispered to Richard. He laughed and steered her toward the opposite end of the long table, where a servant ladled Lamb's Wool into tankards. Mallow stood there, beaming at his son and new daughter. Emil, desperation in his eyes, drew Richard away, intent on gaining his aid in approaching Olwen.

"You dance well, Lord Mallow," she told her father-in-law.

"But not so well as your uncle," he replied, handing her a cup.

She thought a moment, then said, "That's true, but how would you know? I'll warrant you never danced with him."

"Ah, but I have. Sparred with swords. You know what the Irish say."

"I can't say that I've ever met an Irishman."

"Never give a sword to a man who can't dance."

"Oh, bosh. Murdoch's never danced a day in his life, and no swordsman's reputation can touch his." Floating bits of apple bobbed against her lip as she sipped the spicy cider.

"You were too young, Alana, to attend feasts like this. If you only could have seen them—Murdoch and Joy. When they danced, everyone stopped to watch. They didn't even need music. A walk along the parapet, a procession to the church, everything they did was a dance." Mallow sipped thoughtfully. "He wore bright colors then. You can't imagine the pain he must feel, watching others dance. I know that is why he is not here today."

"But it's been so long. Twelve years since she died. Why does he still mourn? Why hasn't he remarried?"

"She died in childbirth, Alana. He blames himself."

"Many women die in childbirth. Many men remarry."

"I am one of his closest friends, and he speaks to me of things he will not tell others. You should know this: As a youth, he swore a vow never to wield a sword or go to war."

"Murdoch?"

"Murdoch. He set his vow aside for love of Joy. Your father made his fighting Sir Brian Borrenough a condition of their marriage, and he was right in doing so. Murdoch was a peasant, a blacksmith, and Joy the daughter of a knight."

"And by defeating Sir Brian, Murdoch thwarted Rolf's plot and ended Velendruch's attack."

"Exactly. He feels Joy's death was his punishment for forswearing."

"But he saved the kingdom! Why should God punish him for that?"

"Who knows the ways of God? An oath is an oath, I suppose."

"But he is a warrior still."

"Your father was a wise man, and a clever one as well. He knew that without Murdoch, the truce with Velendruch might collapse again. As a new-made knight, Murdoch had sworn loyalty to the throne. Galeschin treated Murdoch kindly, and the two men, despite the difference in their stations, were friends, but your father made sure that Murdoch understood that he held his oath as binding, and that the punishment of God for breaking a second oath would certainly not be less than that for breaking the first. I suppose that has held him since your father's death—that and mistrust of Rolf. He is a strange man. No one despises the carnage inflicted with the sword more than he, but no man loves the dance of swordsmanship better."

Mallow's steward beckoned to him. He took his leave of Alana. Shends stumbled up to her, his gray eyes filled with drunken urgency. "My lady, a word in your ear." He grasped her arm and led her roughly from the room.

38

"You nurse a viper in your bosom. Loyalty. Loyalty is what counts. I am forsworn of all my vows." Shends stood swaying, clasping her arm to keep his balance. His speech, slurred and incoherent, raced onward. "I would never do ought to harm my lady wife, or your grace, Your Grace," he mumbled. "No. Not I. I have wronged you." He broke into tears.

"What do you mean? Does this have to do with my uncle?" asked Alana.

"I have sinned gravely," he answered. "You must believe me!"

"In what way? What are you trying to tell me?"

"I am a sinner!" His fingers dug into her arm.

She pulled away. "Please, Lord Shends! You're hurting my arm!"

Wickerts came through the doorway and saw them. "Shends! What are you doing?" He ran to them and pulled Shends away from her. "Highness, I ask pardon on his behalf, until he comes to his right mind." He called for help and two serving men ran to him. They carried Shends, still mumbling, off to his bedchamber.

"Highness, I regret that you must see him thus," said Wickerts. "Over the past months, he has become more and more deranged. At first, it was a small matter, little lapses of memory, but now he is as mad as a forest faery. He drinks more now, and I fear it worsens his condition."

A crowd of servants came past them, their arms heaped with rushlight torches and baskets filled with clappers and small tambours. Alana saw Richard wading toward her through the rollicking chaos. He reached out his hand and clasped hers. "Come, my lady, it is time for the hullaballoo."

Within the great room, each guest received a torch, then lit it from the great Yule candle on the high table. As they passed through the door, the servants handed each a noisemaker. Soon the company stood shivering on the parapet, gazing across the flat expanse of Mallow's domain at the bonfires dotting the land. The midnight cock crowed and they broke into whoops and laughter, waving the torches, rattling the clappers and thumping the tambours on each other's heads. The chill wind brought the faint sounds of the peasants celebrating around the bonfires, rejoicing in the birth of the Christ Child and calling the sun back from the nether regions.

Richard escorted her to her chamber. "Tomorrow, my love, I will hunt. My father's huntsman tells me he has found the grand-sire of all boar for our wedding feast. And the day after that we will marry." He kissed her hand, and they gazed into each other's eyes.

She clasped his hand. "Let the others hunt," she said. "Stay safe with me."

He laughed. "You needn't fear. With so many kinsmen here, there are more than enough of us to best even the greatest boar."

Lord Mallow cleared his throat and the couple startled. He stood, Lady Gwen by his side, holding a taper.

"You're not married yet," Lady Gwen cautioned them. "Come, Richard. Mass is at dawn, and the hunt leaves forthwith."

He kissed Alana's fingertips and followed his parents down the hallway.

Chapter 7
The Hunter and the Hunted

The morning dawned brilliant and crisply cold. Mallow's chaplain knew better than to linger over his sermon, for this marked the first day of the boar-hunting season, and the hunters were eager to begin. The men came booted and spurred to the Mass, then ate a quick breakfast standing.

"Fyan," asked Mallow, deferring to his guest's gray hair. "Will you hunt with us or hawk with the ladies?"

"Hunt, of course," he replied, apparently shocked by the question.

"And you, Lord Hounshel?"

Alana's grandfather smiled and patted his lips with the edge of the tablecloth. "Thank you, but no. I will leave the boar to the younger and stronger. Besides, why should I wish to hunt with you fellows when so many fair ladies go hawking?" His eyes twinkled with mirth, and his face smiled amid a thousand wrinkles.

"And I," said Burrk, tugging his velvet cap over his head, as smooth as a water-rubbed stone. "I could hardly leave the ladies unescorted."

They all laughed at that. Burrk, at eighty years, was no one's idea of a defender. "Strenholm, lad?"

"With the ladies, of course," replied the fourth graybeard. A mere sixty years of age, he had been Burrk's squire before most of the others had been born. "To protect them from you, m'lord."

"I believe I'll hawk today," said Shends. "I fear I drank too much last night to sit a horse properly."

"Oh, bosh, man," said Fyan, thrusting a goblet under his nose. "A stoup of wine will fix that. Hair of the dog. Come along."

"Then we are off!" said Rolf, and he and the rest strode from the room, spurs jingling, spirits high. Richard was swept from the room even before he could turn and bid Alana good-bye.

The beaters had taken their positions an hour before. Now, at the signal from the parapet, the nobles could hear the racket begin as hundreds of peasants whooped, hallooed, and thrashed about the wood. With the start of the noise, the hounds broke into frantic yelping and charged toward the gate in a mad pack. The nobles mounted.

"I'll warrant you reach our quarry first," said Rolf to Richard. "I've never seen a horse like yours for speed and surefootedness."

The head huntsman wound his horn, the gates creaked back, and the dogs and horsemen surged forth.

Mallow's huntsman led the way. Fourteen years he had held his post, and for ten before that he had been apprenticed to his father, learning the ways of all beasts and every twig of the woods of Lord Mallow's domain. The vast quantity of meat needed for the wedding feast was nothing to the importance of this moment. He had delegated that task to underlings. No, for the past month, his keen eyes had focused on the task of finding the boar, of mapping his ways, of strategizing: Where to station the beaters? Which way to direct the beast? Not just any boar would do, only the greatest and fiercest. Was not the young king to hunt with them? And had not Prince Rolf's own huntsman scorned the hunting on Mallow's estate? Let him laugh. For there was one boar in this district that would test any hunter's mettle.

Mallow's huntsman led them down from the ramparts and then swung north by west, out of the flat land by the swamps and toward the rugged hills bordering Amytans. The rest thundered after him, Richard reining in his horse at the huntsman's heels. On they galloped, past the first row of the beaters, ignoring the rabbits and pheasants flushed by the thunderous racket. Ahead, another horn sounded. One of the huntsman's assistants had seen the boar and given the signal. His horn gave the answering call

42

and they turned northward. Presently they reached the edge of the wood and plunged under its eaves. Drent's horse shied as a rabbit crossed its path and Drent slid off to the ground. The horse bolted off. Fyan, Robert, Fynn, and Desney raced past him as he lay screaming imprecations at them. Mallow reined in his horse. The rest thundered past.

"Damn them all!" screamed Drent. "I could have been killed!"

"Are you hurt?"

"Dreadfully. Did you see those fools? Rude as forest faeries. 'Ods body, they could have killed me, and I helpless on the ground!"

Mallow shook his head. "You're not bleeding."

"It's my ankle. I'm sure I've broken it. Damn that horse to Hades."

Mallow dismounted and stretched out his hand. "Here, let's see if you can walk."

Drent hobbled to his feet with groans. He took a step and nearly collapsed, grasping at Mallow's arm. "I pray you. Help me back to the castle. I must be treated immediately lest I be lamed."

Mallow turned his head longingly in the direction of the fading sounds of the hunt. He could not catch up to them now. "Come along then, Drent. I'll set you on my own horse and lead you home myself."

The hunt pounded onward. They were in the thick of it now, surrounded by beaters, the hounds baying. They had scented the boar and the huntsman signaled the dogs to the front. They surged forward, tongues lolling, mouths frothing, baying like the very hounds of hell. Richard let his horse have its head and it surged smoothly to the forefront of the riders. The huntsman, his work done, was now content to fall back into the pack and let the honor of the kill go to another. The country the boar led them through grew steeper, the terrain more treacherous. The roar of the beaters rang in their ears. The hounds had clearly scented the animal, but still the hunters had caught no glimpse of it. Up hill and down dale it led them, splashing across streams, through thickets of thorn. Ahead, the hallooing of the beaters turned to screams of pain as the boar broke through the huntsman's carefully planned route. The hunt roared past like a thunderbolt, catching a glimpse of a peasant groaning, awash in blood while his fellows frantically staunched his wounds.

The boar led them down a ravine so steep that the horses sat down on their haunches to navigate it. Halfway down the mad careen, Fynn's horse veered sharply into Wembers', sending him tumbling into the boggy bracken at the foot of the slope. Wembers recaptured his horse and remounted, only to find the animal lamed. The hunt was over for him. He turned homeward, leading his limping steed.

"I see him!" shouted Richard, and he blew a long blast on his horn. Truly this was the grandsire of all boar. Its bristling back stood nearly three feet high, its snout flanked with tusks as long as a man's hand. The boar squeezed under a fallen tree, held up at one end by its branches. The hounds, nipping at its heels, surged under. Richard spurred his horse and it proved as good at flying as it had at the gallop. It soared over the tree trunk and landed nimbly on the boggy earth beyond. Desney and Valan followed.

Abbersley's burdened horse raced up to the trunk and stopped short. The corpulent Abbersley, in his rich scarlet robes, flew across the barrier like a load of flaming pitch from a catapult. Rolf and the rest bringing up the rear pulled their horses' heads round and detoured past the tree's roots, but Wickerts and Cirgan, close behind Abbersley, hemmed in by the others, were forced to rein in their horses before they could follow him over the log. Abbersley thrashed about in the mud, as if in his death throes, but had not said a word. They peered over the tree cautiously. As they watched, Abbersley raised his head and spewed a torrent of mud, followed by a volley of oaths.

"God's breath, I shall have that horse cut up for stew meat! My garments!" He let out an agonized moan. Cirgan and Wickerts roared with laughter. Still on his hands and knees, and looking like nothing so much as a pig in a wallow, he craned his neck backward to look at them. "Good sirs, help me in my plight. God forbid the peasants should see me so without my dignity."

"Pulling Abbersley from the bog will be much harder work than killing a boar," said Cirgan.

"True," answered Wickerts, "but 'twill make a better story." Still laughing, the pair dismounted.

44

Richard rode, bent low over his horse's neck, close behind the ranting hounds with Desney and Fynn at his heels. He could hear the boar's ragged breath, so close was he to the beast. The remaining hunters lagged behind. The boar reached the base of a ravine and tried to clamber up it. It could find no footing on the hard-packed earth and slid backward. It tried again, to the same end. The hounds were upon the boar in their blood frenzy, nipping and dodging, swirling about it, surging up the ravine to turn and attack from above. The boar swung its massive head. A yelping hound flew, spurting blood. Again, again the boar's head swung, dealing death. Richard dismounted, his spear in hand.

"We are with you!" shouted Desney. He and Fynn sprang from their horses before they were fully stopped. "God's legs, man. Never have I seen such a beast! Have a care."

Richard nodded, his attention focused on the boar.

"Here," said Fynn. "Take my spear. It is heavier in the shaft. You will need the strength."

Richard took it without looking, and his gloved hands could not feel the crack that ran through it. He stepped toward the whirlwind of fang and fur.

"Strike well. We are here at your side," said Desney.

The boar broke loose and charged. With a great shout, Richard struck the boar full in the chest. The animal gave an ear-splitting shriek and lunged at him. The spear shivered and broke and Richard went down under the weight of boar and dogs. He screamed as the tusks ripped into him. Desney and Fynn ran in, throwing dogs aside, stabbing at the boar with their own spears, but the boar fought on, rooting through Richard's body. Valan, Rolf, and Shends arrived and leapt from their horses. Fyan rode up, just behind them. He did not dismount, but sat staring at the scene, eyes wide in shock.

"Milord! Milord!" screamed Shends. He ran at the boar and did what the others had not: killed the beast with one clean thrust. Rolf let out a roar of rage and stabbed the dead beast again and again in a mad frenzy until the others dragged him off.

"I blame myself for his death," said Rolf. "Had I not given him that horse, another would have reached the boar first."

Desney bent low over Richard's mangled body and held his shining blade close to his mouth. It dimmed with a faint mist. "He lives yet, Highness," he said.

* * *

The falcon soared through the clear, cold, air and fetched yet another dove to his mistress. Olwen raised her gloved hand. The bird roosted on it and dropped its prey obediently to the falconer waiting beside her horse.

"Well done, Icarus, my high flier," she said, and fed him the bit of meat the falconer handed her. "Go on, Highness, fly your hawk. Alana?"

Alana turned her face from the northwest. "The horns have stopped, but they've not played the mort." Her eyes strayed northward again.

"Well, she's entitled to long for her bridegroom if she wishes," said Burrk. "I'd just as soon catch a few more of these fat little doves. By your leave, milady."

Alana nodded and he let his gyrfalcon fly.

"Who is that coming out of the wood? Someone's hurt!" said Olwen.

Alana shaded her eyes. "It's your father, Olwen, with—oh, it's just Drent in the saddle. Probably broke a fingernail."

Strenholm snorted. "Lost his horse, in any event," he said. "Well done, Burrk! A fine bird, that."

"Look! Another leading his horse," said Alana, the nervousness rising in her voice.

"It's Lord Wembers," said the sharp-eyed Olwen. "He seems sound, but his horse is limping."

"I cannot wait," said Alana. "I would ride to meet them."

"I'll escort you, my dear," offered Hounshel. The two rode off at a brisk trot.

They reached Wembers and his hobbling steed. "Bad piece of luck," said Hounshel.

"Were you hurt? Where is Richard?" Alana asked.

"I've taken a bruise or two, but nothing serious. Richard's at the head of the pack, having the time of his life."

46

Fyan burst from the wood, whipping his lathered mount. He saw them and reined abruptly. "Milord! Milady! Oh God! The boar! His spear . . . may God have mercy!"

Alana went as pale as chalk. "Richard?"

Fyan nodded. For a moment, the world swam before Alana's eyes, then righted itself. "Go to the castle. Send a cart to carry him. Tell the women to boil water and prepare bandages. Red oil. Thread to stitch him. Tell Cook we will need a tisane of sage to wash the wound, and honey to bind it and stop the bleeding. *Go!*" He spurred his horse. "And cobwebs for poultices !" she called after him.

Alana and her grandfather set off for the wood at the gallop.

* * *

Dusk darkened the room, and servants lit tapers.

"Eat, Alana, please," begged Lady Gwen.

"If the wound does not fester he will live," she replied. She did not take her eyes off the barely breathing Richard, who lay in the high bed she had expected to share with him.

"And you must be strong to nurse him to health," said Lady Gwen. "Eat."

In reply, Alana stroked Richard's cheek. She took the cup and wooden trencher from Lady Gwen and put them on a chest beside the bed.

Shends stood near the doorway, in quiet conversation with his wife, Lady Johanna. He looked haggard, as they all did that day. Hounshel entered and Shends approached.

"A word with you, Milord," he whispered. He looked nervously about, at the maidservant bringing fresh linen, the chamberlain, and Richard's cousins. "Not here. My words are for you alone. In the chapel. Meet me there."

He left. Again, this urgency, this mystery, and for what?

* * *

Richard lay unconscious. Alana sat beside him, his hand clasped in hers. Hounshel returned from the chapel, and went to Lady Johanna, still in her seat in the antechamber, her rosary in her hand. "Where is Lord Shends?"

"I know not," she whispered.

"What is so urgent? What is he trying to tell me?"

Lady Johanna shook her head. "I know not. He said naught to me."

Alana sat beside the bed and stroked Richard's fevered face. "Yes, my love," she said, as gently as a mother to a child. "You will heal. You will return to me. You will heal. We will heal the festering, and you will return to me."

Lady Gwen, sitting across the bed from Alana, shook her head.

All that night, the women sat. Alana said nothing. She held Richard's hand and sponged his forehead. As the weak winter sun rose, his breathing stopped.

"The others must be told," said Johanna.

Lady Gwen beckoned to her servant. "Carl, find Lord Hounshel and His Highness. Bring them here."

Matilda stood and quietly took the blankets from Richard's body. "Bring water, Mary," she instructed the maid. "We must wash him. Help me, Alana."

Alana sat, staring at her bridegroom's corpse. Then she broke into a keening wail. "How can you be so cold-hearted?" she raged.

Matilda faced her. Alana could see the lines etched in her face. "Alana, you forget yourself. We have work to do before we grieve."

Alana could not move. Richard, so full of life and laughter, lay before her, as cold as a clod of earth. Mary returned with two full buckets on a yoke. Other servants entered, bearing wood for the fire, cloths for the washing, and a copper cauldron to heat the water. Hounshel entered and put his arm around Alana. Mallow put his arms around Lady Gwen, and they wept for their son.

Cirgan entered and spoke softly to Lady Johanna. "I cannot find Shends."

Her jaw hardened, but she replied, "Try the wine cellar."

"I have, cousin, and his chamber, and the chapel, as well."

"Ask everyone—the servants, the guests."

He bowed and left.

Gently, the women washed Richard's corpse, and then Lord Mallow laid him in his shroud. The silent women threaded needles and sat, sewing it shut.

There was a soft tap on the door and Cirgan came in. "We have not found him. Fynn and Wickerts put him in his bed last night, but none have seen him since. He was gone when his valet looked in at dawn." He paused. "His horse is in the stable, and the sentries saw no one leave."

"Have you looked in all the dark corners? He could be. . . asleep." Their eyes met in understanding.

"I have already given the order."

They heard the sound of booted feet running in the hallway. Johanna looked up in expectation. A guardsman stood in the doorway panting, his eyes wide with terror. He dropped to one knee before Lady Johanna. "Milady," he said. "Lord Shends has hanged himself in the north tower."

Alana looked from one woman to the other: Matilda still sewing, as though she had not heard; Johanna, motionless as a statue; Lady Gwen, her hand to her mouth to muffle her gasp. A candle guttered and sputtered. Still they did not react. The guardsman got to his feet and left. Mallow bowed deeply. "I will see that all is attended to," he said to the unseeing Johanna. He left the room, pulling the door shut behind him.

Alana put down her needle and knelt before Lady Johanna. "I am so sorry, cousin," she said.

At that, the older woman's face crumpled into tears and she began to keen. Alana embraced her and howled her grief. Behind her, she could hear Olwen's heartbroken sobs. Lady Gwen, weeping, embraced her daughter.

The door opened without a knock. Robert, Fyan's son, stood in the doorway, with his father, Fynn, and Rolf. "Aunt Johanna," he said and went to embrace her. "As long as you live, you may stay with me."

"My lady," said Fyan, his gray moustache drooping. "I am so sorry. I had no idea his madness would carry him to such an end. We should have ordered a servant to stay with him last night. We thought him unconscious when we left him in his bed."

"Come, Johanna," said Fynn. "Stay with us, if you don't want to go back home with Robert. Wouldn't blame you if you wanted a change of scene."

"No need to vex her with these decisions now," said Rolf gently. "She can decide after they are buried, and Robert is invested as Lord Shends."

Alana's head swam as she realized what had happened. Robert's mother was Shend's oldest sister, and Shends had no sons. Robert, already his father's heir, would inherit the title and lands of his uncle as well. She looked at the faces of the three men, but could see nothing other than sorrow in them. Only then did the thought come into her mind, surfacing like a bubble of air from the depths of the sea: *Richard is dead. And I have no heir, nor will I.*

Chapter 8
The Crusader

The wheel of the seasons turned. Easter passed, and summer approached. Each day, the light lingered longer, but nothing could lift the darkness from Alana's heart. She clung to her duties as a shipwrecked mariner clings to a floating shard of wood.

"Uncle," said Alana one morning at breakfast. "Papa had a request for you on his deathbed." This was not precisely true, but she had decided to leave nothing to chance.

Rolf wiped his lips with the edge of the tablecloth and took a sip of fresh cider. "Yes?" he said. "I am yours to command."

"He asked that you found a university. He told me he felt you were the only man in the kingdom who could successfully undertake such a task."

Rolf's eyes widened, and he smiled. "Galeschin. Such a kind man. I regret. . ." Here, his eyes teared and he fought for control. "But what a wonderful idea. A university. I'm sure we could hire Doctor Ablemeister from the University in Benmad. He is energetic and well-connected in academic circles. No doubt he would jump at the chance. And Harbingson, the master mason who built Queen Lothana's chapel in Velendruch. I'm sure he would be just the man to design the building. And the mathematician, Ruus, we must have him."

"And Longinus, the poet," suggested Alana. "Do you think we could get him?" She glanced at her grandfather, who smiled as he buttered his bread.

"Longinus! Of course! He would be perfect to give our students a thorough grounding in classical technique. Excellent!"

He stopped and sighed. "But how can I think of my own pleasure when there the kingdom requires my services as regent? Of course, I will honor my brother's dying wish. I will write letters today to Ablemeister, Ruus, and the others. But you must realize that a project of this magnitude takes time. I will, of course, do all I can at present, but I will always keep my duties to the kingdom foremost."

He knelt on one knee before the astounded Alana. "Your humble servant, my lady." Then he swept from the room with Valan in his wake.

* * *

As the seasons revolved, Gwalhafed's affairs rode as serenely as a swan on still waters, although those of the university did not. Harbingson had accepted a commission for a cathedral in Alantoya and expected to be employed there for the rest of his life. Ruus would be delighted to teach in Gwalhafed, providing Ablemeister were not involved, and Ablemeister wrote expressing similar sentiments. Rolf explained that he was seeking alternatives, as his duties permitted, but the task was far more daunting than he could have imagined.

* * *

The following spring, a papal bull was proclaimed, granting absolution to all who would join the crusade against the heathen in Outremer.

"So, you will represent Gwalhafed on the crusade, Lord Mallow," said Rolf. "I envy you your liberty."

They stood in the courtyard of Gwalhafed Castle beside Mallow's brilliantly caparisoned stallion. Birds twittered in the glistening warmth of spring sunshine.

A smile creased Mallow's handsome face and he shook Rolf's hand heartily. He was tall and big-boned, with gray just beginning to show at his temples. "Thank you, Highness. Perhaps you will join us when your responsibilities have been taken by the princess."

Rolf laughed. "Of course, if you have left any Saracens for me to fight. I count the days!" The two men shared a back-slapping embrace. "So, off to Rhynn to take ship. You'll not make that distance in one day, I'll warrant."

"No, my lord, I and my squire will stay at an inn along the road. There's one called the Lionheart. It seems an auspicious name."

"The Lionheart," Rolf said doubtfully. "I recall staying there once. Most distressing. Crawling with vermin. The Turk's Head is much better. And of course, in Rhynn you must not trust yourself to a public house. Here is a letter to my seneschal, a most able man named Humbert. He'll see you lack for naught."

"Thank you, Your Highness." Mallow dropped his voice, and his face grew serious. "My lord, I must confess I have wronged you."

"In what way?" Rolf's eyes widened in surprise.

"I was one of those who mistrusted you, Highness. After the death of my son, I blamed you, without proof. But I have seen your dedication to duty and reverence toward the princess. I must say that I doubt you no longer. That is why I now feel free to join the crusade."

A spasm of emotion passed over Rolf's face and he fought to control it. "There has been no offense. Your mistrust has been my penance for the sins of my youth. God go with you, Mallow."

* * *

Lord Hounshel had carried out Galeschin's plan. Rolf wrote weekly to Humbert and each letter found its way to Hounshel's study before continuing its journey. But there was nothing to be discovered in them. They dealt only with the conduct of business.

"Anything of interest in his last letter, Grandfather?" Alana's quick hands continued to make flowers bloom on the cloth stretched on the frame before her.

He read from his copy. "The early wheat harvest to be sold to the Benedictine Abbey at Granton, one Sommers in Benmad to be approached regarding the sale of this year's lambs, no more than twelve gold sovereigns to be paid for the building of another warehouse near the harbor, and in postscript, a cask of well-aged brandy to be sent to the Turk's Head from his warehouse. Nothing out of the ordinary."

She sighed. "I don't know. This seems like a waste of time. Perhaps we should simply take my uncle at his word."

"Is that your wish, Alana?"

She sat silent, her needle glinting as it plied the soft woolen cloth. Beneath her hands, a rose as red as blood took shape. "I wish I knew what I want. He has done me no wrong, and his offenses against my father were so long ago, but still. . . ."

"You do not trust him?"

"Is that wrong? Am I indulging in one of those whims Papa used to warn me against?" Hounshel said nothing. His eyes had taken on that far-away look again.

"Grandfather?"

"Yes, quite," he murmured and she wondered if he were answering her question or reliving a conversation he had had years ago with someone else.

* * *

"May I ride with you a ways, my lord?" asked Murdoch, when Mallow and his squire had reached the castle gate.

"We would be honored. But be careful. I might persuade you to join us."

God's legs, how I will miss this man, Murdoch thought. *Of all the nobility of Gwalhafed, he was the first, saving only the king, to see past my low birth. Indeed, some of them have still not gotten over it.* "I have my duty," he said.

"Of course, of course. And you still mistrust the prince, if I read you aright, old friend."

"And you do not?"

"I think he has shown remorse, and certainly he has changed. You did not know him in the old days, before he was forced into exile. Believe me, he is a changed man."

"I knew him better than I would have liked. So did my wife."

"Well, yes. Inexcusable behavior. Still, I am a warrior and a judge of men. Believe me, Murdoch. I would not leave Gwalhafed if there were any doubt in my mind."

Murdoch scowled. Mallow grinned. "Well then," Mallow said, "my stubborn friend, we must agree to differ. For heaven's sake, he's even given me a letter to his seneschal and saved me the torture of bad lodgings at the Lionheart. Who'd have thought a place with that name could be worse than one called the Turk's Head?"

They forded the Eisen and climbed the twisting trail up the further side of the valley. From the top, the way sloped gently down toward the lowland kingdom of Velendruch. Murdoch rode with them to Hirday, Lord Hounshel's estate, where they put in

54

for a fine luncheon of cold venison. They parted there. Murdoch sat astride his horse, Achilles, watching Mallow's armored back glint in the early afternoon sunshine and then he turned to take the uphill way to Gwalhafed.

* * *

Candles gleamed in the well-appointed study. Tapestries and Turkish rugs covered the cold stone of the walls, and the carved chair in which the heavyset man sat was padded with cushions of red velvet with golden tassels at the corners. Had Rolf been in Velendruch, Humbert would never have presumed to sit there, but as he was not, the seneschal regarded the comfort as one of the well-earned prerogatives of his post. He read the letter, made notations in a variety of ledgers, and then turned his attention to the postscript. He singled out the key to the chest beneath the window from the thick bunch hanging from the gold chain he wore about his corpulent neck. He unlocked the chest, but did not open it. Instead, he did something quite unusual for someone so portly and dignified. He huffed down to his hands and knees and pressed a carved leaf on the front of the chest. A drawer popped out the side. From this, he took a narrow scroll and brought it over to the candle.

He unrolled the scroll, laid it on the table next to the letter, and weighted the free end with the ink pot.

"Let's see," he rumbled. "Two casks of well-aged brandy . . . ." He turned his attention to the scroll.

"Cask of . . . amontillado, that would be Strenholm; burgundy, Wickerts; brandy, Mallow—Lord Mallow and a companion. Well-aged . . . well-seasoned is poisoned; well-dressed, kidnapped; well-aged, yes, killed by the most convenient method. Turk's Head . . . not on the list . . . of course, that place on the road from Gwalhafed. And warehoused, yes."

He ran his finger down the list. "Buried, all traces removed."

* * *

Murdoch went to wait upon the princess early the next morning. Rolf was already with her, discussing the mediation of a dispute between Lord Drent and his serfs over the tariff he charged for grinding their grain at his mill—which service he had made mandatory. Murdoch paced the hallway outside her antechamber and listened to the rising and falling voices within. He could not make out the words, just Drent's braying, as irritating as fingernails on slate, and the thick, deep tones of the peasants. Finally, he ordered Alana's page John to find him as soon as the regent had left.

It was nearly noon when John came to the armory to fetch him. Alana sat in her antechamber, studying the tithes ledger. She looked up at him. "You wished to speak to me . . . without my uncle's presence."

"Mallow has left for Outremer. He feels your uncle has reformed himself. Do you agree?"

"He certainly seems to have done so."

"And you trust him?"

Alana sat in thought. "I cannot find reason to doubt him."

He held her gaze and spoke deliberately. "Do you trust him?"

Again, she paused before speaking. "No, not entirely. Do you have evidence of treachery?"

"Perhaps. You read his correspondence."

"Yes, but it only speaks of his commercial dealings in Velendruch."

"Tell me only one thing, Highness, did any letter mention 'The Turk's Head?'"

"Why, yes, this last, but only that a cask of brandy be sent there."

"God's breath," Murdoch muttered and strode from the room. It took him but a minute to pack a change of clothing into his saddlebag. On the way to the stable, he paused, then turned to the armory, where he sorted through a trunk of castoff guardsmen's uniforms until he found a serviceable belt—a plain one, with a slightly tarnished brass buckle. His own belt, with its three silver disks, he stored in the bottom of his bag.

* * *

Achilles' hooves consumed the road to Velendruch like a burning flame. The white fetlock, which had inspired Galeschin to name him, was lost in a thick coat of mud. Murdoch pushed him as hard as he dared, across the Eisen, past Hirday, to the border of Velendruch.

He showed the guards at the border station a scroll, purporting to be a message to Rolf's seneschal, which Thomas the Clerk had written for him. As he suspected, they could not read either and passed him through with a bored wave of the hand after looking at it upside-down. He reached the Lionheart, centerpiece of a village, and stopped there to water and feed Achilles and ask if, against all hope, Mallow had stayed there after all. But no, the red-faced innkeep replied. No knight from Gwalhafed had stopped there last night. Only a wool merchant and three friars. Turk's Head? Yes, five miles up the road, but he'd be a fool to go there.

"Why do you say that?" asked Murdoch.

"Den of thieves," he said. "Charges twice what I do and his cook can't hold a candle to my Mary. Can I get you something?"

Murdoch folded the collop of mutton the landlord brought him inside a trencher of bread and ate it as he paced the length of the stable yard, waiting for Achilles to finish his feed. Then he mounted and left. The road rose over a swelling hill and dropped abruptly into the next valley. From its crest he could see the Turk's Head, on the far side of the stream that meandered across the valley floor. A mill stood nearby, with a line of oxcarts waiting and several more moving toward it on the road. He spurred Achilles to a trot.

A bellow of coarse laughter mingled with the creaking of the mill wheel to his left. *Millers are everywhere the same,* he thought. The Turk's Head, with its truly inauspicious sign—a painting of a dark, ill-favored face impaled on a lance—stood to his right. The gate to its courtyard stood open, and he dismounted and led Achilles through. He stood, sweeping the narrow space with his eyes, taking in every detail. Somewhere. Somewhere in here there must be a sign of Mallow's presence. The ostler, a crabbed old man with gnarled, rheumatic hands, approached.

"See to your horse, sir?"

Murdoch handed over the reins. "A friend of mine stayed here last night, a knight with his squire. Might they still be here?"

The old man shrugged. "Plenty of folk here last night."

"You'd remember the horse. As like to mine as two peas."

The man's eyes stared for an instant. Then he looked away and grumbled. "Best ask the landlord." He shuffled off, leading Achilles toward the trough.

* * *

Murdoch strode through the dark doorway. The room was dim and smelled of stale beer. Half a dozen loiterers sprawled on benches waiting for the miller to grind their grain. The innkeep was surprisingly young, a beefy blond man with an impassive face.

"What can I do for you?" he said, without a hint of friendliness.

"Brandy," said Murdoch.

"Don't stock it," said the innkeep. "Ale or whiskey."

His customers chuckled.

"Odd," said Murdoch. "I'd heard your brandy was fit for a prince."

The landlord met his gaze, his face stone-hard, but his eyes flickered downward for an instant, to Murdoch's belt. Murdoch saw that the man relaxed upon finding no silver disks.

"Room?" he asked.

"Two farthings a night. Ten, if you want the whole bed."

"Mind if I look first?"

"Suit yourself." He waved his hand toward the narrow staircase.

The wooden building creaked with every footstep. There were three rooms above, along a narrow hallway, each the same, furnished with a broad bed with dirty sheets, save that in one the bed frame was bare. Murdoch opened the shuttered window in that room and looked out. It faced south, across a fallow field. Beyond, crows circled a knot of woods, their cries faint and angry.

He turned, and his eye caught sight of something beneath the bed. He knelt and drew it out. It was a deerskin glove, with Mallow's crest embossed on the gauntlet. He stormed down the stairs and thrust it in the landlord's face. "Where is Lord Mallow ?"

The man looked at the glove with mild surprise, but no agitation. "Oh, him," he said. "Came in last night, said he'd take a room. Then said he didn't like the look of it. Wanted his money back. Left. Probably went to the Lionheart."

The ostler held Achilles' bridle as Murdoch mounted.

"Sir," he said timidly. "There was a man here last night with a horse like yours. Didn't stay long. Headed east. Don't let on as I told you. It'd be worth my place."

Murdoch nodded gruffly and left. Behind him, the ostler stood glancing nervously toward the door to the inn. When Murdoch had left the courtyard, the innkeep stepped from the shadows and nodded. Relieved, the old man went back to his work.

Murdoch set off eastward, but the crows drew his attention to the south. A cart came out of the wood, drawn by a brindle ox, with four peasants walking beside it. Behind them the crows continued to wheel and screech. Murdoch reined Achilles and watched the slow progress of the cart. Four men with the cart, but the crows, intelligent birds, had seen more men enter the wood, else they would have settled by now. Murdoch turned Achilles' head and cantered across the field toward them.

He nodded to them, unsmiling, as he passed them, then looked into the cart. It was smeared with blood. His sword flashed out as Achilles wheeled.

"Turn the cart back," he said, his voice calm on the surface, a deadly inflection in its depths.

The serfs, eyes showing white with fear, obeyed. They reached the wood and entered it, following a rutted track. Murdoch glanced from side to side, but could see no mark, neither of wheel nor foot, leaving it. The crows swarmed overhead, their endless cries echoing. The wind picked up, and Murdoch smelled the unmistakable stench of a tannery. At last, the trees thinned and he could see it, the dark, stinking pits dug along the edge of the river, a shed back toward the wood, built of rough planks. Two men strained to pull a bloody hide against a frame while the third pounded nails into the edges of it to hold it taut for scraping.

One of the men holding the hide looked up and saw them. In a moment, the others turned.

"Back so soon, Wat?" said the master, the man with the hammer, his arms stained the same rich brown as his leather jerkin, blood dripping from his hands. "I told your master four farthings a hide, no more." He turned to Murdoch. "Who might you be?"

59

"I'm looking for a friend who lost his way," Murdoch replied. "He rode a horse like mine and wore the mate to this." He held up the glove.

The man shook his head. "This road goes nowhere, save here. He's not come down it today."

"Last night?"

"Wouldn't know."

Murdoch turned to the serfs. "Well?"

The tanner laughed, a harsh, short grunt. "You'll get no help there. They're all mute. Tongues cut out. Lord Silas is strict with his chattel."

Murdoch dismounted, his sword in his hand. "I want to look in the pits." He took a step toward the tanner.

The man shrugged. "Suit yourself. Just use a wooden pole. I won't have you ruining good hides with that pig-sticker."

The serfs turned to go. The tanners went back to their task. Murdoch sheathed his sword and began the hopeless task.

The sun had passed behind the western hills when he finished. It was all around him, as thick and acrid as the tannery stench. Lies. Lies. And no way to prove the truth. He turned Achilles head and spurred him up the slope. East. The only information given to him freely was that Mallow had headed east. Eastward he went, stopping in every hamlet, every inn, at cottage and tavern. No one had seen Lord Mallow.

* * *

On the third day, Murdoch reached the dusky city of Rhynn. The sky hung low, leaden clouds vying with the smoke of a thousand forges to blot the light of the sun. Massive gray city walls enclosed a rambling maze of streets grimed with dust from charcoal brought to feed the armorers of the mighty empire of Velendruch. At last, with many stops for directions, Murdoch found the place he sought. Prince Rolf's house seemed unimpressive from the outside, just another begrimed wooden door in another stained wall of granite, but the manservant who opened it let him into a chamber of gleaming wood. The floor, he noted, was marble, polished to a high gloss. He suspected it would be washed again the moment he departed to remove the soot his feet left.

The servant padded off to seek Humbert. Murdoch paced as he waited, sharply aware of his boots, coated with the grit of the streets of Rhynn, crunching on the shining marble of the floor. He watched them return, the spare servingman leading the massive seneschal, who despite his bulk moved as silently as a dream, slippered feet on polished stone.

"We are always glad to welcome guests from Gwalhafed," said Humbert, smiling as he waved the servant away, glancing toward Murdoch's belt. "It's a pity that you did not arrive sooner. You could have breakfasted with Lord Mallow. Have you eaten?"

"When did he leave?" asked Murdoch, aware of the harshness of his voice compared to Humbert's.

"Quite early," Humbert replied. "Before dawn. His ship leaves on the slack tide."

Murdoch held up Mallow's glove and stared into Humbert's eyes. "I found this at the Turk's Head."

Humbert's eyes widened. Then he smiled. "Ah! He had complained of losing it. I gave him a pair of my lord Rolf's. If you hurry, you may reach him at the pier. I'm sure he would be glad of an extra pair of gloves. I would offer you a stoup of wine, but for the haste you require. Take the left hand turning at the foot of the hill and follow that road to the harbor. If you hurry, you may reach Lord Mallow before the tide turns."

His hand had already lifted the latch. The door stood open. Murdoch could see the servant coming down the hall with four others.

The door closed softly behind him. The latch clicked home with precision. He mounted Achilles and rode down the hill. He had no doubt that Humbert had directed him honestly. Even before he reached the intersection, he could hear the snap of whips and the cries of the carters.

The street was thronged with carts. He fell into line behind one loaded with iron chain, its two oxen straining backward against it, resisting the weight that threatened to send them hurtling down the slope. Murdoch's heart sank. The line of carts coming toward him were loaded with fish, the boats that had caught them borne back to port, no doubt, by the last of the flood tide. The ebb would begin soon, had already begun, perchance.

The din of the street, the rumbling carts and squealing wheels, filled his ears, behind it the ever-present jangling of a thousand, ten thousand hammers striking anvils, forging swords, pikes, spears: the teeth and claws of the army of Ambrahad, King of Velendruch. Achilles flattened his ears against the din. The whites of his eyes showed, and Murdoch felt the tension rising from the great horse's flanks. He patted Achilles' withers and crooned softly to calm him. He looked around him, at the lumbering oxen, the flood of traffic coming toward him, the maze of unknown alleys, like ratholes, emptying into the major thoroughfare. Grimy buildings lined the streets, hemming him on either side. Swirling about him, the acrid smoke of a thousand forges hovered beneath a sky no less gray.

"This is the very bowels of Satan," he whispered.

At last, the road widened a hair. At the crossing of another way, Murdoch used Achilles' broad withers to shoulder a path past the cart and into the faster stream of traffic entering from the right. He guided the warhorse skillfully, taking advantage of each inch of space that presented itself. Watching urchins dodge through the throng, he considered proceeding on foot, but, looking at the rough crowd, he had little doubt that the moment he dismounted Achilles would be the last moment he saw the horse, short of paradise.

The further Murdoch progressed, the higher his despair rose. At last, Achilles passed the gate that let out from the city and stood at the top of the last approach to the harbor. Precious few ships lay moored at the piers, most of them fishing scows or the broad barges that brought pig iron down the River Heire from the mines. Only two were the high-waisted seagoing vessels that might carry crusaders to battle. Worse, the horizon was littered with dots, each one, he knew, a fully rigged ship. The tide had turned. Sighing, Murdoch urged Achilles down the slope.

He forced his way through the crowd, asking, receiving always the same answer, "Crusade ships? You missed 'em. Left on the morning tide."

Finally, he reached the piers where the crusaders' ships had lain, already piled with goods to fill the holds of the ships that would arrive on the next rising tide. He dismounted and approached a gray-headed man lounging on a bench.

"I am looking for word of Lord Mallow. He is tall and dark-haired, his shield argent with a lion rampant, gules, clutching an oak twig in its jaws."

The man looked at him quizzically. "Plenty of lions here this mornin'. Red ones, yaller ones, green, black—all the same to me. Buncha goldurned landlubbers . . ." his voice trailed off into muttered incoherence. "Them lordly lords with them lordly horses leavin' lordly horse apples all over the dock."

Murdoch looked around for better counsel. He spotted a steward supervising the unloading of a cart of dried fish. "Were you here this morning before the crusaders left?" he asked.

"Aye, and a fat lot of bother they were, too. I'm hours behind. Fifty-five more carts to unload before the ship sails. Get *on* with it, you sluggards," he shouted at the sweating crew of stevedores. He had no further words for Murdoch.

Murdoch looked out to sea. All trace of the flotilla had disappeared over the horizon. Yet there, at the end of the pier, he spied his last hope. Two liveried pages sat, dangling their feet over the edge. The elder seemed nearly old enough to be a squire, thirteen or so, and the other a mere child. Leading Achilles, he approached them gently.

"Did you see the crusaders leave?" he asked.

"Oh, yes, sir," bubbled the small one. "It were a grandly sight."

"A goodly sight, Joshua," corrected the elder. "It *was* a *goodly* sight."

"Grandly," replied Joshua. "It were too grand to be just goodly, Curt."

"I'll bet you could name all of the knights and their devices, now, couldn't you?" said Murdoch.

"Of course, said Curt. "There's Prince Idris, of course, dragons' gules on field sable, bend dexter, argent; Duke John of Hadris, Lion restant vert, field argent, bend—"

"Oh, it's easy knowing the ones from your own kingdom. Try this: field argent, lion rampant, gules. Oak twig in its jaws."

The boys considered this for a moment. "I don't think I know that one, sir," the elder confessed.

"Now, I'll give you a hint. He's tall and dark-haired, beginning to go a bit gray. Rides a horse as like to mine as two peas. No doubt you saw him here this morning. Or did you?"

The boys thought. A flock of gulls wheeled above, crying like lost souls.

At last, Curt spoke. "Well, sir, there were quite a few tall knights, sir, most all of them, in fact, and, Joshua, was it five or six of 'em had black horses?"

"Six," Joshua said. "Maybe eight. Ten."

"Where did you say he was from, sir?"

"Gwalhafed."

The boys regarded Murdoch silently. He watched their eyes look toward his belt.

"Are *you* from Gwalhafed? Do you know Murdoch?"

Murdoch smiled. "I am from Gwalhafed. And I have *seen* Murdoch." *In a mirror.*

"He's old, like you, isn't he?" said Curt.

"Oh, I suppose he is, but he's much bigger." He watched their eyes travel from his head to his feet and across the breadth of his shoulders.

"Oh," they said.

"Well, sir," Curt continued. "Should you see him again, tell him that his size won't save him from me, no more than it saved my uncle, Sir Brian Borrenough, from him. I am Curtis Borrenough. You tell him for me."

"Well, Curt, that I will. I may even seek him out to warn him."

"Master Curtis! Joshua! How dare you break your word to me!"

The boys grimaced. "Sudworth. Our tutor. We're in for it now." They ran to him. "Honest, it wasn't our fault. That man wanted to know the devices of all the knights on the crusade. Grilled us for *hours.* Almost as bad as you, Sudworth. But we passed, didn't we, sir? Oh, Sudworth, you would have been proud of us."

Murdoch mounted Achilles and rode into the tutor's glare. "Fine lads. Skilled in heraldry. A top-notch job. Sorry to keep them. Didn't know they were wanted."

And he rode on, not stopping to see if the flattery had had any effect.

Chapter 9
A Dove in a Snare

Alana sat on the window seat, gazing despondently from her chamber window. Under the pretext of needing to rest, she had bought half an hour's solitude in her chamber to be alone with her thoughts.

Olwen married Abbersley yesterday, in accordance with the promise Abbersley extracted from Lady Gwen on her deathbed. She went to the altar with neither a tear nor a smile. Only fourteen, and he older than her father.

I pray every day for word of Lord Mallow. There has been no word from him, not that much news ever comes back from Outremer. Lady Gwen died clutching the glove Murdoch had brought back from Velendruch. It was all she had left of her husband. Murdoch is as full of black suspicion as ever. Lord Burrk has gone to his everlasting reward, his lands and title to his grandson Emil, whom Rolf has befriended.

I shall be crowned in just a month, and then the duties of rule will be mine alone. My uncle has been steadfast in carrying out his duties as regent, and I could not ask for a more able person to fill the post, but he is reserved by nature, and I cannot feel any closeness to him. I should feel more grateful. Murdoch, of course, refuses to trust him. I realize that I must take into account Murdoch's hatred of Rolf and steer a middle path between them. It is so difficult. I cannot afford to lose the support of either man.

Papa, she thought. *And Richard. Why have you abandoned me?*

She sighed and returned to the anteroom. Crickets chirped and wood doves murmured outside the chamber windows, mingled with Matilda Nursemaid's faint snoring as she slept bolt upright in her seat near where Alana's new ladies were sitting. Candles gleamed on the gold circlets the maidens wore as token of their rank. They plied their needles, stitching seed pearls to the bodice of Alana's coronation dress.

"I have a riddle!" exclaimed Serena, Fynn's daughter, the youngest of the new ladies. Her gown rustled as she bounced in her seat. "What goes upon two legs, then four legs, then three?"

"Serena," said Drent's sister Ermentrude. "The riddle is, 'What goes upon four legs in the morning, two legs at midday, and three in the evening?' and the answer is "Man, who crawls as an infant, walks upright as an adult, and hobbles with a cane in his dotage.'" She smiled at Serena with the air of one who is so much wiser and more accomplished.

Hildegard, Fyan's daughter, shot a glance toward the sleeping Matilda before whispering, "Doesn't she sound just like her brother, Highness?" in a passably nasal imitation of Lord Drent.

"Well, I suppose you think you're so smart, your ladyship," said Serena, pouting. "The riddle *I* posed is: 'What goes upon two legs, then four legs, then three?'"

"A pig?" guessed Hildegard.

"A codfish?" said Ermentrude, with no small load of sarcasm freighting her voice.

Alana seethed. *Blessed Mother of God! I will lose my mind if I have to listen to another minute of this drivel.* She picked up her needle and searched her workbasket for thread.

"Do you wish to solve the riddle, Highness?" asked Serena.

Alana shook her head, keeping her eyes cast down to hide her anger.

"A knight!" exclaimed Serena. "He walks as a child, rides a horse as a man, and leans on a cane in his old age!" She looked quite pleased.

"That's ridiculous!" said Ermentrude. "I've never heard such a silly riddle in my life."

"I made it up myself." Serena began to pout again.

God's breath, Alana thought, and wished she knew more barracks oaths. *These women are idiots.*

Serena practiced her pout in the mirror.

"I see you've heard Emil's coming tomorrow," said Hildegard.

"And what of it?" asked Serena, with the sort of bored voice that can only be summoned by one who is fascinated with the subject.

"Well, since you're not interested, I believe I'll ask him to take me hawking."

Serena scowled, a sign that she had taken Hildegard's bait. "Aren't you a little *old* for him, my lady?"

Enough! thought Alana, pushing away her feeling of helplessness and casting about for a way to get rid of these women.

Hildegard smiled. "I don't think he's interested in *little girls.*"

Another nap was out of the question. Alana hated the thought of sitting alone in her room like a prisoner, listening to them bicker.

Serena's face grew red, and her eyes blazed. She opened her mouth.

"I've had enough sitting," said Alana. "Let's play hide and seek. Serena, you're It."

She ran from the room, gratified to hear Matilda's snoring stop with a snort, and her fuddled cry of "Decorum, ladies!" Alana raced up the nearest of the corkscrew stairways that riddled the castle. Her feet, in their soft slippers, made no sound. She stopped at the top, breathless, her back pressed against the heavy door that led to the walk along the parapet, not daring to risk the squeak of the hinge.

"Which way do you think she went?" Hildegard's whisper echoed up the stair.

"The library, no doubt." That was Ermentrude.

"Or the kitchen," said Serena. "That's where *I* would go."

"I *know,*" said Hildegard. The whispers receded down the hall.

Alana cautiously tried the latch ad found it unlocked. She squeezed through, grateful that the hinge was well oiled, and stood, gasping for breath, eyes closed, her back against the door. She could hear the whisper of steel scraping stone.

"Something chasing you, Highness?"

Alana jumped, with a little shriek. Murdoch's daughter, Sophie, sat on the parapet, sharpening her sword. She was dressed in men's clothing, as usual, with her coppery hair pulled straight back into a braid. "Don't see you up here very often."

"No, I suppose not," Alana said, pretending calmness.

"So, who are you running from?"

"Oh, just playing hide and seek with my ladies."

"Hide and seek? I always wondered what highborn ladies did to keep busy."

"It was all I could think of. I couldn't stand another moment in that room with them."

Sophie nodded, wide-eyed in mock surprise. "I can believe that."

"They're supposed to be my friends. They're so . . . so . . . well, stupid."

Sophie stopped honing her blade and leaned forward. "I *had* noticed that."

"They can't discuss the classics—not Virgil, not Plato, not even Agricola," continued Alana. "They'll have estates to run one day. You'd think they'd at least have an interest in Agricola."

"Shocking," said Sophie. "Imagine not taking an interest in Agriwhatsis."

". . . *cola* . You can't know how awful it is to have no friends to talk to."

"I can, Princess." Jaw set, Sophie stood and sheathed her sword.

"I suppose you can," said Alana. "I'm sorry."

Sophie passed by Alana and reached for the door. She opened it a crack. The voices of the ladies echoed up the staircase, growing louder. She closed the door again. "Stand behind the door. Hold in your skirts so they don't show." She took her seat on the parapet again and began to sharpen her dagger.

"Highness?" Ermentrude flung back the door.

Alana pressed herself back against the wall. Through the crack, she could see Serena and Hildegard pressed close behind Ermentrude. Sophie gave the ladies a glare that would have stopped a bull in full charge. Her hands never stopped gliding the blade over the worn surface of the stone. With a chorus of mouse-like squeals, the three turned and scurried down the stairs.

Sophie grinned. "Now, *that* was fun."

"Well done," said the princess. She paused a moment, then said, "It's getting dark."

"I don't suppose we can let you get a chill, Highness."

"I can't go down the stairs. They'll find me."

Sophie stood. Although four years younger than Alana, she stood a full head taller than the tiny princess.

"I'll teach you a new way to get to the library."

She led Alana along the apron, the narrow walkway along the top of the castle wall. Between the crenellations to her left, Alana caught glimpses of the sweeping view to the south. The castle stood atop a gray cliff with rolling downs at its foot, tapering to the flat expanse of marsh and beyond it the merest glimmering of the sea. To her right lay the castle roof, and from that side she could hear the clatter of the courtyard. Abruptly, the walkway ended in another crenelated wall. Sophie climbed up on it and leapt.

"Is this a jest?" Alana demanded.

"Come on, it's only about three feet wide."

Alana peered nervously over the edge. "And a hundred down, I'll warrant."

Sophie shrugged. "Don't look down. Come on. Here, I can reach your hand. On three, you jump, I'll pull. A baby could do it."

Alana stood, looking across the gap, ashen-faced.

"Well, then, I'll go down and get your ladies to fetch you ," Sophie said, and turned to go.

"No, don't. You have the subtlety of a torturer. Here, take my hand."

"Remember, one *big* jump. Two little ones won't do it. One, two, *three*!"

Alana flew across the gap with enough force to knock them both into a heap. Sophie grinned. "Not bad for a highborn lady."

Alana picked up her circlet and set it back on her head. "More fun than Agricola. More fun than Homer, even."

"Homer. That story about the Greek war with all those heathen gods butting in all the time?"

"You've read Homer?"

"Your father used to read it to my father. He'd tell it to me for bedtime stories. The library's down those stairs."

* * *

What a strange girl, thought Alana, as she padded down the empty hallway toward the library. *Of all the people in the castle to know Homer.*

* * *

What a strange girl, thought Sophie, as she climbed up the roof and slid down the other side. *Spends all her time locked up inside with books and those stupid twits to keep her company. Still, she has more spunk than I ever expected. Strange game of hide and seek, with three seekers and only one hiding.* She slid down a rainspout to the top of the wall between the courtyard and the stables, walked the length of it, lifted a loose slate, and dropped into the hayloft.

* * *

Rolf and his guests sat in his chamber, sipping port.

"But my lord," said Fynn, his tremendous moustache quivering, "how could we hope to conquer Amytans? They are ten times our size and, thanks to your late brother, we have practically no army and nothing in the way of armaments."

"I have acquired ten thousand gold ducats' worth of weaponry—enough to outfit three thousand men—which our friend Valan has been kind enough to store in the dungeon of his castle. It should do for a start."

"The princess approves, then?" Fyan asked, running his long, slender fingers through his gray beard, as was his habit when nervous.

"One can hardly expect a woman to comprehend such matters. I did this on my authority as regent."

"But to conquer Amytans with three thousand men?" exclaimed Drent in his nasal voice. "This is madness. They must have twenty times that number under arms."

"Amytans is rich," Valan replied, "but weakened by their recent war against Dorsland. Its army may seem large, true, but it is a hollow shell, full of young recruits, untried in battle and scattered from Dorsland south to Zilgharia. Thanks to our treaties with them, there are no fortifications—no men stationed between here and the king's castle at Arnhem."

"*Carpe diem,*" said the prince, leaning back in his chair and contemplating the cathedral of his hands. "What is the measure of a man, or a kingdom, but that it seize the opportunities given it by fate? Are we of Gwalhafed to remain soft, a land of woolly-pated shepherds, ruled by fear and womanish ways, the laughingstock of Christendom? Or shall we show our manly virtue in acts of daring and courage and reap the rich rewards of power and everlasting fame?"

Alana could hear his voice as she passed the door to his chamber.

70

"Given stealth, and surprise," Valan added, "Amytans can be taken. This is not madness. It is a plum ripe for picking." There was a murmur of agreement.

* * *

"Father?" said Sophie as she burst through the door to their chambers. He sat on a stool before the fire, wiping the fine filings from his sword with a piece of chamois. "Have you ever heard of hide and seek played with three looking for one?"

"Aren't you a little old for hide and seek?"

"It seems the princess is not. I found her hiding on the parapet. She made light of it, said it was the only way she could get rid of her ladies, not that I blame her. But all three of them came up after her."

Murdoch scowled. "Did she go with them willingly?"

"Never had to. I scared them witless. It was wonderful! The way they screamed, you'd have thought I was a forest faerie."

"Where is she now?" He was already on his feet.

"I took her across the parapet to the other end of the castle, sent her down the staircase nearest the library. Where are you going?"

"Out for a walk. Stay here."

The door slammed shut behind his broad-shouldered shadow. She would wait five breaths, she decided, before she followed.

* * *

So that's their game! War with Amytans, of all the bombastic idiocy! At last the viper shows himself. Alana felt the burden of doubt drop from her shoulders. *Grandpapa must be told, and Wickerts, Cirgan, and Murdoch as well. I will find Murdoch now.*

Murdoch strode up the cold stone hallway. He could see Alana, crouched outside Rolf's door, and behind her . . .

"Oh! There you are!" bubbled Serena. "You're It, Highness." She had come up behind Alana as quietly as a cat.

Murdoch stepped back into the shadows. Inside Rolf's chamber, the murmur ended abruptly and Rolf, after only a second's hesitation, said, "And then, Valan, after you roused this covey of plovers—"

"Begging your pardon, Highness," said Drent, "but it is a *congregation* of plovers. Partridges fly in coveys."

"My error, Drent. Ah, is someone at the door?"

Serena, her eyes satisfied slits, pushed it open.

"Alana!" Rolf said. "Ladies, you grace us with your presence. Valan was just telling us of one of his recent hunts, near Amytans' border."

"That was where I was surprised by the plovers," Valan added, "as I stopped in an orchard to pick a ripe plum."

Alana looked closely at each of the men's faces. Valan stared back at her coolly. Rolf showed only a surprised innocence, as though someone had made a joke he did not understand. Drent grinned smugly. Fyan and Fynn looked like pages caught stealing tarts from the kitchen.

"Oh, that was such fun!" said Serena, giggling. "Let's play again, Highness."

"Yes, let's," said Alana. "Uncle, my lords, if you will excuse us."

Murdoch watched from the shadows as Fynn's daughter, joined now by Fyan's daughter and Drent's sister, swept Alana away from him. They chattered lightheartedly, but he could not deny the feeling of foreboding in the pit of his stomach.

* * *

"And where is your daughter, my lord Fyan?" Rolf asked, once the door was shut behind them, his pale eyes burning with controlled rage.

"I . . . I hardly know, Highness."

"My lady is never to be unattended." Rolf's eyes bore into Fyan's like the blade of a dagger. Then he relaxed and leaned back in his chair. "It is unbefitting one of her rank. Leave us now, gentlemen."

They rose and bowed.

"Valan, I wish a word with you." He waited until the others had gone. "Of all the incompetent stupidity!" He railed. "What fool left the door open?"

"I believe Drent was the last in, Highness."

"He is a danger to us all. We will have to deal with him shortly. And I doubt Alana will believe your story about the plum orchard. First, we must deal with the princess. "

Chapter 10
Sophie

The next morning, when Murdoch returned from his walk, he found the castle courtyard humming with guardsmen. He pretended not to notice and climbed the stairs to the top of the castle wall to get as good a view as possible. He stood next to Grimbold, the sergeant-at-arms.

"They're laying wagers," Murdoch said.

"Mmm," the other grunted.

"Who are you betting on?"

Grimbold pointed to the smaller of the two warriors, swaddled in thick practice padding, who had just entered the courtyard from the armory.

"Who is he?"

Grimbold hesitated a moment before answering. "New recruit," he grunted.

Murdoch looked at him suspiciously, but before he could frame another question, the two combatants crossed swords and began to fight. Murdoch watched with an appraising eye. The recruit fought surprisingly well, Murdoch thought, with quick reflexes and a fluid unity of body and blade. The other seemed a lumbering carthorse by comparison. He would make note of this young warrior's name.

As the fight progressed, Murdoch noted that the smaller swordsman, with considerable skill, was slowly directing the larger in the direction of the watering trough. At last, the larger man stood less than a pace before it, his back to it, unaware of its position. The recruit parried the blow aimed at him, darted under his opponent's guard, and the other, turning to follow, tripped over the edge of the trough and fell headfirst into it.

The courtyard erupted in a burst of cheers and laughter. Guardsmen raced to the trough and pulled the sputtering swordsman upright. They pulled off his helmet and water gushed out.

"Stimms!" called Murdoch from above. "My daughter could do better than that."

The smaller warrior removed her helmet.

"Thank you, Father," she called back. Murdoch rolled his eyes and glared at Grimbold.

A shower of high-pitched giggles descended on the courtyard like a gray drizzle of rain. Alana's ladies had watched the contest from the windows of her chamber.

"Oh, look! Daddy's little girl," Hildegard said with a giggle.

"Oh, no! Daddy's little boy," said Ermentrude.

Sophie heard them, but refused to give them the satisfaction of thinking she had. She removed her protective padding and ran up the stairs to her father's side, breathing heavily from the exertion, glowing with victory. Her height and her honesty, both deemed excessive for a woman, came from her father, but she had her mother's large, dark eyes, abundant copper-colored hair, and dancing grace.

Murdoch looked at his radiant daughter, her hair straying from its warrior's braid, and shook his head. *What have I done? She can neither cook nor sew, and she can best any man of Gwalhafed at sword, saving only myself. By God, a son could have done no better. But still. . . .*

"You dance well," he said.

She laughed and kissed his cheek. "And why not? You taught me."

He shook his head in mock dismay and tousled her hair. *So I have*, he thought, *and to what end?* "Where will we find you a husband who won't mind being beaten at sword?"

"I best an opponent twice my size and all you can talk of is marriage?"

"Why were you fighting him?"

"The pig insulted me."

"Insulted you? How?"

"He called me a *pretty*." She scowled. "*Little*." Her thumb and forefinger showed just how small. *"Thing."* Her eyes widened in amazement. "Can you imagine?"

74

Murdoch sighed. Her mother would have known what to say. *Her mother.* The darkness began to seize his heart and he veered away from it, to safe ground.

"Strategy lesson," he said. "What is the best response to a forehand cut from a left-handed opponent?"

She thought a moment. "Step back, bringing your sword up to block, and then step in and strike quickly once the sword has passed."

"Good," he replied. "But here's a better. Step well back and pivot away, then shift your weight forward as you come around. It lends more power to your arm."

She considered this for a moment, and then grinned. "My future husband won't stand a chance so long as you're around to advise me."

* * *

Alana had noticed that her ladies were especially attentive that morning. Led by Hildegard, they all rose early and came to her chamber twittering like birds. She had little patience with their prattle, and was relieved when the duel in the courtyard caught their attention and she was able to slip out the door unnoticed. She grabbed her page John, now eleven and nearly as tall as she, by the hand and, hushing his protests with her finger to her lips, dragged him with her.

Later that stifling, cloudy morning, she burst out of the counting house clutching a scroll of parchment. Behind her, as the door flapped on its hinge, Thomas, the aged clerk, perched wide-eyed on his tall stool, like an astounded crane. John scurried behind her, burdened with more parchment, an ink bottle, and a sheaf of quills. She did not return to her chambers, but went to a small room near the chapel. There, she wrote three letters and sealed them. Then she sent John to fetch Murdoch. She paced the length of the narrow room.

"My lady," Murdoch said as he entered.

"Close the door," she snapped.

He did so and crossed the room to the end farthest from the door, where she stood, and waited for her to speak, one eyebrow raised quizzically.

She began to speak, then stopped and turned to her page. "You must leave now. If anyone asks, you were playing in the dungeon all morning and have not seen me."

He looked at her uncertainly and bowed. She waited until the door's latch clicked behind him before she turned to the warrior.

"My uncle intends to attack Amytans. I overheard him plotting last night. I have spent the day in the counting house, examining the records. Ten thousand gold ducats are missing. I suspect it is part of my uncle's strategy. Only you, my grandfather, Wickerts, and Cirgan are left of those who count themselves my friends. Give these letters to your most trusted man. Tell him to place each one in the hands of those men, and none other, and to await their reply."

Murdoch smiled grimly as he took the letters. "Is that what you learned at Rolf's keyhole last night?"

"You saw me?"

"Sophie told me of a very strange game of hide and seek. I feared for your safety. You were found out before I could reach you. You are not safe here."

"What can I do?"

"Rolf has the upper hand. If we can get you to Hirday, under your grandfather's protection, we may be able to act from there. Contrive a way out of the castle. Go hawking this afternoon. Sophie and I will help you get separated from your ladies. After that, it is only a question of who has the fastest horse."

She nodded. Then Murdoch continued. "I will prepare a diversion. Go to the chapel. If anyone finds you there, it is where you have been all morning."

Murdoch stuffed the letters inside his jerkin. Cautiously, he opened the door and looked out. The hallway was empty.

He left the room, shutting the door behind him without a sound. *So many deaths,* Murdoch thought, *all to Rolf's benefit, and none, it seems, his responsibility. Richaard's death. Shends' suicide. Strenholm to old age, after the death of his dear friend Burrk. Two years and no word from Mallow. And no connection to Rolf. Perhaps it is, as some say, that God Himself opposes a woman's ruling the kingdom.* Murdoch sighed. Such speculation was not the realm of the warrior. He had sworn to Galeschin that he would protect the princess. If God wished otherwise, that was God's business.

A young page dressed in the green and gold of Gwalhafed came skipping around the corner of the corridor. He looked up to see Murdoch watching him and instantly stopped and began to walk as a proper page ought. He stopped in front of Murdoch and bowed. "Sir, the prince requests your presence."

How unusual, Murdoch thought.

"Tell His Highness I will be there presently." He turned toward the guardroom to dispatch the letters. The page scampered off to deliver the message.

* * *

The regent sat in his chambers with his companions of the previous evening. Murdoch entered and bowed. Although a chair stood opposite his in front of the empty fireplace, Rolf made no motion for Murdoch to take it. He sat, regarding the warrior coolly, with that gift he had of making any companion, no matter how much larger, feel that he was being looked down upon from a great height.

"I want you to take the Hills on the Amytans border."

"Why, my lord?" the grizzled soldier replied, crossing his arms.

Rolf sipped wine from his goblet. He placed it on the small table beside his chair, next to an empty goblet and full carafe. "There are great stands of timber there, quite valuable."

"Blood for firewood is no bargain," replied Murdoch, eyeing the empty goblet and remembering the hundreds of times he had sat in this room with Galeschin, discussing Gwalhafed's affairs over a cup of claret.

"And their heights overlook Amytans," Rolf continued. "We need to control them for our defense."

There was a hum of agreement from the others.

"Our treaties with them have stood for twenty years."

"Perhaps, but Amytans is a warlike state. Now that they have humbled Dorsland, I fear we are next."

"The terrain is rugged and not uninhabited."

"Forest faeries? Surely you don't believe those children's tales." Rolf reached for his wine. As he leaned back contemptuously in his chair, Murdoch noticed the flash of gold on his chest. Rolf wore a medallion on a heavy chain, its jewels picked out, Murdoch recalled, by Joy's father, in his descent into drunkard's hell. Murdoch knew that Rolf was baiting him, and determined not to give him the satisfaction of an outburst. His jaw clenched.

"Sword master Beecham told me they can ride on the wind and the trees carry messages to them, whispering from branch to branch," Murdoch said. For all he knew, it could be true. Beecham owed his life to them, and to the old woman, Dunwadi. He owed his life to Beecham, for training him to face Sir Brian that long-ago day. And now he would close the circle, by stopping an invasion of their land before it started.

Rolf leaned forward suddenly. "Are you telling me you believe that superstitious prattle?" he snapped.

Murdoch's hand moved toward his sword hilt. They glared at each other, a satisfied smile playing on Rolf's lips. Murdoch said nothing. Drent chuckled and nudged Fyan's ribs with his elbow.

"Don't be a fool, Murdoch. If Amytans controls those heights, they can swoop down on us like a hawk in a henyard."

"If," Murdoch replied. He took a long, slow breath. Rolf watched with half-closed eyes. "The taking would be no easier for them than for us," Murdoch said. "If they are foolish enough to try, let them wear themselves out."

The nobles grumbled among themselves.

Rolf leapt to his feet and strode to Murdoch. "I am giving you a direct order!" he shouted. "You will leave in the morning and take those hills."

Murdoch met his eye. "I will not risk my men to obey an order given by a fool," he said in a level tone. It hardly qualified as an outburst, but, for Rolf's purposes, it was enough. The others, Drent foremost, burst into angry protest at this *lèse-majesté*.

"You are relieved of command and restricted to quarters." Rolf motioned to the guards flanking the doorway. "Escort him."

"I know my way," Murdoch growled as he strode away, the guards scampering to keep up. Behind him, the angry voices rang in his ears and above them all fluted the high tenor of Drent, praising Rolf's wisdom and strategic sense.

* * *

The castle slept, except for the guards on the outer wall and Rolf and Count Valan. They sat before a small fire, kindled for light, not warmth, in Rolf's chamber.

"Prince Roderik's knighting comes at an opportune time," Rolf said, as he refolded the invitation. "You will represent us at the ceremony. Enjoy yourself at the feast. I understand King Ulrik lays a bountiful table. Don't get hurt in the jousting. And when you return, bring this." He held up another document, richly beribboned in blue and yellow and sealed with a mighty lump of red wax. "They tell me Prince Roderik is quite a catch. It would be impolitic for my niece to refuse such a proposal of marriage, especially if she understands that it would avert a war."

"Highness! I had long thought that as your most trusted vassal, you would reward me with her hand in marriage."

"And let you breed a competing heir? I think not."

"And Roderik would not? What will Amytans do when she lands on their doorstep?"

Rolf smiled, his white teeth shining amid his dark beard. "Why do you think I would let her reach Amytans?"

Chapter 11
The Minstrel

As Rolf spun his webs in Gwalhafed Castle, a slight, graying, mouse-haired man slept beneath an apple tree, wrapped in a patched brown cloak. His name was Phillipe, and his craft was storytelling. Word of Prince Roderik's knighting had reached not only the flower of the realms of that part of the world, but also, so to speak, its roots. Phillipe was one of throngs of minstrels, jesters, acrobats and prestidigitators who flocked to Amytans to add to the luster of the festivities. He had heard of the event late, and lagged some days' journey behind the others. A man of modest talents and means, he walked, and slept in the open when he could not barter his services for lodging. This day he had passed no tavern, and was condemned to spend his night on the ground and to sup on wormy apples.

He woke in darkness, to find the upper half of the crescent moon risen well into the sky. He gazed at it in sleepy puzzlement, wondering where its nether half had got to, and rubbed his eyes.

"Young man," a voice whispered.

He sat bolt upright to find that the moon had merely been hiding itself behind the bent figure of an old woman dressed in a shapeless shift.

"Oh!" he yelped. "You frightened me."

"Have you any food for a poor old woman?" she asked, her voice as soft as a breeze through a meadow.

Phillipe patted his pockets for a moment and then smiled sadly. "In truth, old woman, I don't even have food for myself." He got to his feet. "There are apples in this tree, though. I can pick some for you."

"You are a kind young man." The woman sat and regarded him expectantly.

Young man, thought Phillipe. *Such flattery.* It had been ten years and more since anyone had called him that. Still, it made sense for her to do so. Her long, loose hair shone white in the moonlight and her back was bent like a shepherd's crook. He climbed the tree, picked half a dozen apples, and tucked them into his jerkin. Then he descended cautiously and gave her four of them.

"They're not much," he said, biting into the first of the two he had kept for himself . "Look out for worms."

To his surprise, the apple was sweet and juicy, with a hint of tart spiciness, not one of the poor, bitter, worm-riddled things he had eaten earlier. "Oh!" he said in surprise. "Here, take this one. It's good."

"Kind and generous, both," she whispered. In the darkness he could barely see her dark eyes regarding him. "Thank you, but no. All apples are the same to me."

Puzzled, he continued eating. Her apples were gone, which added to his confusion. How could she have eaten them so quickly?

"Where do you journey, young man?"

He tossed the core across the road. "To Amytans, for the grand feast. I am late, but if I don't stop anywhere along the way, I will be there in time."

"You are a kind young man, and I will reward you." She stood straight, and her hair gleamed white, with a faint radiance of its own. "You are about to begin a quest. Your greatest work is at hand."

Phillipe stood slack-jawed before her.

"You must continue your journey," she said. "But you must refuse no opportunity to perform. You must stop at every castle you pass."

"But I will be late for the feast!"

"That is of no import."

"But—"

"Do as I say and all will go well."

"But . . ."

She turned her back on him and began to walk away. Before she had taken two steps, he was alone and wondering if he had dreamed it all. But there, in his hand, was the last apple.

* * *

The next morning, as Valan, with a troop of attendants, rode out the gate, the slight, graying man was among the peasants who stepped aside to allow the noble to pass. Unlike the others, he did not bow, but stood quietly watching the scene with interest. When the traffic resumed, he continued on his way.

"State your business," said the grizzled guard at the gate.

"I am a teller of tales, my friend," the man replied. "Am I to gather that the lord of this castle has just left?"

"No," snorted the guard. "That's just his shadow. The regent's home, as always."

"The regent. And the prince, as well?"

"Prin*cess*. You're not from these parts, are you?"

"No. I am Phillipe, from Albi, far to the south and west."

The guard grunted. Had the man said he had come from the moon or Timbuctoo, it would have meant as much to him. "I suppose you'll be trying your luck at the castle."

"It is always the courteous thing to do, to offer one's service first to a noble lord or lady."

"Well, if you've a tale or two for us common folk, the place to go is the Cock and Bull. Ask for Saul, the innkeep. He's an honest man, pours good beer and spreads a fine table."

"Thank you, my friend. I shall do that. Your name, if I may, so that I may send word to you when I perform there."

"Grimbold."

"Ah, a fine name for a warrior. I shall remember that for my next tale."

The old soldier's weathered skin reddened, if such a man could be said to blush, and he smiled.

Beyond the creak of wains and the rustle of grain being poured into storage bins, there was little activity in Gwalhafed Castle, and no visitors. Consequently, Phillipe found a warm welcome. After he was shown to a small bedchamber and fed in the kitchen, a page led him to the solar.

The princess, the regent—Phillipe's quick eye took them in. A chessboard lay between them, the pieces in disarray, the black king prone.

"Highness," he gave her a sweeping bow. "My lord." This bow was more restrained, befitting the difference in their rank. His

82

eyes met Rolf's, and for just an instant Phillipe thought he had given offense, that this man was not content to be second to any-one, but then the noble was looking at him with an expression of amused benignity. Perhaps it had been a trick of the light. He looked at the princess, so wrapped in sadness she seemed not to notice him.

"What is your pleasure this evening, my lady? A tale of adventure, of knightly deeds? A song, perhaps, of love?"

Alana looked up . She looked entirely despondent and Phillipe could see that had the bard Taliesin himself stood before her, she would have no heart for stories, nor poems, nor songs.

"Good minstrel," she said, "I am sure any little thing would please me."

Phillipe turned to the regent. "My lord?" he inquired.

"You have traveled far?"

"Yes, my lord."

"And seen many things?"

"It is unavoidable, my lord."

"Have you been through Velendruch?"

"Just, my lord."

"Are they building many ships?"

"As I recall, every slip was filled with a ship abuilding."

"Hmmm . . ."

It was by far the strangest evening Phillipe had ever spent in his entire career. Not one story, not one song, not even a single rhyme or jest passed his lips. He was glad of it, at the end, since Rolf's relentless questioning about affairs in every place he had ever set foot had left him feeling as drained as a grape at the bottom of a wine press.

The princess said nothing, only sat looking at him with her large, sad, slate-blue eyes. She had the most remarkable hair, utterly red. Not the coppery orange that most people call red, but dark, absolute, intense as blood, with lighter strands that glimmered like the light of the fire in the hearth. That alone might be worth a song. *I'll have to leave out the freckles, though.*

At last, Rolf seemed satisfied. "And where do you journey next, minstrel?"

"To Amytans, my lord, to perform at the celebration of the prince's knighting. It is said that every knight in Christendom will be there."

The princess, although she had not moved, now seemed wholly awake and present. As he watched the pair, Phillipe had the dizzying sensation that he was drowning in invisible currents.

* * *

He was awakened the next morning by a young page conveying the princess's invitation to breakfast. He dressed quickly and followed the boy to a cheerful garden where a table for two had been laid.

"Most beautiful of ladies," he said as he bowed.

"I am utterly alone and at the mercy of my enemies," she replied, speaking quickly and in a low voice. "During my uncle's regency all but three of my supporters have died, changed allegiance, or fallen into disgrace. Only yesterday Murdoch was stripped of his rank and put under house arrest. There is no help for me within these walls."

"My lady, surely things cannot be so bad as that."

"Don't waste my time with reassurances. You don't know what you're talking about. I need your help."

Phillipe blinked in surprise. This was hardly the abstracted maiden of the previous evening.

"In any way I can, my lady."

"Good." She suddenly stopped. "Would you prefer wine or ale with your sausage, my good minstrel?"

He heard footsteps on the flagstone path behind him. "Wine," he said, delighted at the opportunity. "Well-watered," he added quickly, so as not to seem too eager.

"Breakfast in the garden," Rolf said, beaming at them sunnily. "What a splendid idea! May I join you?"

* * *

After breakfast, during which the princess had seemed as dispirited as the evening before, Phillipe went in search of his friend the guardsman. At the barracks, he was told that Grimbold's duties would end at the dinner hour, and he left word that he would be at the Cock and Bull. As he turned to leave, a page, who had been quietly waiting, cleared his throat and caught his attention. "Master Phillipe, the regent would have a word with you."

He followed the boy back to the garden where they had break-fasted. The table had been removed and Rolf paced as he waited. He smiled at Phillipe and gave the page a wave of dismissal. "Sit, please," he said.

They sat side by side on the plain stone bench. Rolf sat silent, watching the ants dispose of crumbs from the recent meal. Then he sighed heavily and turned his eyes to the minstrel.

"I am concerned about my niece," he said. "These past years have weighed heavily on us all. Our kingdom has been beset by disaster. My royal brother, her betrothed, and then, one after another, our trusted vassals have been taken from us, by illness, by ill chance. I am afraid it has affected her mind. You can see for yourself how despondent she is. I fear for her. She sees enemies where only good will exists. I fear for Gwalhafed if she gains power.

"Now, I know there are those who speak against me. I will admit, in my youth I was as rash a fellow as could be imagined. How little do the young know their deeds will cling to them. For seventeen years I have repented sorely. I have given offense to none, but still some hold me to blame for the calamities of the kingdom. I have done all in my power to make amends, humbled myself to those I had offended in the days of my foolishness, and yet there are some who still bear me no love. It just shows the need of Christian forgiveness in the world." He shook his head, as if to throw off his weary thoughts, and then looked at Phillipe. "But I did not mean to burden you with my troubles. I ask a boon."

"Yes, my lord."

"There are those who say that it is against the will of God for a woman to rule. I cannot read God's mind. I can but do my sworn duty, to hold the kingdom in trust until she reaches her majority." He sighed again and regarded Phillipe sadly. "You intend to go to Amytans. And every knight in Christendom, they say, will be there. Many are noble, no doubt, but there are those, I am sure, who would see their opportunity to gain a kingdom by marrying a madwoman. Make no songs of Gwalhafed, I beg you! Or better yet, avoid the celebration entirely. Here," he said, as he removed a small purse from within his doublet. "This should recompense you for any loss." Rolf stood. "I must attend to my duties."

Phillipe stood, bowed to the regent's retreating back, and then sat heavily again on the bench, his head swimming, weighing the purse in his hand.

* * *

"It's the black arts, I'm sure of it," said Grimbold as he sipped at a flagon of Saul's good beer. "Accidents happen, life is short, but for all the accidents to happen to Alana's side and none to Rolf's is stretching things a bit. Do you know how her father died? Plague. Only man in the kingdom to die of plague. And so convenient-like. Rolf no sooner announces he's coming back than his brother drops dead."

"But when he spoke with me, he seemed so kind, so concerned for your kingdom's welfare."

"Concerned that she might not be fit to rule?"

"Well, yes."

"Concerned that she might find a husband who would stand up for her?"

"That is not quite how he put it. 'Gain a kingdom by marrying a madwoman' is what he said."

"You've seen her. What do you think?"

Phillipe sat silent, running his finger along a crack in the table-top. At last, he looked at Grimbold. "I do not think she is mad."

"She's not mad, nor a fool. Did he try to bribe you?"

Phillipe started, then said, "Yes, and but for you, my friend, successfully."

Grimbold snorted and took a long pull at his beer.

"But is there no way to see that he is stopped and punished?"

"Punished for what? For being a lucky man in an unfortunate world? He's done nothing that anyone can see. And how can he be stopped from doing nothing?"

"She asked for my help."

"No offense meant, Master Phillipe, but you hardly seem a match for the regent."

"No. Of that I have no doubt. But she knows that I go next to Amytans, and that any number of heroes will be there for the knighting of the prince. I wonder who she wants me to speak to."

86

Grimbold frowned and shrugged.

In the bustle of the tavern, they did not notice as yet another drunkard left his seat nearby and stumbled out the door. The man was careful that they did not see him become suddenly sober outside the doorway before running in the direction of the castle as if pursued by a pack of hounds.

"Grimbold, you old dog!" Saul, the amply-stomached innkeep, said as he came toward them with his hand outstretched in friendship. "What news from the castle?"

"Only that one of the finest minstrels in all Christendom has come to visit."

"Really? And who might that be? I thought they'd all passed through last week on their way to Amytans."

"This man, right here," said Grimbold, thumping Phillipe on the back.

"Really, he exaggerates," Phillipe said.

"Modest, too. Never trust a man who brags about his work. What do you say, will you let him ply his trade this evening?"

"If you're willing . . . ."

Phillipe nodded. Even without the advice of the old woman, the idea appealed to him. The crowd held many a sturdy yeoman and burgher and was, on the whole, far better dressed than those in most of the establishments where he entertained.

Saul went to the counter in front of the beer kegs and pounded on it with his fist, bellowing for their attention. "We have tonight among us one of the finest minstrels in all Christendom." A hush fell. "And we have persuaded him to perform." Clapping and cheers from the crowd. "I give to you. . . . What did you say your name was? . . . Phillipe of Albi!"

The applause, which was prepared to be thunderous, expired quickly as the crowd realized the name held no meaning for them.

Phillipe stood and began to sing in a passable tenor as he walked toward the counter:

I sing to you of a knight so bold
From a far and distant country,
That his name still lives in the stories told
About him and his errantry.

This knight one day journeyed far away
Seeking dragons and other villains,
What he found that day was a maiden gay
In a pink and white pavilion.

"Good sir," quoth she, "won't you rescue me
From this horrible fate I'm bound to?"
"Fair maid," he said, "I'll cut off its head,
I'm so happy to have found you."

"Alack," said the maid, "that is not what I said,
Or not what I intended."
She said "Prithee, come away with me
And your error will be mended."

She bid him stand, took him by the hand
And they to her chamber wended.
He put up no fight on that balmy night,
And so his quest was ended.

I sing to you of a maid so bold,
May her name live on in glory.
And such a one may you find, my son,
And happ'ly end your story.

As the crowd chuckled and warmed to him, Phillipe silently
thanked the crone for her good advice.

* * *

Hours later, his pockets fatter, Phillipe left the tavern with
Grimbold. They passed through cobbled streets that were silent
save for the songs of late revelers scattering homeward through
the darkness.

"The castle gate will be barred," Grimbold told him, "but I've
the password."

They walked onward, footsteps echoing against the fronts of
houses lining the narrow way. The voices of two roisterers, raised

in drunken disharmony, rang down the street ahead of them. They passed a cross street, then a darkened doorway.

"Hist," said Grimbold. "Are you armed? There are footsteps behind."

Phillipe drew his dagger. He made no pretension of being a warrior, but life as a solitary traveler had brought its lessons, not all of them pleasant.

"We'll try to catch up to those singers ahead. I don't think we'll be attacked if there are enough of us together." They hurried around the corner into a welcoming circle of torchlight.

"Hallo, friends," the torchbearer hailed them, swaying as he stood. "Care to join ush for a drink?"

"I think not, my friend. I wish only to rest my bones."

"Then it's rest you'll have." The voice lost its slur. The torch flew from his hand at them, and they heard the steely hiss of blades leaving their sheaths. The flame passed between them as they dodged. Phillipe heard Grimbold draw his sword and the footsteps that had pursued them hasten.

"Back to back!" Grimbold shouted. There were four surrounding them, swords glinting in the faint moonlight. Suddenly all four leapt forward and he heard the ring of Grimbold's sword as it parried the first blow. He tried to deflect the sword slicing toward him with his dagger, but missed his chance. The blade slid up and over the dagger's hilt and cut deeply into his hand, where the thumb joins. He bellowed in pain and his knife fell from his hand. Then there was a fire in his ribs and he crumpled to the ground. Pain and nausea flooded him, and he almost wished for death.

What faint sight there was left his eyes, but he could hear with an unnatural clarity. A man cried out and toppled at his side. Grimbold's sword rang as he continued to fight. Another set of footsteps ran up and a new voice cried out, "Stop, you thieving pigs!" and a second sword joined Grimbold's before the clatter suddenly ended in bellows of pain and the pattering of retreating feet.

"Grimbold! Are you hurt?" said their rescuer.

"No," he replied, puffing hard. "Only a little."

"Can you walk?"

"Yes."

"Who is he? Does he live?"

Damn that old woman. I am dying, Phillipe thought, as his awareness faded into dim unreality. *Or going mad.* Why else would the voice of his rescuer sound like that of a woman?

Chapter 12
Phillipe

Phillipe was first aware of the feel of clean linen next to his skin. Then his vision changed from black to the dull red of candle-light seen through closed eyes and the throbbing began in his hand and in his side. He moaned. There was a soft rustling, and a hand touched his forehead.

"There, ducks. Rest easy now. You're among friends."

He opened his eyes and saw a plump woman of middle years looking at him, concern clouding her brow. He opened his mouth to speak, but she held up her hand. "I'm Mary, Saul's wife. Grimbold brought you back here. You must stay quiet. We can't let it be known you're here."

He looked about and saw that he lay on a pile of straw in a garret. About him sat casks and boxes of little-used belongings, covered with dust. Slender spears of sunlight glimmered through the cracks in the closed shutters.

"Do you think you can eat? I've brought barley gruel."

Phillipe nodded and she spoon-fed him, as one might an infant.

"Grimbold?" he asked as she caught a drip on his chin with her spoon.

"A cut, but not a bad one. He will come if he can."

"There was another who came to help. I was far gone. His voice sounded like a woman's."

"Sophie."

"A strange name for a warrior."

"But not for a woman. You were not as far gone as you thought."

A land of surprises, this Gwalhafed, Phillipe thought as he accepted another spoonful of gruel. He heard a soft tapping from somewhere beyond the large chest that guarded his feet. Mary stood and set the bowl down. She bustled off in the direction of the sound. Phillipe heard the squeak of a hinge. A square of morning sunlight, obscured by the shadow of a figure, flashed briefly on the rafters above his head, and then the shutter squealed shut again. There were brisk, booted footsteps and a young woman peered over the chest at him.

"Feeling better?" she asked. He nodded. "It might interest you to know that the men who attacked you were all hanged at dawn."

"Justice is swift here."

"I don't know about justice, but dead men cannot tell who hired them."

"Do you really think someone paid them to attack me?"

"My father does, since I told him what you and Grimbold were discussing at the Cock and Bull. In public! Two grown men! 'The regent tried to bribe me, but I've changed my mind.' Stupid. Really stupid."

"Your father? Who are you?"

She came around the end of the trunk and hopped up to sit on it. She was dressed as a huntsman, with brown leggings and jerkin and a white shirt. A sword hung from her broad belt and a long knife, in its sheath, was tucked under the belt as well. Her coppery hair hung in a thick braid to her waist. "I'm Sophie, and my father is Murdoch, so lately disgraced by our good friend, the regent."

"Murdoch!"

"You have heard of him, then?"

"But of course! The tales of his exploits are always the most popular wherever I go. I am indebted to him for half my livelihood. . . . and to you, fair maiden, for my life itself."

She shrugged, ignoring the compliment. "A warrior does what must be done. Now, listen. Here is the plan. Mary says it is a clean wound, and will heal in a couple of weeks. We must get you out of here and off to Amytans, as soon as you can travel. We'll see to it that you leave the kingdom safely. After that, it is up to you.

"You must interest some knight in coming to Gwalhafed. You must find one of good heart, yet clever and subtle—not some ignorant, sword-swinging lout. You cannot speak too clearly of Rolf's part in this, at least until you are sure of your man. Rolf has spies everywhere, and the chiefest of them, Lord Valan, is attending the celebration. Have you got that?"

Phillipe sighed and nodded. "But why doesn't your father send you?"

"It would be too obvious. Besides, he needs me here to be his eyes and ears and to carry his messages. He is under house arrest. I am the only person who can come and go there, except for the guards."

"But why would Rolf let you go free?"

"I think he underestimates me." She spoke lightly, but the set of her jaw told Phillipe that she took this as a slight. "And he has me followed—the better, I think, to find out who my father's allies are. You will not see me again. Grimbold has frequented the tavern downstairs for years. He may come up and visit you now and again, but the less anyone sees of you, the less chance of anyone else finding you."

She slid off the trunk and stood looking down at him. "I must be off!" she said. "I must find Rolf's spies and let them follow me around for a while. I will go to Emmet the fruit seller and purchase a single apple. I will do that every day for, let's see, a week, and then I will purchase a pear. Won't they have fun trying to ferret out the deeper meaning of that!"

Phillipe shook his head in puzzlement. "And what *is* its deeper meaning?"

"Emmet is a pig and overcharges. Maybe they'll take him in for questioning and everyone will buy their fruit from someone else."

* * *

Many times in his life, Phillipe had wished for peace and quiet and time to simply create rhymes and tales without the constant need to perform. Now he had it, in abundance, and more than abundance. Although his wounds still pained him, they had not festered and in just over a week he was able to sit upright and feed himself clumsily with his bandaged hand. Grimbold came to him twice, the first bearing the news that the arrangements for his journey had been made and only awaited his mending, and the second with a message that Phillipe found totally puzzling.

"He's beaten her at chess!"

Phillipe lay on his pallet and blinked as he wondered which question to ask first. He finally settled for "What?"

"The regent. Rolf. He bested the princess at chess."

"This upsets you?"

"Don't you see? It's never happened before. For over a year, they've played almost every day and she's always won."

"Perhaps the practice has done him good?"

"He won on the tenth move. He's been letting her win, don't you see?"

"And?"

"He's up to something. He wants to intimidate her. Can you travel?"

Phillipe shook his head. "I stood yesterday, but my side burns like fire when I try to walk."

"Well hurry it up, will you? She's in danger."

* * *

Phillipe lay or sat for endless hours as darkness gave way to a shadowy gloom that many hours later faded back to darkness again. At first, he hardly noticed, as his body gave itself wholly to the task of mending, but shortly after Grimbold's second visit, he realized that he was bored.

"A good sign, that," said Mary with a laugh, as she changed the dressing on his side. "You'll be fit in no time and ready to go. How's the poetry coming?"

"It comes."

Although there may have been other ways to recruit a champion for Alana, the one that naturally occurred to him was to write a song about her. If any knight were intrigued by his description of her charms, he would quite naturally ask for more information and Phillipe would have the chance to sound out his worthiness for the task. At least, that was how he conceived it. A simple, straightforward job for an experienced poet, but he was having trouble with it.

Never had so much depended on any work of his, and that seemed to frighten the muse away entirely. Never had his metaphors seemed so flat, his similes so barren. It was no worse than his usual output, but perhaps the importance of the task made him more critical. And then there was the difficulty of his revealing too much, or saying too little to stir interest in the princess and her plight.

One morning, not quite three weeks after his wounding, much to his astonishment, he found himself pacing the floor.

To be accurate, *he* did not find himself; Mary did.

"For heaven's sake!" she whispered as she came bustling up the stairs. "You'd think a horse was stabled up here! Stop that! You can hear it in the room below. I think you are healthy enough to go. I'll tell Saul. Wait here. And sit still!"

A few moments later, Saul tiptoed up the staircase, bearing a dull brown cloak. Mary followed with a broom and began to swiftly bundle linens and toss the straw bedding out of the back window.

"Here, Master Phillipe," said Saul, "cover yourself up and follow me. The guest in the room below just went out, which is odd, because he just came in. It may mean nothing, but who's to say?"

Phillipe did as he asked and followed the innkeep down the stairs, along the corridor and down the back staircase to the kitchen. They left by the back door, which opened into an alley laden with refuse and perfumed with the contents of chamber pots. A blizzard of straw drifted through the air as Mary continued her cleaning. Saul turned to his right and scurried along the passage with Phillipe at his heels. Three houses down, they turned right again, into an alley that was more like a tunnel, as the houses on both sides overhung it.

"I must go back. It will not do for the innkeep to be absent. Fare well! Keep moving downhill and you will come to the city gate. Do not stay in the city. Someone will come to you on the road." Saul turned and left him.

Phillipe walked slowly toward the opposite end of the alley, where passersby hurried on the street beyond. He was still three paces short of the end when a squad of guardsmen raced past in the direction of the tavern. As he stepped into the street, he heard them pounding on the tavern door and their captain calling Saul's name. He did not turn to look, but hurried away down the street.

The streets were busy, but not crowded, and he walked as quickly as he felt he could without drawing attention to himself. His side ached. He reached the gate without incident. Grimbold stood in his accustomed place.

"Guardsmen are at the tavern. I had to leave," Phillipe said. "I don't know how far I can walk."

Grimbold's eyes opened wide. Then his face changed. "Move along, move along," he said, but he looked Phillipe in the eye and nodded.

Phillipe walked slowly along the road that led down from the city. It descended the rolling meadow in wide sweeps and at its base joined the east–west road that linked Gwalhafed with its neighbors, Amytans and Velendruch. The eastward road was broad. It led through fertile farmlands to the nearest harbor, at Rhynn in Velendruch, and most of the trade of Gwalhafed passed over it. The western road was little more than a trail. Less than two miles from the junction, it plunged into forest and slowly began to climb. Few traveled here, save woodsmen bringing firewood and lumber to the city and hunters bringing meat and pelts. Although the road led to the rich and mighty realm of Amytans, little trade passed this way. The products of Gwalhafed were quite mundane and Amytans could obtain their like—and things much more exotic—at lesser cost from its conquered provinces.

Philippe made his slow way along this road, hungry, resting at whiles far back from its edge. The sun began its descent and still he had seen no one. At last, a jingling of harness warned him of the approach of a cart from behind him. He slipped off the side of the road and hid behind a tree. A strong black horse with white forefeet and blaze toiled up the slope, pulling a stave-sided cart. A canvas covered the top, but below its edge Phillipe could see a row of barrels.

"Damn," the driver said, mopping his face with a greasy red rag. "And nary a word as to how to find him. What do you think we should do?" He said this in such earnest that Phillipe almost expected the horse to answer. Instead, a mumbled reply came from inside the cart. He could not make out the words.

"Well, if he had any sense, he'd not stay on the road. He'd be off in the bushes somewhere."

A head pushed up the canvas just behind the driver's seat. "Well, he hasn't shown any so far, William."

Phillipe knew the voice. He stepped out from behind his tree. "But one can learn," he said.

Sophie smiled. "Quick now, hop in. We've miles to go."

"Get up, Nightingale," said William.

96

The cart jolted and clattered along the rough road. Still, it was respite from walking and they had brought food. Phillipe gnawed a chicken leg in the lurching hollow between the barrels and then dozed as well as he could, his head pillowed on his folded cloak. As the sun came level through the trees ahead of them, they halted.

"This is as far as we go tonight," the carter said. "There's a stream down the hill."

They had stopped on a level place next to the road, barely wide enough for the cart. William's horse stood patiently, waiting for her harness to be loosened and dinner to appear beneath her nose.

"I'm going to get a drink," Sophie said.

"Take this," the carter said, handing her a wooden bucket from beneath his seat. "Nightingale needs watering."

Phillipe, stiff, thirsty, his face sticky with chicken fat, joined her.

They had stopped at one of the few places along that road where a wain could pull off without striking a tree or overturning, so although there was little traffic on that road, the path from the road to the stream below was worn hard and smooth by the feet of travelers seeking water for themselves and their animals. They followed its twisting course downward until they reached a brook tumbling into a small pond contained at the lower end by a rude dam of rocks and fallen branches. The slopes surrounding it were lined with ferns. Thickets of brush and bramble obscured their view of the top of the slope. Phillipe removed his shoes and woolen stockings and dabbled his feet in the water as he scrubbed his smeary face. Sophie filled the bucket and stood it on the path, well back from the water's edge, beneath the bramble hedge. Then she cupped her hands and drank and splashed water on her face and the back of her neck.

"What of Saul and Mary? I am torn with guilt."

"It was close, but no trace was left for the guard to find. No thanks to you."

"I am sorry. I was not thinking of my footsteps. I did not even realize that I was pacing."

"Footsteps can belong to anyone. Mary told them she was cleaning the attic. I mean this." She drew the purse Rolf had given Phillipe from within her jerkin and held it with its drawstring between her forefinger and thumb, as though it were a rotten fish. "Just how have you managed to live long enough to have gray hairs on your head? You might as well have written your name on the rafters."

"I cannot write."

"You have answered my question. Blind luck."

Phillipe dried his feet with his cloak and put on his stockings and shoes. "How far is it to Amytans?"

"By noon tomorrow we will reach a village, if you can call it that. There's not much to it besides a tavern—the Fallen Log it's called—and a few houses. William Carter will deliver a barrel of beer to them and then take the road south, toward the Swanswater ford. We will leave him just short of the inn and go westward on foot. It's little more than an hour's walk uphill and then, once we pass the crest, we will be in Amytans and I will cut across the woods and meet William on the southward road. From there, you must care for yourself."

"I will do my best," Phillipe said humbly.

"You will have to do better than that," she replied and then stopped. "Listen!"

Phillipe heard the clop of hooves and jingle of harness on the road above.

"Ho, there," a deep voice hailed the carter. "Where are you off to?"

"Delivering beer to the Fallen Log and to the Feather down at Swanswater. And yourself?"

"Chasing a cutpurse, not that it's any concern of yours," the voice answered. "Search the cart," he added in a lower tone.

Sophie listened carefully. "There's at least three of them, maybe four or five."

"Did you see anyone along the road?"

"No."

The voice lowered again. "Look down by the stream."

They could hear footsteps on the path above, but they could not see past the bushes. Sophie slipped into the water.

98

"Quickly," she hissed and tugged at his sleeve.

He swallowed hard and followed her. The water, which had felt so refreshing to his tired feet, stole the heat from his body almost instantly. The pool was just over four feet deep and about six across, but the upper end, next to the freshet that fed it, was thick with overhanging ferns and he followed her toward them along the slippery muck of the bottom.

There they crouched, pressing themselves back against the steep side of the bank, hearing the footsteps grow louder. Suddenly Sophie inhaled sharply, but softly. "The bucket," she whispered. It sat proud and full in the shade of the brambles. They watched the dim shapes of two guardsmen descend the path behind the screen of leaves. Then the pair reached the last bend, stopped, and gave a perfunctory glance around them. The water plashed. The hardpacked trail showed no footprints. Satisfied, they left. Had they come another step, they would have seen the bucket. Had they come two more, they would have tripped over it. Sophie and Phillipe found themselves breathing again.

"Blind luck is not so bad, eh?" Phillipe said.

Sophie sighed.

* * *

Phillipe counted that night the most miserable of his entire existence. His clothing, from cloak to shoes, was soaked and his spare set sat in a bag in Gwalhafed Castle. Although he took his clothing off one item at a time and wrung it as dry as possible before putting it back on, and draped his cloak over a tree branch near the fire to dry, it made little difference. Sophie, for her part, seemed to notice neither wet nor cold, but Phillipe could see the gooseflesh on her arms. Before she took any thought to dry her clothing, she borrowed William's rag and carefully dried her sword and then her knife. She laid them to one side and put her belt and the sheaths near the fire to dry. She chattered cheerfully with William as they ate, and then, as the darkness grew, curled into a ball by the fire and fell quickly asleep with her cheek pillowed on her hand.

As the sky lightened to gray, William and Sophie awoke. Phillipe had no need to wake, as he had hardly slept all night. They breakfasted on dried fruit and fresh water and then were off, with Phillipe and Sophie tucked safely away among the barrels. The sun warmed them, even under the shade of the tarp, and the heat from their bodies warmed the small space. Both slept. William guided the cart up the rutted trail calling words of encouragement to Nightingale when the going grew rough. They climbed through forests of oak and beech and then descended again into a shallow trough of valley. Here and there even rougher tracks left the road, leading to hamlets too obscure to even possess names.

They passed only one house on their way. It sat near the road, behind a rough, waist-high, unmortared stone wall. A path of beaten dirt led from a gap in the wall, from which hung the remnants of a gate, to the front door. To the left of that path stood an oak tree of such age and grandeur that three men could not have encircled its trunk with their outstretched arms. Its roots embraced a stone well with a winch above and a wooden dipper hanging from a peg on the winch housing. An area of perhaps half an acre was cleared around the house, part of that in garden, but all grown to weeds. Green moss covered the walls of the house and even the thatch of the roof, and only a thin stream of smoke fluttering from the chimney showed that someone lived there. As they passed it, William crossed himself and clucked to Nightingale, urging her to hurry. Sophie and Phillipe slept.

At last, about an hour before midday, William reined in Nightingale and woke his passengers. Phillipe lay silent and bleary-eyed. Sophie sneezed.

"Well," said William, shaking his head, "a fine escape this is turning out to be."

Sophie crawled out of the cart, took a sip of water from her flask and wet her face. "Come along, Master Phillipe," she called with more vigor than she felt. "Adventure beckons."

Phillipe groaned and followed her.

"We'll have to climb this slope and skirt the village. William and his cart should draw their attention." She picked up the bundle containing their food. "You'll need this for your journey."

She slung it over her shoulder and began to climb. Phillipe hastened behind her, puffing as he tried to keep up. She stopped and turned. "Would you mind breathing a little quieter? You'll set the dogs off."

"My apologies," he answered with forced dignity. "I have spent these last weeks lying in bed with a sword wound."

She said nothing, but he noticed that she eased her pace after that.

As Sophie had known, William's arrival with beer and gossip was a major event in the life of the village and all of its few inhabitants were drawn to the carter as naturally as water runs downhill. Just beyond the Fallen Log, the road curved to the left and downhill, running south now to the Swanswater ford. Another track, narrower and grassy, kept on west to the border, and a footpath wandered up the hill northward. This they climbed, and then turned west and cut along the edge of a ridge for an hour. Sophie led Phillipe down a steep slope, across a boggy stream, and into a dell where a tremendous log, the last remnant of a huge beech, lay covered with velvet-soft moss. He sat gratefully on this while she crept up the other side of the dell to see if anyone might be on the path.

"You never know," she told him. "Rolf could have sent troops to man the border."

But it was not so.

Sophie returned after too short a time to suit Phillipe and they left the dell by a path that led up to the main trail. Once again, they climbed, the trail winding to and fro on the steep slope until finally, after another three miles, they crested the ridge and looked down upon the realm of Amytans.

The trail slanted down a cliff of about one hundred feet in height, but from there the slope was less steep on the Amytans side, falling into a series of rolling, wooded hills that diminished into upland pasture. On the far horizon, something twinkled in the haze, a gleaming white dot.

"Arnhem Castle," said Sophie, pointing. "This road will take you to it."

She handed him the food and the pouch containing Rolf's gold. "Good luck," she said. "We are all depending upon you." Then she turned and strode down the road toward Gwalhafed.

Phillipe stood watching her. *What a remarkable young woman,* he thought. *But how will she prosper? What man would marry her?* He watched her as she turned from the path and entered the trees. The wind brought the faint sound of her sneeze.

Chapter 13
A Hero Is Found

Prince Roderik lounged in his seat at the center of the table on the dais, one hand clasping the stem of his goblet, the other absent-mindedly stroking the wolfhound whose head rested on his knee. He was dressed as befits a prince of a great realm, his blue silk jacket studded with pearls and slashed so the yellow lining showed boldly. He had unfastened it in the wine-induced heat of that crowded hall, and fine embroidery showed on the front of his white shirt. The gold and gems of his belt glinted in the candlelight. It was hours past midnight on the last night of the celebration, and he regretted its ending.

In the life of a feudal lord there are two events of supreme importance. The first is the knighting of his eldest son, the second the marriage of his eldest daughter. In the life of King Ulrik of Amytans, there could only be one such event, and it came to pass in the autumn of that year, as his only child, Roderik, became a man and a knight. The festivities had lasted a full month.

Each day, warriors from Amytans and every kingdom beyond displayed their skills on the field. The prince cut a fine figure on the field by day, newly made golden breastplate and helm shining like a meteor, his swordplay adequate, although no one pushed him very hard—it would be unthinkable to damage the only son and heir of such a generous and powerful host as Ulrik of Amytans—and all agreed that none could match him in horsemanship. Each night, trestles in the Great Hall of the palace creaked with their savory burden and the stone walls rang with laughter and song as minstrels recounted the events of the day and of legend.

It's over. Roderik looked out over the hall, where the flower of chivalry lay wilted by wine. *What's left? There will be parties, of course, but not like this one. Father will go on about my royal duties. Mother will go on about my marrying some princess. At least the hunt-*

ing season is about to begin. That's something. He ran his fingers through his tousled blond curls and yawned.

"Shall we leave, Highness?" asked his cousin Tolsturm, son of a duke, and the most able at keeping pace with the prince in his cups. He was a tall young man in his middle twenties, with a worldly air and a light brown goatee. The others of Roderik's boon companions lay snoring beneath the table or dozed with their heads by their cups.

"No," the prince replied. "I don't want it to end. Have some more wine. Are there any minstrels awake? I want to hear a song."

Tolsturm snapped his fingers at a servant nearby, assuming the man had overheard their conversation, which he had, that being his chief duty. The man went off, yawning and stretching, and returned a few minutes later with a minstrel Roderik had not seen before. The man was of middle height with a simple, honest face and mouse-brown hair beginning to gray. His clothing was stained with the grime of travel and there was a dirty bandage on his right hand. He looked exhausted, but that was of no concern to the prince. The minstrel had come to perform, and was now being called upon to do so.

"Surprise me," said the young knight. "Sing to me something I have never heard before. Sing to me something that does not involve fighting or the saints." He leaned over and whispered to Tolsturm, "Gold piece says he can't do it."

"Agreed," the noble replied.

Phillipe sighed. All his haste, all the sweat and danger of his journey, two gold coins gone to bribe his way into the celebration and a third just now to the servingman, and all for this: two elegant young sots in the mood for poetry. They seemed the only men still capable of sitting upright in the room. It hardly seemed worth his time, but he reasoned that one must make a beginning somewhere. Much to Roderik's surprise, the minstrel bowed, cleared his throat, and immediately began to sing:

Maidens there are many
Of beauty dark and fair,
But none can match Alana
Of the flame-red hair.

But beauty counts as nothing
If lacking wit and grace,
For even lesser maidens
Can be fair of face.

Alana, noble lady,
Daughter of a king,
Whose mind is like a ray of light
Darkness overthrowing.

Alana, like a goddess
Come from days of Rome
Worthy of men's worship
Seated on her throne.

Her voice as gentle as a dove's,
Her heart as warm and kind,
Her face as pale as yonder moon,
Yet brilliant is her mind.

Maidens there are many,
Of beauty dark and fair,
But none can match Alana
Of the flame-red hair.

"Pay up, my lord" said Tolsturm.

Roderik fumbled absently in his purse. "Come here," he ordered the minstrel. "Have you met this lady?"

"I have, my lord. I have just come from Gwalhafed, where she rules under the regency of her uncle."

"Gwalhafed—of course. Not much of a place, I'm told."

"A land of peace. Doubtless of little interest to the heir of such a mighty land as Amytans."

"Is her hair really as red as a flame?"

"My words are but a poor reflection of reality."

The heir to the duchy of Brent raised his head from its position to the left of Roderik's cup. "What about her tits?" he inquired good-naturedly.

The minstrel eyed him sternly. "It goes without saying that her bosom would be as lovely as the rest of her." He paused to appraise the young man's rumpled shirt and the wine stain on the front. "It goes without saying that a gentleman, a *preux* knight, would not make such an inquiry." Brent shrugged and sagged backward in his chair.

"And what would the *preux* knight do?" Roderik asked. He winked at Tolsturm.

"Knowing of such a lady, he would immediately begin a quest to offer her his service and to perform bold deeds for her honor."

"Really."

"Of course. It could only make him more *preux*, more valiant, more renowned, this quest. It is more exciting than hunting even the wild boar." Phillipe shut his mouth. *What am I saying? I am a babbling fool.*

Roderik stroked the edge of his firm jaw. A twinkle began to replace the blurred look in his blue eyes.

"More fun than hunting, you say?"

Tolsturm rolled his eyes.

"You may leave us, Tol. Come with me . . . what did you say your name was?"

"I did not, my lord. It is Phillipe, of the far-off city of Albi."

Roderik stood, towering over the minstrel. He drained his silver goblet and tossed it aside. A servant caught it and placed it carefully on the table. The wolfhound grunted his dissatisfaction and stretched out on his side beneath the table. As the two men left the hall, the few who were still able stood to show respect for the prince. Those who could not raised their heads from the tables as he passed. The remainder continued to snore.

"Tell me more of these quests, Master Phillipe. How does one begin? Does this quest have a name?"

"Yes, my lord. It is called Courtly Love." He found himself hurrying to keep pace with the prince's long strides.

"And the forms?" the prince asked. "A quest for the sake of a woman. This game is new to me. What are its rules?"

Phillipe stopped still. "This is not a game! It is dangerous."

"Of course, of course, but I am a knight. What sort of danger? A dragon perhaps?" he said, his eyes twinkling with mirth.

"An uncle," muttered Phillipe.

"Foul villainy. How wonderful."

"I do not think you are the knight for this job. It requires subtlety."

Roderik shrugged. "I have my sword. So, tell me the forms."

"My lord, I do not think you will like them."

Roderik's eyes blazed. "Get on with it, will you?"

Phillipe stepped back a pace, surprised to strike steel beneath the gold plating. "Firstly, when one undertakes a quest for the sake of a lady, one must be true. One's head must not turn for any other."

"I can deal with that. Continue."

I have my doubts. "And one cannot refuse any request she might make," Phillipe said aloud, "from the smallest token to the giving of one's life."

"Of course. What else?"

"One must be cheerful and courteous to all."

"I always am. Is there anything else?"

My God, Phillipe thought to himself. *What have I done?*

* * *

King Ulrik paused, his breakfast cake halfway obscured by his opulent mustache. The early sun illuminated the room through a casement, throwing golden coins into the fountain on the tapestry filling the opposite wall.

"Good morning, Father. Good morning, Mum." Roderik bent and kissed his mother's hand cheerfully.

"Up early this morning, I see, Roddie. Hadn't expected to see you before noon. Coming to see me dispense justice?" Ulrik hardly expected an affirmative answer, but felt obligated to remind his son, however unsuccessfully, of his duty.

"I," Roderik announced grandly, "am beginning a quest."

"Good lord," Ulrik rumbled.

"Oh, Roddie," Queen Rowena moaned.

"Roderik," his father began, in a speech well-polished by endless repetition. "Someday, I will not be here—"

"And I will be called upon to rule." Roderik accepted a filled plate from the servant.

"Yes. The well-being of the entire kingdom, the survival of the empire—"

"—will rest upon my shoulders. Please pass the butter."

"Roderik, please!"

"Sorry, Father. Jam, please?"

"Roderik, this is important."

"Of course it is, Father. But it is also well in hand. The army attends to the provinces quite effectively. Our administrators are honest and efficient. You have the best years of your life ahead of you. It really won't make any difference if I go off for a few days."

"Roddie, dear. Listen to your father."

"Mother, I have. Repeatedly. But this quest might interest you."

"Roderik, what interest could it possibly hold, other than endless worry for your safety?"

"It concerns the princess Alana."

"Who?" his mother replied, raising her finely arched eyebrows.

"Of all the ridiculous, self-indulgent . . ." Ulrik muttered.

"Alana of Gwalhafed."

"Gwalhafed!" said his mother. "Good heavens, Roddie, why waste your time in Gwalhafed? By treaty they form a buffer between us and Velendruch. If you were to become involved with Gwalhafed, Velendruch would consider it a threat and we would need to draw men from the south to guard the eastern frontier. Why not Tremaria of Alantoya? She would bring a claim to the throne of Caeland and access to the harbor of Vaniar—"

"Or Gondaron," his father interrupted. "What's her name. . . . Gisella. Brings the rights to the castle. One of the best defensive position in the west."

"Or that Beldanian girl, Carinna. Not much land there, but fantastic wealth from their sea trade."

Roderik knew better than to mention Alana's uncle problem. That would result in the entire matter being handed off to Archduke Whisted and his army. He'd be shoved to the side with no say in the matter at all. "The princesses of earth, air, and ether. No, thank you. I'll try the princess of fire. Besides, I'm twenty-one years of age. A man. A knight. And I've never been outside my

108

own kingdom. If I am to rule, as you so often remind me that I am, would it not seem wise for me to travel, to meet some of these people who would be my allies and adversaries?" He looked at his mother the way he had looked at her since before he had learned to toddle. It had never failed to get him what he wanted, and it served him still.

"Your father and I will discuss the matter."

Prince Roderik stood, and bowed, and went off whistling to order his servants to pack.

* * *

Arnhem Castle rose above the surrounding city, its seven white marble towers glistening in the sunshine. Blue pennants with the lion crest of Amytans embroidered in yellow fluttered from the top of each. In the courtyard, which was large enough to hold all of Gwalhafed Castle and a bit of the town besides, servants packed the prince's gear onto his snow-white horse, Dreyfala, the fastest mount in three kingdoms, and one of the most beautiful.

"Highness!" called the groom, a lad of about sixteen years.

"Yes, Fred."

"If it please Your Highness, come see the new trick I've taught Dreyfala." He walked a few paces from the horse and snapped his fingers. Dreyfala went to him. "Good boy. Smart horse. Isn't he a marvel, Your Highness?"

"Best horse in the world, Fred. Let me try." He snapped his fingers and Dreyfala ambled over and nosed his pocket for a treat. "You're a wonder," he told the horse, stroking his mane.

* * *

Roderik roamed the castle, bidding farewell to the people he loved most. His grandmother, Queen Mother Edwynna, sat, as usual, in the sunniest corner of the garden, working at her embroidery. It occupied nearly all her time, and had done so since she was widowed thirty years before. It was now nearly one hundred twenty-two feet long and sat in a huge bale, as big as a cart wheel, next to her seat, with one end trapped in an embroidery hoop. She smiled as he stood before her, so tall, so strong, and so terribly, terribly young.

"They tell me you're leaving today."

He nodded, eyes glowing with excitement.

"You'll be very careful?"

He shrugged. "This is a quest, Grandmother. There are always dangers."

"Yes, yes." She nodded and patted the bench next to her. "Sit with me a moment." He obeyed. "Now which direction do you think you'll go?"

"East," he replied, twinkling with suppressed excitement.

"Into the Hills?" she asked with some alarm.

"Oh, no. I'll cross the pass into Gwalhafed."

She raised her eyebrows. "Gwalhafed? Why there?" She smiled as though she already knew the answer. He blushed. "Take a look at this," she said, pointing to her needlework. It showed two figures on horseback: one a warrior and the other a petite woman with crimson hair.

"That must be Princess Alana!" he said.

"That's what I thought," she replied. "No one else could have hair that color."

"But what does it mean?"

She shook her head. "The images are given to me, but their meanings are not."

"Is it true, Grandmother, that everything that has happened in the kingdom since Grandfather died is shown on your tapestry?"

"I suppose so, dear," she replied, drawing out a length of thread.

"But how? You never leave the castle."

"When your grandfather died, I missed him terribly. I wanted to follow him, and I very nearly did. Here, thread this for me. My eyes aren't nearly what they used to be." She sat, gazing absently at a rosebush as his square warrior's hands grappled with the tiny needle. "I wanted to be with him, and I followed him to the Gate of Death itself, but I could not bear to cross it. There was a woman there, you see. She said nothing, just looked into my eyes, and I knew that I wasn't ready. She kissed my forehead and I returned. She visits me still, in my dreams, and shows me what she chooses."

She looked at Roderik, and noticed his struggle with the thread. "Here, let me do that. Your hands were not trained for such work." He handed the needle and thread back with obvious relief. "So," she continued, "this quest involves the princess Alana?"

"Yes," he replied with enthusiasm. "She is the one for me."

"The one for you? You've never met her."

"Grandmother, I just know."

"You really shouldn't narrow your choices too early, you know. How about Gisella of Gondaron?"

"Grandmother, she belches."

She smiled a little at that.

"Or Tremaria of Alantoya?"

"The one with the wart on the end of her nose? Oh, please."

"Now there's Carinna of Beldania. She's perfectly presentable."

"She fancies herself a poet."

"Such accomplishments are not unbecoming in a lady, you know."

"Such beauty blushing like a rose, from dainty ear to pointed nose," he quoted.

His grandmother gave him a mischievous smile.

"Grandmother, you're doing this to vex me."

She chuckled and patted his knee, then turned to him. "Promise me one thing, Roderik."

"Anything."

"Do not go into the Hills."

"For fear of forest faeries? Oh, Grandmother, that's all superstitious blather."

"Promise me," she said, with authority.

"But how can there be any truth to it? No one really knows. No one ever goes there."

"Men have gone there. The important point is that no one ever comes back. Anselm, my older brother, was one of them. He was a fine, strong, young knight like yourself. He never came back."

"But, Grandmother, that was fifty years ago!"

"A company of twenty knights went after him and were swallowed up and never seen again, and a company of fifty men at arms followed them to perdition. Promise me that you will not go there! It would kill me."

She looked into his eyes. He lowered his for a moment and then looked at her and nodded.

Chapter 14
The Quest

Dreyfala pranced as Roderik sat upon him, listening to his father's farewell speech. As usual, it utilized the word *honor* an astounding number of times. Rowena, his mother, stood at his father's side, her fair hair pulled smoothly up, shining as brightly as the crown that sat atop it. She made frequent use of her handkerchief.

". . . and so," King Ulrik concluded, smoothing the right side of his graying moustache, "may you embark upon this quest, this journey into the unknown, not for your own amusement but for honor." Here, Rowena's sniffles redoubled. "For the honor of your family, the noble house of Arn; for the honor of your city, Arnhem; and for the honor of your country." He paused, his eyes glaring hawk-like from under his bushy brow. "For the honor . . . of Amytans," he concluded with great feeling.

Rowena blew her nose, as if to punctuate his speech. He shot her a look out of the corner of his eye and she immediately dropped her handkerchief and resumed looking at him with worshipful eyes.

The throng in the crowded courtyard burst into cheers. At last, the formalities were over and Dreyfala was free to prance out the main gate, his mane and tail floating like white clouds in the wind, carrying his master into the unknown.

Prince Roderik rode through the crowded streets of his city followed by his entourage. First came his closest friends, the heirs to the duchies of Perwicke, Brent, and Tolsturm, then a round dozen of the other lordling sons of Amytans. This vibrant procession concluded with three wagonloads of equipment and provisions, twenty-seven servants, and a cook to see that all went smoothly. As they rode, a path opened before Roderik as the people pressed themselves to either side of the passage and bowed deeply. Women curtsied after the fashion of the time, bowing low to display their tightly-laced bodices to advantage. His companions enjoyed the sights, but the prince, devoted to his quest, ignored them for once.

First, they passed through the castle gate, through which throngs of carters brought wagonloads of provisions: squealing pigs, squawking hens and honking geese, casks of wine, baskets of bread and vegetables for the feeding of the royal family and their many retainers and servants. Scattered through the crowd moving toward the castle he saw warriors, an occasional troubadour or jester seeking patronage, and well-fed merchants with sturdy ponies loaded with luxuries seeking wealthy buyers. Beyond the gate, down several streets, lay the market, full of the bustle of tradesmen and servants.

Below that, on the way to the city gate, the beggars sat, their positions assigned by order of the king, a few of them women with children huddled about, but most of them men of varying years, missing eyes, missing legs or hands, wearing the badges their sacrifices had won them in the wars that had enriched the kingdom and extended the domain of Amytans. All eyes turned to Roderik as he entered the beggars' street. The men looked up expectantly and the women waved the faded fragments of their husbands' livery, setting the chains pinned to them jingling and the badges fluttering. Roderik reached into his fat purse and flung a handful of coins at those lining each side of the road, receiving a chorus of thanks and praise in return. Finally, he crossed the bridge at the city gate, reached the crossroads, and took the little-traveled road toward Gwalhafed.

* * *

Late that afternoon, they entered the woodlands surrounding the approach to the Hills. Their progress had been leisurely, with plenty of jests and song. The grandfathers of these men had ruled by conquest. Their fathers ruled by administration, and were likely to do so for the next twenty years. The prince and his friends spent their days pleasantly, fending off boredom until their turn came.

"Constanzia," said Brent, who was riding behind the prince.

"Ten gold pieces says Irene," Perwicke replied calmly.

"Oh, come on. Constanzia's the eldest."

"Since when has Roddie ever considered things like that? He'll come back from this little camping trip and marry Irene. She laces herself tighter."

"So, what's this Alana like?" Tolsturm asked the prince.

"Beautiful and brilliant, I am told."

"By whom?"

"By that minstrel who sang for us at the feast."

"Take it with a grain of salt. I once heard a song about Tremaria of Alantoya that didn't mention warts."

"No," Roderik replied. "I feel it in my heart. She's different."

"Do tell. They're all the same, these fine ladies. Embroidery hoops and piety. You'll see."

"No, Tolsturm. She has red hair, so she must have spirit. She is graceful and smart and beautiful and . . . oh, you'll see. I just feel it in my bones."

* * *

The afternoon progressed and the servants, as they drove, began to look for a place to make camp.

"Irene," said Fred the groom, who drove the lead cart.

"Constanzia," Ernest, the cook, snorted. "If his mother has anything to say about it. Anyhow, they're twins. You can hardly tell 'em apart."

"I've seen them together. Irene's got bigger . . . you know." He held his hands cupped in front of his chest. "What about that spot over there?"

Ernest craned his neck. "Too boggy."

"Well, we can't go on much longer. I don't fancy gathering firewood in the dark."

"There's a place half a mile on. Higher ground and plenty of room for the horses and pavil—" He cut himself off. "What was that?"

A white stag burst from the wood to the south of the road and leaped northward like a bolt of lightning.

Prince Roderik's heart leapt. He was an educated man, having read all the tales of Arthur's knights, and knew that the appearance of the white stag heralded the true beginning of his adventure. Without a thought, he spurred his horse after it, his companions struggling to keep up. He intended to lose them, as the forms demanded, and be swept up by events that would inexorably lead him to Alana's side, to find her alone, just in time to save her from something ghastly.

Dreyfala galloped up the slope, following the ghostly form of the stag. Roderik bent low to the horse's neck, and the branches of the pines whipped them as they flew through the forest. The cries of his companions grew fainter, until all the prince could hear was Dreyfala's snorting breath and the thudding of his hooves on the soft forest floor. As the sun sank and the forest grew darker, mist began to rise, obscuring Roderik's vision. Ahead, the white stag slipped silently through the trees, seeming at times to change its form to that of a woman, and at others to take the shape of a great, white bird. Then Roderik lost sight of it altogether.

He reined in Dreyfala, and sat scanning the forest around him for a sign of the deer. Failing to see any, he dismounted and carefully searched for its track. He was justly proud of his huntsman's skill. In a moment, he remounted and followed the stag's trail. He reached the end of the forest, where cold, gray cliffs of granite took root and soared in creviced grandeur, marking the boundary of the realm of Amytans. He reined Dreyfala in, looking about warily in the silence. There was no sound—not the call of a bird, not even the sigh of the wind. To his left rose the cliffs, and to his right a dense thicket of bramble and wild grape intertwined. The fog grew thicker. He had come to the end of the trail.

Suddenly, the stag burst out of the thicket, not a yard away. Dreyfala, squealing in terror, skipped sideways as nimbly as a goat and reared. Roderik toppled off with a shout and a clatter, thankful that no one was around to see. His gratitude did not last long, however. He was without food, drink, or any item save his horse, his sword, and the clothing on his back. He was also without any clue as to his location.

Chapter 15
The Bride

In due time, Lord Valan returned, bearing his forged tidings. Rolf found Alana in the garden, surrounded by her ladies. With a wave of his hand he sent them scurrying like bright leaves in the autumn wind. He held up four letters. Two were those Alana had written herself.

"My lady," he said softly. "Lord Hounshel is dead."

He let the first of the letters drop into her lap. She sat frozen in her chair.

"Shot dead by a poacher's arrow while hawking. His assailant was, regrettably, killed in the taking."

She sat stunned, staring at a bee as it hummed amid the clary sage.

The second letter fluttered from his hand to land atop the first.

"Cirgan is prisoner in his own dungeon, for withholding his tithe. Your messenger was not permitted to see him. Wickerts sent this."

He opened the third letter and read it aloud: "'My lady, I am shocked to the depths of my soul by your accusations. Surely the treachery of Cirgan must account for the shortfall. . .'"

Rolf's voice seemed as meaningless to Alana as the humming of the bee. *Grandfather. Grandfather dead?* She struggled to make words of the sounds coming out of her uncle's mouth.

"What?" she said.

"The treachery of Cirgan must account for the shortfall," he repeated, with insulting slowness.

"The treachery of Cirgan?" Alana said, fighting the fog enveloping her mind. "My lord uncle, you know as well as I that he pays his tithes in kind, not coinage." She seized the facts and pulled her drowning mind from its grief. "One hundred carts of grain; forty barrels of wine; twenty horses, well-broken; and a vial of rose petal oil no smaller than a man's thumb." She totted them up on her fingers. "All are accounted for."

He resumed his reading without comment. "'I leave tomorrow to inspect my new domain at Hirday, and will counsel with you further upon my return. . . .'"

"Hirday! That is my grandfather's estate, and mine by right of inheritance. How dare you!"

"'I must warn you in the strongest terms against any rash action you may attempt against your honorable uncle, and remind you,'" he said, raising his pale blue eyes from the parchment and observed her with feline satisfaction, "'that your well-being rests upon his good graces. Signed Wickerts, of Mannol and Hirday.'"

"Alana," he asked, his voice full of limpid concern, "what can this mean?"

"It means I have been a fool these past years."

"My lady!" he said. "You are too harsh! I am ever vigilant for your welfare. Perhaps this letter will be of more cheer to you. It has just arrived from Amytans." He handed it to her.

There, swathed in yards of verbose formality, was a request for her hand in marriage from Prince Roderik. She felt dizzy. *The prince himself. That minstrel did his work well. This prince is a masterful strategist. What better way to get me away from my uncle without his suspecting anything? I'd best act surprised . . . and none too eager.*

"I suppose this puts an end to your little war," she said.

"Marriage is as much a tool of politics as war," Rolf replied.

Opportunist, she thought. "I cannot marry someone I have never met."

"You are a princess, not a farmgirl. Your desires carry little weight in this matter."

"I am a princess, not a broodmare. Your desires carry no weight at all."

"Alana," he said, as patiently as a father to a wayward child. "The times change, and Gwalhafed can no longer remain isolated from its neighbors."

"If I ally with Amytans, it will upset the treaties. You know that, Uncle. Velendruch will rearm its borders, Amytans will try to enforce its claim to Gwalhafed, and the work of my father will be for naught."

"Not at all. I have approached Ambrahad of Velendruch for the hand of his eldest daughter. Your marriage to Amytans will strengthen my suit. You will bear children by your prince. Carlona will bear my children, and, some day, another match will be made, one that will unite all three kingdoms and end this dispute forever. Surely your father would have approved of that."

It all seemed so reasonable. The vision stretched out before her, of peace, stability, and her part in it so simple. But for a year she had seen every bit of correspondence that left Rolf's pen, and none of it concerned marriage. *The minstrel has succeeded, but given my uncle an idea for a new strategem. Still, it removes me from him, and that is good enough.*

"My uncle, this comes as a surprise. Why did you not discuss these arrangements with me?" *You lying viper,* she added mentally.

"I must beg your pardon. This solitary habit of mine is old, well-used, from my friendless days in exile." He looked at her, his pale eyes sorrowful, and she realized, with a sudden shock, that even while knowing that he was lying, she felt a pull of sympathy for him.

He has missed his calling. He should have been a traveling player. Well, perhaps that talent runs in the family, too. She set her jaw angrily. "And this was your plan from the start, was it not, Your Highness the Prince Uncle Rolf. To marry me off and take the throne for yourself." She let her voice grow shrill. "And now you think you can force me to go to Amytans. . . ."

The sugar-coating melted away from his voice when he spoke: "You must stop and consider political realities. In a month, you will be twenty-one and the council of nobles will reconvene. How many do you think will swear fealty to you?" He continued, his voice gentle once again. "If you marry, you will have a crown. You will be mistress of your own estates, a mother to children. If you do not . . ." He let the sentence hang unpleasantly.

She looked down at the letter in her lap, the better to appear defeated, the better to hide the triumph in her eyes. "I will go."

"A wise decision. A company of soldiers will escort you."

She glared at him. "I do not trust my welfare to anyone who takes orders from you. I will go with Murdoch, and none other."

He smiled slightly as he bowed. "As you wish, my lady."

"His Highness Prince Rolf requests your presence."

Valan bowed formally, and Matilda Nursemaid curtsied before replying, "I should be honored."

He grasped her arm to steady her as she recovered from her curtsy. She smiled her thanks and smoothed the pleats of her wimple before resting her hand on his arm to allow him to escort her to the prince.

Rolf sat in his chamber. "Lady Matilda," he said with a smile.

"Your Highness," she replied, and curtsied to the floor.

He continued to smile as she struggled to rise. Neither he nor Valan moved to help her. "I have news that will interest you," he said, when she had nearly regained her balance. "My niece is to be married to Roderik of Amytans."

"Sire!" she said, staggering back a bit, her wrinkled face flushed pink. "My little highness to be married! And to Amytans! I had not expected her to do half so well. I will go to her immediately. We have so much to do! The guest list, the dress, her trousseau. . . what date has been set?"

"You need not concern yourself," Rolf replied, still with the same benign smile. "She is to be married; your work here is done. I have arranged a place for you at the convent of Saint Agnes. You will leave forthwith."

"Sire?" she said.

"My servants have packed your belongings. The cart awaits. Valan, escort her."

"Sire! But she needs me now! The preparations! How can—"

"*Now*, Matilda! Begone, you prattling hag. Guards!"

Matilda stood stunned, her mouth agape. "How *dare* you!" she said at last.

"I do so because I can," he replied, with that same gentle smile. He nodded to the guard.

"You'll not treat me —" Matilda thundered, her words cut short by the guard's cudgel on the back of her skull.

"Take her away," said Rolf. "You know what to do."

* * *

". . . and Prince Rolf has commanded that I alone go with her, Sophie." Murdoch said as he laid his saddlebags on the broad, high bed of his chamber. "Get my shirt out of that chest, will you?"

"That snake. All the more reason for me to go." She opened the chest and rummaged through it. "Here's the linen shirt, and take the woolen one as well. The nights grow cold."

He stuffed them into the bag.

"With you gone," Sophie said, "I'll have no reason to stay here. Take me with you." She put three pair of woolen stockings on the bed.

"This journey holds more danger than you realize."

"Do you think my training inadequate?"

"No. I could not have asked more from a son."

"Then let me go with you. I'll disguise myself as her maid. I'll keep my hood low. No one will know it is me if I wear a dress."

* * *

It seems my deliverance has come. Rolf has paid Matilda's fee to enter the convent of Saint Agnes. I should be happy, but only feel alone. She did not even say good-bye. Alana packed the last of her belongings in the saddlebag.

Her page John buckled the bag and carried it to the courtyard. In the chill, gray light before the dawn, he and the stable boys were the only ones who bid Alana and Murdoch good-bye. The party was the sole spot of color in the deserted courtyard. The princess wore the colors of her kingdom, a dark green woolen cloak nearly concealing her emerald dress with its gold embroidery on bodice and cuffs. Meadowsweet champed at the bit as the groom tightened the saddle girth. Murdoch's clothing was dark, as always, with the three bright silver disks on his sword belt newly polished, but his warhorse Achilles, the strongly built black, bore blood-red trappings. Sophie's horse and the brown pony that carried Alana's clothing and the two dower chests were unadorned. Sophie came out of the door beside the armory, the bright rose-pink of her dress peeping from beneath the chestnut-brown cloak that had swallowed her. She had braided her hair with bright ribbons and pinned the ends of the braids atop her head so that they would hang down and conceal her face when she assumed a maidenly downcast pose. Murdoch nodded to her and casually

120

reached up and put his hand on her sword, which hung from his saddle .

"Highness. May I present your maid?"

Alana smiled at her and then, recognizing her, stared.

Sophie shrugged, clearly not comfortable in her garments .

"The color becomes you," Alana said. *Why, she is beautiful*, she thought. *Who would have expected it?*

Sophie frowned and bobbed an unpracticed curtsey.

The stable boy helped Alana onto Meadowsweet and then helped Sophie to mount. They had given her a bay gelding, a sorry animal, suitable for a servant.

Alana turned Meadowsweet's head toward the gate. *What a strange girl, who clumps about in men's clothing when she could be so lovely if she chose, but then, she's always been so. Who would think such a disciplined warrior as Murdoch would so indulge his daughter?*

When they reached the narrow gate, only wide enough to admit one rider at a time, Sophie fell back with the pony. A pikeman—one of Valan's, not a castle guard—stepped in front of her horse. The honed edge of his weapon gleamed coldly in the gray light.

"Murdoch and none other," he sneered, "by command of the regent."

He stood, blocking the passage, and leered at her as the others reined their horses and turned to see what the matter was. Under normal conditions, Sophie had no doubt that she would have kicked his teeth down his irritating grin and ridden on. Weaponless and enwrapped in flowing, bulky clothing, she felt helpless.

"What is this?" Alana's voice held a note of command. "Allow my maid to pass."

"The regent has ordered that none go with you but Murdoch."

"The regent rules in my name. Stand back," she ordered, but the man did not move.

Murdoch rode up beside her. "Highness, shall I teach him manners?"

There was a rustle in the passage, and the soft clink of chainmail. Pikemen, all of them in Valan's livery, materialized from the guard room and stood between Murdoch and Sophie. Sophie heard footsteps behind her and glanced back, relieved to see

Grimbold and a group of the castle guard. Murdoch looked through the forest of blades at her, realizing that it would take a bloodbath to win her passage.

"I cannot risk your life and hers for this," murmured Alana. "Daisy," she called, "it seems His Highness the Prince Uncle Rolf wishes me to braid my own hair. You may return to my chambers. Tidy them up and then report to the housekeeper and see what she would have you do."

"As you wish, Highness," Sophie said, in what she hoped was a maidenly falsetto. "Please, help me dismount," she said to Grimbold, who gaped at her as he did so. She went to the pack animal and unstrapped her bundle from its back, being careful to carry it as though it held only clothing, not weighty chainmail.

Bewildered, she turned back. She put her bundle in her room, transformed herself back into a hoyden, and then climbed the stairs to the top of the wall. From there, she could see the road leading down the hill from the castle, and she watched the pair's progress, wondering how she could manage to follow them. She stood watching the travelers until they had shrunk to dots and been swallowed by the forest. Steely clouds billowed to the west. The grass was losing its green, the leaves beginning to fade from the nighttime cold.

It is the dying time of year, she thought, and shivered. She turned and looked into the castle courtyard. The usual morning activities were going on: guardsmen drilling or lounging about polishing weapons, servants dealing with laundry and bringing food to the kitchen, stable boys grooming horses. *So, I am to be left behind, am I? Best play the part of the dejected girl.* She walked listlessly down the stairs to the courtyard and flopped down on the bench next to Grimbold.

He looked at her out of the corner of his eye. "I remember when Alana's mother came to be married to King Galeschin. It took ten carts to carry her dowry. She brought eight ladies to wait on her and was escorted by twenty-five mounted warriors and one hundred foot soldiers. And she was only the daughter of a lord, not a princess."

When Sophie, wrapped in gloom, said nothing, he continued. "You could tell that *she* was going off to be married, not being sent into exile."

Sophie stared at him, wordlessly.

"Strategy lesson," he said, getting slowly to his feet. "Think about it."

* * *

At the third hour after sunrise, Sophie carried a basket of washing down toward the postern gate. She was wearing a blue woolen dress and walked with a noticeable limp.

"Here, ducks, let me carry that for you," said a broad-faced serving woman.

"No, no, thank you, Sarah, you've got enough to do, I'll carry it down."

Sarah stopped, and her jaw hung slack. "Sophie? In a dress?"

"Flame threw me into a mud puddle. I've nothing clean to wear. Oh, Cook was asking for you. Something about the aprons."

"Thank you, miss," the good-hearted laundress replied. "But are you sure I can't help?"

"It's nothing. I just need to walk a bit and get the stiffness out."

Sarah grinned with relief and went off to the kitchen muttering, "Lovely child, not a proud bone in her body. Not like some around here."

Sophie continued to the postern gate, where a stout man-at-arms kept watch. "Cook's baking tarts," she teased.

"And you didn't bring me one?" he complained.

"They're not out of the oven yet," she replied, smiling, "but I'll do you one better. I'll stand watch for you while you go get one."

"Would you?" he said.

"Give me your pike and the key," she said, "just to make it official."

He did so with obvious gratitude and hurried up the walk.

"Bring one for me," she called after him. When he was out of sight, she quickly unlocked the gate and dragged the basket through it.

As was common in those days, the town clustered at the bottom of the hill with the castle standing guard on the heights above it. The main gate of the castle opened into the town, but the postern gate, or bolt hole, opened into a ravine in the cliff behind the castle. Sophie carried the basket down the ravine and set it at the end, just behind the ancient holly bush that concealed the opening in the castle's defenses. She pulled a dress and several pieces of bed linen off the top of the basket and dumped the rest—helmet, chainmail, saddlebags, and a cloak—on the ground. Then she pulled up her skirt in a most unladylike fashion, undid her sword belt, and dropped it onto the heap along with the sword and quiver of arrows that hung from it. She took the end of her bow out of her boot and slid it out of her dress, cursing softly as the other end caught in her hair. She bundled the clothes back into the basket and carried it back inside.

When the guard returned, munching pastry, she was waiting demurely for him. As she handed him the key, she told him, "I'll tell you what. I won't tell anyone you left your post, if you won't."

He gave her a conspiratorial look and nodded.

Sophie continued down the passageway toward the laundry.

"Well, well, well. . . Murdoch's daughter in a kirtle. Who knew you could be so lovely?" The voice chilled her to the bone. She turned. Valan stepped into the passage, a smirk on his face. "And your father sent off without you. You must be lonely."

"Not so lonely as to wish your company." She turned and strode off. She heard his footsteps behind her, his long strides growing closer. Only three steps to the entry of the laundry. She lengthened her stride and ducked into the doorway. Then she turned, and when Valan reached the threshold, she jammed the handle of the washbasket into his midsection with all her strength. He gasped for breath.

Sophie dumped the basket on his head, dodged past him, and raced to the stable where she ordered a groom to saddle Flame, the nimble, white-footed chestnut mare whose coat matched Sophie's hair. While he did so, she stripped off her skirts, revealing her normal attire. She told the stable boy that Flame needed exercise and rode off through the main gate.

124

Chapter 16
The Forest

Facing a chill, damp wind, Murdoch and Alana followed the road through the forest. They kept a slow pace on the uphill track and said little. Murdoch rode, senses alert, watching the forest for signs of movement. *The forest is thick here. Half an army could hide behind these trees, never mind enough to ambush a girl with an escort of one.*

Meadowsweet laid her ears back and startled as the wind blew dried brown leaves across the path, skittering like crabs. Alana soothed her mount and tried to keep her mind on her strategy, how she would present her cause to the prince, wondering if he really were as handsome as rumor reported. She rode with her eyes cast down. She had traveled before, through the meadows and villages of Gwalhafed, through tamed and tended countryside, but she had never taken the road to the west. Trees towered above the narrow track they followed, seeming to lean toward her, prepared to crush her with their weight. She glanced up at them, only to see, with a nauseating dizziness, a canopy of leaves shutting out the sky, and, it seemed to her, all light and air.

By noon, they reached the carter's camping place. "I'm hungry," Alana announced.

Murdoch scanned the forest and decided it was safe to stop. "Yes, Highness," he replied, then dismounted and helped her down from her horse. He took the leather sack containing food from their packhorse while she stood, looking in vain for a seat. There was neither chair, nor bench, nor even so much as a fallen log that would serve.

Murdoch turned toward her, watched her dilemma, and, with a sigh, removed his cloak and spread it on the ground. "My lady," he said, indicating that she was to sit.

"I cannot sit on the ground," she said.

"With all due respect, Highness, time advances, the weather worsens, and we have many miles to go before we reach the nearest shelter. It would not be wise to stop longer than need be."

She sighed and sat heavily on the cloak. Murdoch pulled a loaf of bread and half a round cheese from the sack. The princess's silver goblet had been included in the packing, but there was nothing to drink. He left the goblet in the sack and began to cut slices of bread and cheese for their meal.

"Pour me some wine, please."

"There is none, Highness."

"What? Preposterous." She seized the bag and began to rummage in it. "Here," she said, handing him her cup. "I can hear a stream nearby."

"My lady, I think it would be unwise to leave you unguarded."

"Please, Murdoch! I'm thirsty!"

"Princess, if we reach Amytans you may have me flogged for insubordination, but I am not leaving you unguarded."

"Of all the stubborn. . ." she began and then faltered as the import of his statement struck home. "Why do you say 'if'?"

"My lady, does it not strike you odd that the daughter of a king should set out to marry with a retinue of one?"

"It is what I commanded. 'Murdoch, and none other.'"

"But not so much as a groom or maidservant? No lady accompanies you. I have not the skill to braid your hair and cannot dress you."

"Rolf wishes to embarrass me, to send me to my wedding barefoot, like the goose girl in the fairy tale."

"Why will no nobleman of Gwalhafed let his sister or daughter go with you?"

"You know that they all support my uncle. Besides, they are an empty-headed lot of ninnies. I'm glad to be rid of them. The prince expects me. Rolf thinks he has found a way to turn my marriage to his advantage. He wouldn't dare harm me."

"Do you know that?"

"I have seen his letter, and held it in my hand."

Murdoch seemed unconvinced. "You hold a claim to the throne, and I know every detail of the defense of Gwalhafed, and here we are, set off alone for a kingdom Rolf wishes to war against."

"He no longer thinks of war. He sees this marriage as a part of a new strategy."

126

"And you believe him?"

Alana did not reply.

Murdoch stuffed the loaf and cheese back into the sack. "Highness, we are leaving." He stood and towered over her. "Now."

* * *

The sun hovered above the mountain ridge when they stopped at the dismal cottage in the valley. It looked no different than it had when William Carter had passed it with his passengers the week before, except that a broken-down cart now sat in the yard in front of it, to the right of the path that led to the door. Behind the cart they could barely see the top of a dark head and could quite clearly hear its owner pounding on the cartwheel he was repairing. They stopped at the gap in the wall.

"You there, boy," called Murdoch, "bring water for us and our horses."

The figure stopped its hammering, turned, and stood. When he had unfolded himself, he was nearly as tall as the warrior, or would be if he straightened himself. He held his shoulders clenched, as though he expected a beating. He wore a torn shirt and battered leather jerkin. His leggings were baggy and tattered at the knees and belted with a piece of rope. His straight hair was tousled and his face gaunt and smudged.

Without a word, he went to the well and drew water for them. He dipped out water for Alana, then for Murdoch, with a wooden ladle that hung by the well, and let the horses drink from the bucket. The powerful arms revealed by the torn shirt sleeves showed that he was no child, yet there was a childlike gentleness in his manner as he stroked Meadowsweet's head while she drank.

"Thank you," said Alana. She looked at him closely. His hair was black and his eyes so dark that the pupils were nearly invisible, his nose long and narrow, and his cheekbones prominent. His skin was tanned from a life lived out of doors. He looked different from anyone she had ever seen. "Who are you?" she asked.

"Boy," he replied.

"Boy?" she said. She would be hard-pressed to find a name more at variance with this young man's appearance. "You deserve better," she told him.

His large eyes opened wide and he looked at her, awestruck. She seemed to him like an angel, seated far above him, the narrow gold circlet she wore like a halo.

"Murdoch," she said, "let us go." She did not look back to see Boy standing, watching them until they disappeared around a bend in the road.

* * *

The storm clouds grew heavier as the afternoon wore on. As sunset approached, the wind gathered force and it began to rain. Their horses plodded on through the looming darkness, their breath misting in the cold. The rain soon soaked through the riders' cloaks.

Alana shivered uncontrollably. She was beyond trying to distract herself with thoughts of strategy or of daydreams about her handsome prince. Either the darkness or her imagination caused the trees to seem bigger, more threatening, and she thought they had perhaps left the paths of this world entirely and wandered on the road to Hell. When the dim, decrepit outline of the Fallen Log appeared before them, with its sounds of revelry and its promise of warmth and food, it seemed to Alana as welcome as a palace. They dismounted at the door, the wind tearing at their clothes.

The ceiling of the Fallen Log was low and grimed with wood smoke, the light scarcely better than the dimness outside. The air was hot, stale, fetid with the smell of unwashed bodies, and filled with raucous voices.

Murdoch looked around cautiously and then bade Alana wait by the door. "Stay in the shadows. Keep your hood up and your face down. With luck, they might think you my grandmother." He waded into the crowd of merrymakers.

A huge young man staggered up to Alana and leered at her. She shrank back toward the door. "Well, what do we have here?" He pulled her hood back. The slender gold circlet slipped off into the hood as he swept it from her head. "Oh, ho," he growled. "Looking for a place to stay the night, wench? I've got a place for you."

128

"No, thank you," she replied stiffly, glaring at him.

"Oh ho, not interested, are we? I bet you think you're too good for the likes of me." He moved closer to her and his hand reached under her cloak.

She twisted away, stepped nimbly past him, and called out, "Murdoch!"

The inn fell silent. Murdoch turned from his negotiations with the landlady and replied, "My lady?"

Women craned their necks to see him better.

The huge young man beside Alana turned and nervously asked, "Are you Murdoch?"

"Yes, I am." The warrior pushed back his cloak, so the disks on his sword belt would show. "And you are?"

"Garn, sir," came the meek reply.

"Garn," Murdoch said. "I'll remember that." He studied the young man's face for a moment, then turned again to the landlady.

Garn turned again to Alana. "Carry your bags, miss?"

* * *

Sophie, despite her best efforts, had not overcome her late start. By the time the sun set, she had only reached the dismal cottage. The rain whipped into her face and soaked her clothing. She left Flame at the gate and knocked at the door.

It creaked open from the force of her knock. In the darkness, she could see what appeared at first to be a moving pile of rags. Slowly, as the mountainous thing approached, she was able to make out a frazzle of gray hair and a stub of a nose, like that of a pig. As it approached Sophie, the apparition emitted what might be taken for a gurgle of delight.

"Ooooh! A visitor! Look, my darlings, at what the road has brought us tonight!"

Sophie shrank back half a step. She saw nothing that could be described as a darling, not so much as a cat. "I wondered if I might buy a bowl of soup for my dinner."

"Buy? Buy! The thought! A young one like you alone in such a storm. Of course not. Buy! Fah! Come in, come in. You'll stay to dinner and then have a warm bed for the night. Buy? Fah." The figure turned and retreated back into the house. "Don't mind your horse. The boy will take care of it." The woman stuck her nose out a window and bellowed, "Boy! Move your lazy carcass! We've company. See to the horse."

* * *

Boy dumped an armload of firewood into the box by the door, tugged his tattered cloak around him, and stumped off through the mud toward the gate. When the soup was ready, the woman shoved a bowl out the back door into his waiting hands and slammed the door in his face. He ate his soup in the stable, with the pigs, chickens, and Sophie's horse for company. After his meal, he peeked through a crack in the shutter. He could see Sophie, sitting by the fire, laughing and joking with his mistress, the witch. The girl was the second most beautiful woman he had ever seen, the most beautiful being the one who had spoken to him so kindly only that afternoon.

* * *

Midnight approached. The rain had stopped, blown away by the piercing wind. It was dark as pitch inside the cottage, save for a brilliant blade of moonlight stabbing through a crack in the shutter, and stiflingly warm in the great featherbed that the old woman had given Sophie for the night.

Sophie heard a scuttling noise and opened her eyes. Something just outside the window was trying to come in. She reached for her sword. The thing was poking a stick through the crack between the shutters, lifting the latch. The shutter swung back, creaking faintly, and she saw him silhouetted in the moonlight.

He saw the gleam of her sword and stopped. "Lady," he whispered. "Lady, are you awake?"

"Who are you? What do you want with me?"

"I'm Boy. I took care of your horse. I'm rescuing you."

"Rescuing me? From what? Go away. I can take care of myself."

"From the witch. Hurry. You don't want to be here after midnight."

"What? Don't be ridiculous." She rolled over and turned her back to him.

"Please!" The urgency in his voice drew her back. She sat up and looked around her.

At first, the place seemed as it had been, but then, could it be? She was sure that the plates on the sideboard had eyes. Eyes! Yes, and they were watching her. She dared not move. She must be dreaming. Dreaming, yes . . . but the scuttling noise came again, and this time, she was certain that she saw the teapot scurry across the table.

"Hurry, it's almost time!" He reached out his hand to her.

Again, the teapot moved, apparently carrying messages to the other household objects, and all the furniture seemed to emit a faint growl and draw closer to the bed . . . except the chair holding her bow and the quiver of arrows, which sidled away. Sophie bolted awake. The fireplace tongs hopped off the hearth and strode boldly toward her.

"AHHH!!" shouted Sophie as Boy knocked the tongs across the room with his staff.

"Run!!" Boy shouted, pulling her from the bed as it tried to swallow her. Sophie grabbed her boots and sword as she fended off hostile household objects. The chair cantered across the room, carrying her bow and arrows out of reach. Boy and Sophie tossed her belongings out the window and she leapt through, running barefoot for the horse.

"Come back!" the hag cried. "Oh, dear, did my darlings frighten you? Oh, please, come back."

She was answered by the sound of galloping hoofs.

"Drat," the witch growled. "Curse that boy."

* * *

They had slowed to a walk by the time they got to the Fallen Log, quiet now in the moonlight. They passed it and continued through the silent stillness under the waxing moon.

* * *

Murdoch and Alana spent the night in what passed for a room. It was, in fact, a pantry in the back of the tavern near the stables—and it stank. Alana slept in her dress on a plank laid on top of two of the barrels William had delivered, a pile of her spare clothing serving as a pillow. Murdoch paced the dirt floor to keep awake and at times looked through the shutters into the stall where their animals slept in greater comfort than they did themselves. Murdoch trusted the inhabitants of the inn as little as he trusted Rolf and kept the two dower chests beneath Alana's makeshift bed.

They left before dawn and passed the crossroads. The road to their left ran downhill toward Swanswater ford, in what had been Lord Mallow's domain. Now, thanks to Olwen's marriage to the bloated Abbersley, it was his. No ally to be found there.

Murdoch looked longingly to the right, the twisted path that led to the humble cottage where Beecham had trained him in sword. Beecham, dead five years past. No ally there, either.

He thought of the old woman, Dunwadi, who had come to Beecham and persuaded him to take on the task of training Murdoch. Was she still alive? He had repaid her by refusing to follow Rolf's order to invade her home. Of course, she would never know that—or would she? She'd known when Beecham was injured and sent help to him then, and knew when he had arrived at Beecham's hut. Was she still alive? Would she remember him?

Did it matter? They would go to Amytans, where Alana would marry her prince, he hoped. He hoped with all his heart that this was not some new stratagem of Rolf's, but in his heart, he could not believe it. He shook his head and followed the westward path, toward Amytans. They were already climbing the lower slopes of the mountains when the sun rose. As the gray light gave way to pink, he noticed the fresh tracks of a horse.

"Who would be traveling at night through these parts?" Alana asked.

"No one on honest business," he replied. "Keep your wits about you."

The trail ran along the bed of a shallow stream. At times, there was room for them to ride beside it; at others, the horses waded through, wet to their hocks. After a few miles, the stream veered to the right and the trail continued westward, up a steep rise. The tracks of the single horse left the path and followed the stream, trampling the bracken on its banks, going into a dell.

"Should we follow it?" she asked.

He looked around, at the increasing steepness of the grade, and at the ravine the path followed. *A good place for an ambush*, he thought, *but there's only one and I'm expecting him*. He slid his sword out of its sheath and spurred his horse cautiously up the hill. In the dell, just out of sight, Sophie and Boy slept, wrapped in their cloaks as Flame cropped the sparse grass.

Murdoch and his charge had not gone too much farther when three armed men wearing the blue and yellow of Amytans blocked their path. Alana sighed with relief.

"Good day, gentlemen," Murdoch said.

"And good day to you," replied the leader, a tall, squint-eyed man with a scar along his cheekbone. "What be your business?"

"I am escorting the princess Alana to Amytans for her marriage to Prince Roderik."

"Good," the man replied coldly. "We've been waiting for you." He moved toward them.

These soldiers know little of courtesy, Alana thought bitterly. *It seems I have traded the tender mercies of my uncle for a bridegroom who thinks me a broodmare, or a pawn in some imperial game.*

Murdoch's horse took a step forward and turned its flank toward them. He held his sword concealed beneath his cloak. These were not men of Amytans. He recognized one of them as Garn, the oaf from the tavern.

Garn whispered something to the leader, who seemed to falter. "Murdoch?" he whispered back and looked up at the figure on horseback.

Murdoch smiled at them beneath steely eyes. They dropped their swords. With a shake of his head, he ordered the men to stand to one side. Their leader gave a quick look toward the south side of the ravine. As Murdoch's eyes followed that glance, a dozen men dressed as Amytans soldiers leapt down the embankment.

He turned his horse toward Alana's, and his sword flashed as he went about his deadly work. The first to reach him fell, blood spurting from his throat. Murdoch backed his horse into the three on the road, who had stooped to pick up their swords. Achilles, trained to battle, brought his heavy hooves into play against them as Murdoch's sword flashed in a great arc, sweeping a path clear to the princess. Two more of the attackers lay crumpled, red stains spreading over their yellow garments. Behind Murdoch, two of the assailants slunk toward the south side of the road, one clutching his limp arm, the other, the leader, unhurt and intending to stay that way. Garn lay in the road, the side of his face black and crumpled, blood trickling from his ear. Alana turned her horse and tried to ride back down the path, but the suddenness of the attack overwhelmed her.

Four of the men made straight for her. Two seized the bridle, and one went sprawling as Meadowsweet's back hoof thudded into his chest. Nearby in the dell, Sophie's horse answered the screams of their horses. The pack horse, squealing in terror, escaped back down the path and ran into the dell, following the voice of her stablemate.

Sophie and Boy were startled from sleep and heard the ring of swordplay.

"Come on!" Sophie shouted and grabbed her sword. Boy picked up his staff and followed her to the top of the dell.

Five men lay groaning, or ominously silent, in the narrow space around the warrior. Murdoch's sword flashed in glittering, deadly arcs, but great as his prowess was, it would not allow him to be on both sides of Alana at once. Three soldiers now hung on her plunging horse's bridle as a fourth dragged her from the saddle. Four others faced Murdoch as he tried to reach her. The leader skulked behind him. As Boy and Sophie reached the top of the embankment, the man saw his chance and swung at Murdoch's left arm. Murdoch let out a roar of pain as the sword bit.

Sophie shouted and leapt from the embankment. The squint-eyed man threw his sword at her and ran. Another stood his ground, but in two swift, flashing strokes, she toppled him into a lifeless heap.

Boy, unused to battle, hesitated. His cry, as he jumped, came as much from sheer terror as warlike intent. His staff crashed into the head of the man clawing at Alana and in quick succession he felled two of the three men holding her horse. The third, eyes wide in fear, bolted back the way he had come.

Boy helped Alana to her feet as the surviving attackers quickly clambered into the forest on the south side of the road.

"What in Hell are you doing here?" Murdoch roared at his daughter.

"Aren't you glad to see me?" Sophie asked.

He dismounted carefully, favoring his wounded arm. He closed his eyes and took a few deep breaths. "Yes, Sophie, I am. We'll need to get off the road in case these motherless curs have any friends."

Sophie saw his blood-soaked sleeve. "Father, you're hurt!"

He looked annoyed. "We can bind it when we are well hidden. Lead my horse. My lady?"

Boy was still supporting Alana. Her cloak was muddied, her dress torn, and he could feel her tremble. He was shaking as well, from the thrill of the fight and from the awe of touching her. The scent of lavender from her clothing filled his nostrils. Her hood had fallen back onto her shoulders and her hair come unbound and he could see that what had seemed to him a mass of scarlet flame was in reality a cacophony of color, from darkest mahogany through every conceivable shade of red to pale strands that shone like polished copper. It came to him that even death would be sweet if he could reach it by being engulfed in that fire.

"Come, Lady, we can't stay here," he said, and began to lead her after Murdoch.

She looked at him, her face blank with shock. Then her eyes focused on him. "Boy!"

He stood, dazzled that she should remember him.

At that moment, a flurry of hoofbeats burst from the forest farther down the hill. Murdoch and Sophie clutched their swords and Boy stepped in front of Alana. It was the soldiers, but instead of attacking, they pelted down the road toward Gwalhafed.

Sophie led them around to the dell by the path. Murdoch sat on the fallen beech.

"Why are you here?" he asked Boy.

"He rescued me," said Sophie, with unaccustomed shyness.

"Well, then, I am twice in your debt." He eyed the young man appraisingly. *He's as filthy as a blacksmith,* he thought, and then he smiled. *What a promising young man.* He glanced sidelong at his daughter.

"You'll need better clothes if you're going to travel with us— that is, if you've nothing better to do."

Boy grinned with delight.

"There, in my saddle bags," Murdoch said. "Find something that will suit you."

Sophie tended Murdoch's arm. The sword had sliced nearly to the bone and the flesh hung in a jagged flap. As best she might, she laid it back together and bound it tight with a strip of linen torn from Alana's underdress. Murdoch gritted his teeth against the pain. The makeshift bandage quickly soaked with blood.

After the sudden clatter of battle, the wind's sighing and the birdsong sounded strangely loud in their ears. Boy took the bag with Murdoch's spare clothing behind a hazel bush by the stream.

Sophie was tying off the bandage on Murdoch's arm when the woodland quiet was broken by clattering hoof beats from up the path. Boy ran up from the stream and picked up his staff. He was wearing Murdoch's leggings and his own footgear. His skin was clean and moist and his black hair clung sleekly to his neck. Alana's eyes stayed on him, on the way the lean muscles of his back moved as he waited, restlessly holding his staff ready. He was as thin and as taut as wire.

At Murdoch's gesture, Sophie crept up the slope to lie flat at the top and peer over the embankment. A beautiful white horse bearing the lion crest of Amytans on its saddlecloth burst into the ravine, checked, and reared. Its rider's weaponry glinted with gold in the sunlight. Sophie gasped. She had spent her life among warriors, but she had never seen one like this. She could not take her eyes from the breadth of his shoulders and the way he and his horse moved as one. He removed his gleaming helmet and the curls that tumbled out shone no less brightly in the clear morning sun. His eyes glinted as blue as the sky. *Surely this man must be a warrior of renown*, she thought. She studied his gleaming mail coat and the gilded breastplate. *His armor is worth a king's ransom. What great deeds has he done to be so rewarded?* A thrill of danger ran up her spine, mingled with anger that one so noble-looking should resort to cowardly ambush.

The rider dismounted, his blue cloak swirling gracefully, and studied the scene, turning over bodies, removing helmets, and looking at the faces of the dead.

"Look at this, Dreyfala," he said in puzzlement. "Nine soldiers of Amytans dead. What were they doing here? They wear the em-

136

blem of the castle guard." None of them looked familiar, but, he reasoned, one could not be expected to know all one's retainers. Dreyfala snorted and pawed the ground.

Roderik stood, shaking his head, and then searched the ground for footprints. He read the marks of the struggle. He was now close enough for Sophie to hear his words.

"They leapt from here," he said, looking at the south side of the ravine. "And some, at least, escaped the same way. They attacked three horsemen coming up the ravine. Two more attacked from this side." He scratched his head. "A warrior, quite young, or at least with very small feet, and. . . . a peasant?" He snapped his fingers and Dreyfala trotted to his side.

Such mastery of animals, Sophie thought.

He remounted and rode slowly down the hill, bending low to see the tracks. "Another puzzle, Dreyfala. One horse ran into the dell and then the other two horses went into the dell at a walk and with them the two warriors, the peasant and. . . a lady! They walked—not ran, Dreyfala—this way, and at least one is wounded." He looked a bit farther down the road. "And here the attackers, quite a few of them, left in a panic for Gwalhafed."

Sophie crept along the ridge, watching him and planning her defense of the dell. She was both appalled and impressed by the ease with which he read the tale of the battle from the footprints. *In a moment, he will find us and finish the work his lackeys began. He is formidable. With Father wounded, he might well have his way.* Silently, she moved to the end of the ridge, where the path to the dell split off from the main track. She drew her dagger and crouched, waiting. His back was to her, and he was scarcely six feet away.

He sat silent, as motionless as a statue. *Why would Amytans guardsmen attack a lady and her escort? No doubt they are spies sent from Velendruch, and our spies found them out.*

Four courses of action competed in his mind. The first would be to turn back and bring news of the attack to the castle. He discarded that notion outright. Amytans soldiers would travel with a pigeon, two pellets—one black, one white—fastened to its legs. If all went well, the bird would return home with a white pellet; if events went ill, with the black. If the bird returned with both pellets, it meant that things had gone totally awry and help would be sent at a gallop. No doubt the bird had already reached Arnhem Castle. The second course would be for him to wait there or turn back in hope of meeting the reinforcements. He discarded this as the act of a coward. The third alternative, to follow the trail into the dell, he reasoned, would be the act of a fool. Warriors who had killed nine and put another half dozen or so to flight could hardly be challenged by one. There remained the alternative of following the surviving guardsmen into Gwalhafed, rallying them, and leading them back against the foe. If he could do so before reinforcements arrived from Arnhem Castle, he would show his valor and have tales to tell at parties for at least the next year. At the conclusion of his reasoning, he spoke.

"I'll rally them and bring them back to victory. What say you, Dreyfala?" The horse stamped his hoof and whinnied. Roderik nodded and then followed the tracks of the soldiers.

Sophie sat openmouthed. She returned to the dell and reported to her father. "A knight, coming from Amytans, with their colors on his saddlecloth. Half-witted, I think. He asked his horse for advice. He looked at the dead and then followed their companions. He plans to bring them back to finish us, the pig."

"We must leave here now," Murdoch said. "Unload the pack horse so Boy can ride." Sophie unstrapped the dower chests and Boy lowered them from the pony's back. Alana watched him, her mind preoccupied with more serious matters. The muscles of his arms and chest stood out in clear relief as he took on the weight of the chest.

"What's in these things?" grunted Boy as he staggered, attempting to lower the first chest gently to the ground. It landed heavily, with a metallic jingle.

"My dowry," Alana replied.

"All that money," he said in awe. "Should you leave it here?"

"It won't do us much good in the Hills," Murdoch said.

"The Hills!" Boy dropped the second chest and it cracked.

Alana blanched. "Murdoch, are you sure?"

"Your uncle and Amytans are in league against us. Where else would you have us go?"

"But the forest faeries—"

"I've never spoken of this, lest others think me mad," he said. "But I met one, long ago, when I was sent to Sword Master Beecham to train. Her name was Dunwadi, and she said I will play a role in some prophecy they have. If we can find her, I think we will be safe."

"And if we do not?"

"Where else would you have us go?"

Boy looked nervously up the slope.

"You don't have to come with us," Murdoch said. "You have done us great service already."

"No," Boy replied, looking at Alana. "I will not leave you." He picked up Murdoch's shirt from where he had dropped it, brushed off the dried leaves, and put it on. The shirt of a larger man, it concealed all evidence of the body within it.

Chapter 17
Prince Roderik Learns a Thing or Two

An infant could have followed the trail the soldiers left. They made no attempt at evasion or concealment, but pelted down the road toward Gwalhafed and made for the Fallen Log, the first tavern in their path.

Roderik dismounted and tied his horse to the rail, next to theirs. He studied the chaotic mass of hoofprints behind the tethered horses. Lifting the near hind foot of one of them, he confirmed that it was the one with the nicked horseshoe that he had followed from the ambush. He followed the scent of stale beer to the door.

Inside, he stood for a moment, blinking, as his eyes grew accustomed to the gloom. The place was deserted, but for a slovenly barmaid and a group of men clustered around a long table in a back corner. He could just make out the yellow of an Amytans jerkin crumpled in a heap beneath the table. He strode toward them.

"One old man and a woman," one of the men growled at the leader. "You lying, misbegotten son of a cur. That 'old man' was Murdoch!"

"Garn knew, but—the halfwit—he didn't tell me until it was too late."

"You told him you'd cut off his ears if he snuck off to the tavern—"

"At ease, men," Roderik commanded, seating himself on a stool at the end of the table.

Their heads snapped toward him. "What in hell . . ." said one. Another spat on the floor.

As his eyes roved the table, Roderik realized that, like those of the dead on the road, not one face was familiar to him.

"What has befallen you, men of Amytans?" he began grandly. They said nothing and their stares grew colder.

They shifted in their seats and he knew they were reaching for weapons. "Who's your captain?" he demanded.

"I'd not ask any more questions, pretty boy," their leader growled. "I'd be leaving if I were you."

"Not until I get some answers, soldier. I'm Prince Roderik and it's time for you to start talking!"

The leader leapt to his feet. Roderik stood and reached for his sword. Before it was half out of its sheath, the leader had grabbed his end of the trestle and upended it. Flagons flew and beer sprayed across the room.

"None of that!" screeched the barmaid. "I run a respectable place here!"

Roderik stepped back and tripped over the fallen stool. The two men nearest the leader heaved the table. Sparks flew in Roderik's vision as his head met the beer-drenched flags of the tavern floor. The last thing he saw was the tabletop as it rushed toward his face. He threw up his arms to protect himself, and the world dissolved in a blaze of pain.

* * *

Roderik crawled out from under the table, blood dripping from his nose, his ears buzzing like a hive of bees. The barmaid stood over him, demanding payment for the beer and broken crockery in a voice that had the insistent force of an unoiled hinge. He gave her a silver piece from his shrinking purse and staggered out the door. The highwaymen and their horses had disappeared, scattering this time in as many directions as possible.

This, I see, is the price of being distracted from my quest, he thought.

Head pounding, determination firm again, Prince Roderik continued his journey to Gwalhafed. Soon he reached the witch's dismal cottage with its inviting well. He dismounted, tied his horse to the gate, and entered the yard, hallooing. Hearing no reply, he hauled up the bucket and dipped water with the ladle. He drained it quickly, then washed the dried blood from his face.

The witch came around the corner of the cottage with a basket of grain in her arms and a flock of poultry at her heels.

"People interrupting you all day it's a wonder I get anything done around here drat that boy," she grumbled, the words billowing around her like a cloud of acrid smoke. She spotted the prince.

"Oooooh!" she gurgled. "And how may I be of service to you, your lordship?"

"I just stopped for water." He sat heavily on the bench next to the well and dropped his aching head onto his hands.

She put the basket down and regarded him. "Headache, eh?" she said. "Bet you stopped at that tavern up the road." She filled the dipper with water, dropped a pebble into it and sidled up confidentially. "Just between you and me," she whispered, "I think they water their beer."

He grunted and took the dipper from her. "You wouldn't know of a remedy, would you?" he asked.

"I might," she replied. "For a generous young man." There was an unmistakable emphasis on the word *generous.*

"Mmph," he grunted. He handed back the dipper and pulled out his jingling leather pouch. As he rummaged in it, she leaned closer to peek in. He noticed her and turned away quickly. He handed her a large copper coin. She accepted it with some satisfaction and waddled into the house. She returned with a wooden cup filled with a vile green liquid.

"This will do the trick," she said, giving him a toothless grin.

"Are you sure?" he replied, sniffing at it.

"Of course," she replied, her voice testy. "I make the finest potions in these parts. Guaranteed. All of 'em."

He brought the cup to his lips, then took it away again. "You make a lot of these, you say?"

"Every day. All kinds. Headache potions, potions for the chilblains, for colic in babies . . . love potions." She leaned round and gazed up coyly into his face.

He leaned back and set the cup down on the bench. He smiled, his white teeth shining like stars. "I have no need of love potions, old woman."

"So you say," she returned. "And it may be true, but one cannot always be too confident in matters concerning love."

Dreyfala snorted.

"You keep out of this," the witch retorted, and then turned to the prince again. "A handsome young knight, alone, on the road to Gwalhafed Castle. Might this journey concern the princess Alana?"

"I . . . ah, well . . ."

She nodded. "And are you aware that this same princess is about to be married?"

"Married? To whom?"

"Oh, some prince, not a mere knight without entourage." She looked scornfully at Dreyfala. "It will take more than a handsome face to win her hand."

"And you can help?"

"Now you sing a different tune," she said, cackling.

"Can you really make a potion?"

"For a price."

"Any!"

He held out his pouch and she took it, hefted it in her hand, and slid it beneath the layer of rags at her bosom. She reached under another part of the rag pile she wore and took out a minuscule leather pouch.

"That's it?"

"This is very powerful," she hissed. "Only a pinch is needed."

"Are you sure?"

"Would you like to try it out right now?" she said, advancing toward him amorously.

"No!" he barked as he jumped to his feet. The cup fell to the ground and the liquid oozed out. "Thank you very much. I'll be going now."

He leapt into the saddle and put the spurs to Dreyfala, who seemed as glad to leave the witch's house as Roderik was.

The witch stood laughing at his panic, her chickens pecking the ground around her feet. As she turned to pick up her basket, she noticed one chicken eyeing the pool of slime next to the fallen cup.

"No! Shoo!" she shouted as it pecked at the potion. "Stupid bird!" With a startled squawk, the chicken turned into a large and scabrous toad.

* * *

Grimbold and Samson stood guard at the city gate, the afternoon sun in their eyes. "Now, what do you suppose that is?" said Grimbold, pointing at the golden spark that had just emerged from the forest and was pelting down the road toward the castle.

Samson shaded his eyes and squinted and the wind brought Dreyfala's hoofbeats to their ears. "I hope it's friendly."

The mounted figure grew larger, until Roderik sat before them on his prancing mount.

"Halt, sir, and identify yourself," Grimbold demanded, as he and Samson blocked the way with their pikes.

"I am Roderik, prince of Amytans," he replied, removing his helmet.

Samson and Grimbold exchanged glances. "And your business?"

"I seek audience with the princess Alana."

"What?" Grimbold shouted.

Prince Roderik was taken aback. "What?" he echoed. "How about, 'Enter, Your Highness, we will tell her you are here?' The forms, man, the forms!"

"She left yesterday, for Amytans, to marry *you*," Grimbold said.

"What?"

"I'd hurry, if I were you," Samson drawled. "Wouldn't want to miss your own wedding."

Roderik gaped at the men and cursed himself for his stupidity. He set his spurs to Dreyfala. The great horse backed away from the pair, spun around, and galloped away from Gwalhafed Castle as if it were an haunted place.

He rode through the night and reached the scene of the attack early the next day. The bodies were gone, and the tracks hopelessly muddled. He followed the trail to the dell, where hoof and boot prints were everywhere in the boggy soil. The chests were gone, but their marks remained. It took Roderik some time to find the faint trail leading out of the dell, toward higher, drier ground: the prints of four horses, obscured at the base by others that had followed a short distance and then turned back when it became evident that the tracks led directly toward the Hills. He reined in Dreyfala, who stood pawing the earth, and looked about, as if expecting monsters to leap out of the trees and devour him.

144

"Lady of Dreams," he whispered. "Please don't let my grandmother see this." He began to climb the hill.

* * *

The messenger departed, carefully closing the door after himself.

"I am surrounded by incompetents!!" raged Rolf. The chessmen shivered as his fist landed on the table next to the board.

"Fifteen men were sent, as you instructed," Valan said calmly. "Your move, I believe."

"Fifteen cowards! I should have gone myself. All these years, all this work, to be thwarted by fifteen fools."

"Murdoch and the princess have gone into the Hills, Highness. They are as good as dead for your purposes."

"Don't tell me you believe those stories."

"Of course not, my lord, but what better reason to mount an expedition into the Hills? Those warriors loyal to Murdoch and the princess will be the most eager to volunteer. They can take the Hills in the name of finding Alana, while we solidify your position down here."

Rolf nodded thoughtfully and moved his knight to threaten Valan's queen.

"And if the stories are true, and none of them ever returns, so much the better," Valan continued.

"It is also possible," Rolf answered, "that they would find them. Murdoch and half the army on the heights at our border is hardly to our advantage."

"I did not say to send them off unsupervised, my lord," Valan continued. He pondered his move and the prince waited. "The hazards of the Hills are notorious. If a squad or two, or even an entire regiment, disappear, there is precedent in the legends, and certainly no blame would attach to you." He took Rolf's knight with his rook.

Rolf smiled. "How would you like to be commander of the army?"

"I think not, sire."

"You think not?"

"I am ever content to be your vassal and right arm, sire, but the Hills are an unknown factor. If things should go amiss, it will be necessary to fasten the blame to someone, and I must decline the honor. May I recommend the sterling Lord Drent as an alternative?"

Rolf nodded. "Excellent. I shall send you along to supervise." He moved his remaining knight. Valan's logic was impeccable. He needed to be reminded of his place, before he could develop notions about hatching plots of his own.

"Don't you think that would be a bit obvious, my lord?"

"Obvious?"

"The grieving uncle stays home? Your going would solidify your support among the peasantry and allay their suspicions." He drained his goblet.

Rolf seized his opportunity and nudged a pawn forward. "The peasantry? Valan, since when have you given any thought to the opinions of the lower classes?"

"My lord, they are a long-suffering lot and will undergo any amount of privation if they support its cause. They hold your niece in high regard, and would no doubt pay additional levies if it would help to bring her back." He moved his bishop.

Rolf took Valan's bishop with his rook. He leaned back in his chair, his fingers steepled, and then smiled at his only friend. "Valan, you are a wonder. Oh, check. And mate, if I'm not mistaken."

* * *

"Grimbold, you old fool, why are you dragging me down here? The place is full. I've got business to attend to." They stood in the cellar of the Cock and Bull. "Ow! Now look what you've done." Wax from the candle Saul held dripped over his hand.

"Saul. Yesterday, the princess is sent off to be married with an escort of one and not so much as a serving wench."

"But it was Murdoch went with her. What harm could come to her?"

"Saul, listen. This afternoon, the bridegroom rides up, big as life, says he's come to see her."

"What? Are you sure?"

Grimbold nodded. "Big blond-headed lad. Blue and yellow trappings. Fine horse and the sort of armor an ordinary knight can't afford. Said he was Prince Roderik of Amytans. I believed him."

"God save us all." Saul sat heavily on a keg. "What does this mean?"

"It means Alana's been sent off to be killed, you bloody fool."

"But Murdoch—"

"One man can be outnumbered. Worse yet, the prince came up the road they went on. If he met them on the road, he'd have stayed with them, wouldn't he? She must be. . ."

The door above them creaked. Footsteps stumbled on the stairs. "Ow! Damn. Grimbold?"

"Sams!"

"Orders," he panted. "We're to search for the princess. They're calling for recruits."

"There goes your theory, Grimbold."

"Grimbold," puffed Samson. "She was attacked by Amytans troops at the border."

They all sat silent, trying to make sense of events.

"It makes my head swim," Saul said.

"When are we to march out, Sams?"

"Next week."

"Next week! What in blazes?"

"Grimbold," said Samson, "She's gone into the Hills. They're gathering an army to go in after her."

Saul crossed himself.

Grimbold sat on the keg next to Saul's, his hands on his temples, as if that would help him think more clearly. "Wait . . . wait. No one knows about the prince except us. So, what would it look like if we didn't know that the wedding was a sham?"

"That Amytans was treacherous."

"And how would the regent's behavior look?"

"Like he wanted her back."

"But to wait a week? She could starve to death in that time."

"They said Murdoch was with her. They said there would be safety in numbers and encouraged all those who love the princess to join the search. "

"All those who love the princess. . . that's it, Samson. He wants to get rid of all of us who might oppose his rule."

"So, what do we do?"

"We're under orders. We'll have to go. And we'll walk into a trap. If the princess is dead, I suppose we would want as few of Rolf's opponents to go into the Hills as could be. If she lives, we must send in as many as possible, to fight for her safety."

"Do you think she lives?"

"I don't know, but we can't take the chance."

Chapter 18
Into the Hills

Alana and her companions passed beyond the lower hills, where the cliffs diminished into the sloping tongue of land that separates Gwalhafed from Amytans. The beeches and oaks gave way to tall pines and then gnarled firs, and even these failed as the ascent became steeper and the soil parted to reveal the bones of granite beneath. They now followed a ledge along the east side of the ridge, barely wide enough for a horse, with a sheer drop of increasingly dizzying height to the right.

On the left, the rock was as flat as a wall, broken occasionally by rivulets that trickled down and disappeared in fissures that crossed the path and threatened to trap their horses' hooves. They rode with downcast eyes, each looking toward the gray wall of solid rock to their left, as a guard against the terror of the view that spread below them.

Far below, the cliffs ended in great barren hillocks, and even farther below that, the Eisen wound through its great dish of valley, sweeping past fields of golden stubble and the bright green of newly sprouting winter wheat. They came at last to a hollow in the mountainside, sheltered to the north and west, a pocket of meadow with a sparkling stream and enough room for their horses to graze. There, on the eastern side of the mountains, darkness fell early, and so there they spent the night.

The dawn woke them, but as great as their need was, they could not leave the meadow. The horses needed a good feed to be of further use. Murdoch's arm tormented him. He felt giddy from loss of blood. They sat and shared rations, hoping that the terror of their destination would guard them from pursuit, wondering if they themselves dared go further. Their view soared over the breadth of Gwalhafed and they could see Valan's castle, inside its wall of red rock, and beyond it Alana could see her home, like a dull gray tooth, near the southeastern horizon. Compared to that staggering view, the dense, shadowed forest through which they had passed seemed as safe as a castle keep.

Sophie unwrapped the bandage on Murdoch's arm and noted that the wound seemed clean, at least at the surface, and the bleeding had slowed to an ooze, but there was a redness surrounding it that she disliked.

"This worries me," she told her father.

He grunted. "There's nothing we can do now. We can poultice it later, if we can find the right herbs. I've survived worse." He smiled grimly.

Sophie scrubbed the bandage in the stream and rewrapped her father's arm.

Alana sat shrouded in her hooded cloak, looking toward her kingdom. Boy watched her, but she did not notice.

"Why are you named 'Boy'?" Murdoch asked.

He turned toward the warrior. "I was never named," he replied. "My mother died when I was born and my father refused to give me a name. When I was three, he traded me to the witch for a milk goat."

"Traded his son for a goat?" Murdoch said. "That's inhuman."

"Oh, no. She was an excellent milker."

After they had paused a moment to digest that bit of information, Sophie asked, "And since then you have lived in the witch's house?"

"In her barn."

"How cruel!"

Boy shook his head. "She was good to me. She fed me every day. Twice, sometimes."

Sophie deftly unbraided her hair. "And you never tried to leave?"

He thought a moment and shook his head, as if trying to dispel cloudy thoughts. "I never thought to until *she* told me I deserved better." He looked toward Alana. "I never even peeked through the window before that."

"Lucky for you, Sophie," Murdoch said.

"What would have happened if she had caught me?" Sophie asked as she combed through her hair with her fingers.

"She would have cut out your heart."

They shuddered.

"Why?" Murdoch asked.

150

"She wants to be beautiful. . . ."

"I can understand that," Sophie said, shivering again.

"And she needs the heart of a beautiful young maiden for the potion."

Murdoch held up his hand for silence and raised his head, listening. "Hoofbeats!"

He, Boy, and Sophie grabbed their weapons and stood in front of Alana. The sound grew louder until, with a great flourish, Dreyfala rounded the bend and burst into the meadow, mane and tail waving proudly. The horse stopped abruptly and reared.

"Unhand that lady, churls!" Prince Roderik shouted, sweeping his sword from its scabbard. It was a magnificent, if inappropriate, entrance.

Murdoch sighed. He stood, arm throbbing, blade ready. His opponent was fresh, unhurt, well-armed, with a longer reach and the voice of a young man. Murdoch's best weapon, he judged, was his reputation, and he decided to try that first. "Allow me to make introductions," he said coolly. "I am Murdoch, champion of the princess Alana. . . ."

To their astonishment, the rider sheathed his sword, tore off his helmet, and dismounted, leaving the helmet to tumble across the ground and off the cliff's edge. He strode toward Alana, a broad smile on his face, only to be stopped by Murdoch's and Sophie's swords, pointed at his chest.

Roderik held his hands out, palms down, in a gesture of appeasement. "My lady," he said to Alana, ignoring the swords as much as possible. "I have been seeking you to offer my service."

Murdoch was dumbfounded. For the past sixteen years, the mere mention of his name had inspired instant—at the least—respect. Since his childhood as the foundling son of a blacksmith and through the long years of his fame as a swordsman, he had been challenged, insulted, reviled, and honored, as fate and his opponent of the moment determined, but he had never been ignored. He decided he did not like it—nor did he like this foppish young man.

Roderik, for his part, gazed lovingly at Alana. For this moment he had come. He had wandered alone, on short, foraged rations. He had ridden all night. He had suffered assault, hunger, fatigue.

The wisps of hair that floated from beneath the princess's hood were, indeed, as red as could be imagined, her eyes as pale as the dawn sky, and there were freckles on her nose. *A pox take all minstrels,* the prince thought. *He didn't say anything about freckles.*

"And who might you be?" Alana said.

"I am Prince Roderik of Amytans," he told her, drawing himself up and giving his most charming grin.

The rumors of his looks are not exaggerated, Alana decided. *In his golden armor, he looks like the Archangel Michael.* She could still hear the clanging of the helmet as it dropped down the cliff face. *Here stands a man lacking in attentiveness,* she concluded. *His connections may prove useful, but he himself will take looking after.*

Sophie glowered at him. "You low, two-faced, treacherous *pig!*" she muttered, her voice rising to a murderous crescendo on the last word.

Murdoch's sword flashed to parry hers. Roderik leapt backward, caught his spur on a corner of his cloak, and sat heavily, gazing awestruck at the enraged amazon towering over him. Her cheeks were flushed with anger, her eyes blazed, and her hair billowed about her head like a bonfire. He had never seen anything like her. Her intensity burned into his soul.

My God, he thought, *who is she?*

He sat on the ground, at her mercy. He felt a broad chasm open deep in his soul. Then he remembered the forms that Phillipe had taught him. *My head must turn for no other. This woman is a danger to my quest.* He tore his eyes from her and looked at Alana. Boy ran up to him and held his staff ready, in case Roderik should decide to draw his sword again.

"Hold!" Murdoch shouted. "Put up your sword, Sophie." He stood over the unfortunate prince, the point of his sword uncomfortably close to his nose, and began to question him.

"Why did your men attack us on the road?" he demanded.

"They were disguised as men of Amytans, but were not so in truth."

"Liar," snapped Sophie. "You met with them."

"I followed them, but when I found them, they would not answer my questions or obey my orders. I tell you, they were not men of Amytans."

152

"Then why do you follow us now?"

"I left Amytans on a quest to seek the princess Alana and offer her my service." He moved from his seat to the customary position for such offers, on one knee. "Which I do now."

"Why?" Alana replied. "Since you well knew I was on my way to Amytans."

"My lady, I did not. A minstrel came to the celebration of my knighting and sang of you. I was told of this supposed marriage by the guards at the gate of your castle."

So, this is my hero, she thought. *What could that minstrel have been thinking?*

"My uncle!" she said in disgust. "What a fool I've been."

"Come with me to Amytans," Roderik said. "You will be safe there and we can take counsel as to how to deal with this usurper."

She nodded and they mounted and turned their horses' heads back down the path. They had only traveled a few paces when a dull rumbling ahead gave them warning.

"I'll go look," Boy offered, already off his horse and squeezing between the rock wall and the flank of Murdoch's horse. Murdoch looked nervously up the cliff. "Back the horses into the meadow. There may be more loose rock above."

Boy returned a few minutes later. "The path is completely blocked. It's strange, though. Most of the rock on the path is different from the rock here. It's round, as though it were taken from a river, not broken off a cliff. Could there be a river above?"

"Can we move the stones?" Roderik asked.

"Some of them, yes. Others. . . I don't know. Come with me and look."

The moment they turned to walk down the slope, there was another rumbling, nearly above them. Roderik looked up, but Boy, without waiting to see the danger, leapt backward, dragging Roderik with him. A boulder twice the size of a bushel smashed into the ground at their feet, bringing a cartload of scree down with it. They scrambled quickly toward the others in the meadow. It was quite clear to all of them that there would be no passing this newest roadblock.

"It seems we cannot go down," Murdoch said, shading his eyes and scanning the cliff top for sign of their adversaries. "But do they wish us to stay here or to climb the path?"

"Lovely," said Sophie. "How are we supposed to find out?"

"We can't stay here forever," said Alana. "We have very little food. If they wanted to kill us, I'm sure they'd be throwing rocks at us this very moment. I say we continue." She looked to the others for agreement.

"They could be planning to loose another avalanche upon us further up the trail," Roderik said doubtfully.

"They could already have done so," Murdoch replied.

Roderik swallowed hard. "I take your point."

* * *

The path skirted the cliff's edge for several more miles. At the top, they found themselves at the rim of a bowl-shaped plateau, their view into it obscured by a thick forest of pine. It was late afternoon, and they followed the slope inward, seeking a sheltered place to spend the night away from the dizzying edge of the cliff. The sun had already dropped behind the western rim of the plateau when they reached the end of the forest and saw an open meadow stretching in shadow under the still-bright sky.

"We'll stop here, under the eave of the wood," Murdoch told them. "We'll be harder to see." *Not that it makes much difference,* he thought. All through the day, as they traveled, he had neither seen nor heard any trace of forest faeries. *Faer,* he reminded himself. Still, after their experience on the path, he had little reason to doubt that their presence was known and their position precisely noted.

They ate the last crumbs of their rations and drank some of the water they had brought from the spring on the trail. Murdoch's wound, when Sophie changed the dressings, was an angry red and his entire upper arm had swollen and was hot to the touch.

"In the morning," he replied to her concerned look. "We'll lance it and look for herbs. Who will take first watch?"

* * *

The gibbous moon hovered above the western rim of the mountains, signifying midnight. Murdoch, unable to sleep for the throbbing in his arm, sat watch. He knew the wound was festering

154

badly, both by its dull ache and by the feverish lightheadedness that kept threatening to turn the world into a dream. He gazed down over the open meadow and then peered back into the wood, keeping vigil over the whole. When he looked down the slope again, a solitary figure stood there, ten paces distant, silhouetted in moonlight.

The sight struck him like a fist. There had been no sound. The meadow seemed as bright as day under the radiant moon, with no cover from which the man could have sprinted in the short time that Murdoch's gaze had been elsewhere. The two stared at each other—or at least, Murdoch stared at the figure and had no doubt that it was looking unwaveringly at him as he sat in the darkness at the verge of the forest. He wondered how many more of these watchers there were. He glanced quickly back toward the wood, to see if they were surrounded, but his eyes, accustomed to the brightness of the open field, could see nothing. As brief as the glance was, when he looked back into the meadow, the figure had vanished.

For once in his life, he did not know what to do. His hope for their survival rested upon one woman, a woman already aged, white-haired, when he'd met her, half a lifetime ago. The fever muddied his thoughts, and the fearless warrior felt the hair rise on his nape and the cold taste of fear on his tongue. He despised both and, in the twisted maze of his feverish mind, felt the need to defy them. He staggered to his feet, drew his sword, and walked unsteadily toward the place where he had seen the figure. The ground sloped smoothly downward, but it seemed to him that it was rutted, that unseen hands grabbed at his feet as he passed. Silently, he counted his paces until he reached ten. Swaying, he looked at the ground before him, expecting trampled grass and some vestige of tracks. What he saw instead made him laugh in amazement. There was a hole.

He was still laughing when he fell into it.

Chapter 19
The Faer

"Father?" called Sophie, awakened as much by the abrupt end of the laughter as by its beginning. She sat up and looked around her, something like panic beginning to grow in her stomach. Murdoch was nowhere to be seen. She stood, sword drawn, and turned slowly, every sense alert. She saw no one but her companions.

"What is it?" Alana whispered.

Sophie could see that both Boy and Roderik were awake, but had not moved.

"Father's gone. I could have sworn I heard him laughing." Sophie continued to turn. She completed another circuit, seeing nothing, but then, as she turned again toward the meadow, the solitary figure was there.

She gasped, and her companions sprang to their feet, Roderik with his sword and Boy with his staff held ready. The figure neither moved nor spoke and, as they looked about them, they could see dozens of others surrounding them on all sides. All this time there had been no sound save the sighing of the breeze: not a footfall, not a single crackling leaf or snapping twig.

Alana broke the silence. "We come for refuge and throw ourselves upon your mercy." She spoke loudly and clearly, that all might hear. "In token of this, we put down our weapons."

The others looked anxiously at her. "Go on, drop them. We wouldn't last a minute in a fight against them all," she whispered.

Boy slowly bent and laid his staff on the ground. Roderik, after a moment's hesitation, laid his sword beside it. At last, Sophie, having considered the distance to the spare sword on her father's saddle, dropped hers as well.

156

The figure spoke in their tongue, with a strange accent. "You will come with us," he said; it was neither a command nor a request, but simply a statement of fact. As they stepped into the moonlit meadow and looked around them, they noticed, with shock, that the others had vanished. Seeing this, Roderik was tempted to pick up his sword from where it lay, but Alana, laying her hand on his arm and giving him a warning look, stopped him.

They followed their guide and passed, unknowing, the hole Murdoch had fallen into. They crossed the meadow and entered another band of forest, this one quite steep, and their path followed rugged ravines. After an hour's wordless walking through a land of silver-gilt beauty, their captor turned up one of these ravines and followed the glow of firelight through a crevice opening into a cave. They entered through a narrow passage five paces or so in length, and then, rounding an outcropping, came into a large chamber, lit by torches. Their guide led them in, his back to them. Sophie fingered her dagger and thought it a stupid gesture of excessive trust until she had gone three paces into the passage and realized that several of their captors walked behind her. The leader pointed to the center of the chamber and they sat. A steady stream of people entered, seating themselves in a double, then triple row around the edge until the travelers were completely hemmed on all sides. There were no less than fifty in the space, most young men and women, with a few gray-headed men as well. All of those that had surrounded them on the hillside had come. They had made no sound along the way.

The four sat in the middle of the circle, backs together, wondering what would become of them. Gradually, a murmur started, and worked its way around the circle. Their captors craned their necks, but it was not, as might be expected, Alana's vivid hair that drew their comment, nor Roderik's gilded armor, nor even Sophie's boyish garb. They were looking at Boy. He looked about.

"Why are they all staring at me?" he whispered to Alana.

She looked at the faces surrounding them, at the dark hair and eyes, the strong cheekbones and long noses, and then at Boy. "You're one of them."

"What?" he said with a start and all the dark heads turned to stare at him. He smiled at them nervously.

Finally, one of the elders, finishing a conversation with the other grayheads, stood. The rest fell silent and waited. The elder walked to Boy and peered at him closely. "What is your name?"

"Boy," he replied. There was a stir throughout the group.

"Have you no memory of us?"

"No." Again, a rustle of talk.

"Where do you live?"

"Nowhere now, but I lived in the witch's barn and was her servant ever since I was a child."

The murmur rose to a roar. All around them, their captors spoke excitedly to their companions, some with animation, others in tears. The man interrogating Boy grasped his hands and pulled him to his feet. Boy looked around in terror. Tears streamed down the old man's face. He held up his hand, and the talk subsided. "The child returns full-grown. The time that was spoken of is here."

The group sat silent, staring at Boy. Some looked fearful, some eager, some angry or sorrowing, but there was not one among the *faer* that did not show deep emotion.

"Please," said Alana softly to the elder. "What does this mean?"

"Dunwadi told us, many years ago, that when the stolen child returned, we would end our isolation."

"But I wasn't stolen," Boy sputtered. "My father traded me for a milk goat."

The elder looked at him strangely, but did not argue.

"Who are you?" asked Alana. "How can you live in this place, haunted by forest faeries?"

The elder's eyebrows rose. "Faeries?" he said.

"No one will come here for fear of them. No one who comes here has ever returned."

"But you came."

"Danger drove us and the trail was blocked behind us. Was it faeries who dropped those stones?"

"*Faer*," he corrected. "We are the *faer*."

* * *

Murdoch saw blackness and then a bright, blurred light. He heard the trilling of a lark and breathed the heavy scent of roses. He shook his head and tried to focus his eyes. He lay on a stone

158

bench. His body felt weightless as he stood and looked around. He was alone in a garden filled with flowers and fruiting plants surrounded by high, gray stone walls.

He stood, enraptured by a rose, blood-red, so dark as to be black near the edges. He felt drawn into it, closer and closer, new details showing themselves as it drew him into its fragrant petals. He stopped himself, pulled back, withdrew from the rose, the task taking all his concentration, and immediately found himself drawn into the next one, pale as ivory, with a golden blush. Again, he resisted. This time, he managed to look further, beyond the tangled beds of flowers.

A door stood closed at the far end of the garden. He walked to it and put his hand on the sun-warmed metal of the latch.

He felt a woman's touch and looked down. Her hand rested on his. He looked at her face and was captured by her dark eyes. She said nothing, but he felt those eyes cut through his flesh, his bone, his marrow, and into his soul as no sword had ever cut him. His eyes blurred and the light returned. The face, with its dark eyes, remained, but changed: older, less ageless, beautiful, but less awe-full.

"You're going to live, you know," she said.

"What?" he sputtered, trying to sit. She pressed her hand gently on his chest and he sank back onto the bed.

"Hush," she said, like a mother soothing a sick child. "You're still weak. You are safe here."

"You were in the garden. You stopped me from opening the door."

She raised her eyebrows, then lowered them and, smiling, shook her head. "You have seen the Lady, and she returned you to us. Rest now." She started to stand.

He grasped her hand. "Who are you?"

"My name is Mirna. You are a guest in my home."

Mirna, the healer Dunwadi sent to Beecham. "And the others?"

"They will be cared for."

"And Dunwadi. Does she live still?"

She looked at him, surprised. "Yes."

"I must speak with her." He tried to sit up again.

"All in time," Mirna replied. "Rest now." She stood and left him.

The chamber was small, with pale stone walls and a tapestried floor. Bright sunlight poured in from above and there were more tapestries with geometric designs in bold reds, ochers, and browns hanging on the walls. He moved his arm, and found that all pain had left it. Then, exhausted, he slept.

* * *

Most of the *faer* had returned to their posts, leaving only a dozen young ones and the head elder with the lowlanders. Alana and her companions rose well after dawn and were fed fruit, water, and flat bread. Midmorning, they were shepherded down the trail. Now, they walked on well-defined paths through woodlands that seemed neither wild nor quite what any of them were accustomed to think of as gardens. There were fruit trees and berry bushes, small patches of wheat and vegetables all mingled together. Unlike the fields of the lowlands, there was not a fence or a straight line to be found anywhere, but there was beauty and order. It took them half the morning to cross this strange, yet rich, garden world. Then they passed through a belt of tall pines, came into a clearing, and stopped, facing a limestone cliff about forty feet in height and overgrown with vines. They were alone, and then, in the blink of an eye, they were not. What seemed at first an empty space of bare earth was the center of a village of two hundred people, who appeared as if by magic from behind trees and on the ledges that lined the pale gray cliffs overlooking the clearing. The elder led them to a path concealed by bushes that followed a winding course up the cliffside.

When they were twenty feet up, the path doubled back sharply, broadened, and leveled. As they passed the villagers standing on the ledge watching them silently, they caught glimpses of chambers behind them: tapestried floors, dim light coming in by some means from above, a world of order and simplicity, with richly colored tapestries hanging on the walls and covering the floors. Again, they climbed steeply and doubled back to another tier of dwellings. There was no one before the third entrance in the row. The elder swept aside the flowering vines that hung before the doorway like a curtain and stood back for them to

160

enter. There, in an alcove cut out of the limestone wall, looking rested and comfortable, lay Murdoch.

"Father!" cried Sophie as she ran to where he lay. He lifted his uninjured arm and hugged her. The others followed, crowding near the bed to hear his tale. The elder went to the doorway of the room to the left, where Mirna tended a pot of broth on the small hearth cut from the rock wall. He spoke to her softly, and she let out a short, sudden cry and pushed past him through the doorway.

She ran to the group of newcomers and singled out Boy. She stopped before him, clasped him in her arms, and burst into tears. Boy, stunned by her outburst, could think of nothing to do but pat her shoulder awkwardly.

The elder joined him in this and, when she had quieted, said, "He has no memory of us."

She released Boy from her embrace, dabbed her eyes with a cloth and smiled. "This must be very confusing to you." He nodded. She smiled again and her luminous eyes took them all in. "I am forgetting my manners. My name is Mirna. Welcome to my home. Sit, please. You must be hungry from your journey."

She served them broth with more of the flat bread that seemed to be a *faer* staple. There were crisp, raw vegetables: pungent scallions, sweet slices of some sort of tuber, and tangy green leaves rolled around a savory stuffing. Fresh apples and a hot tea scented with mint followed. All this time, she conversed with them, drawing them out and making them feel as comfortable as if they had known her all their lives. When they had filled themselves, the elder took his leave.

"Dollon," she asked, as he turned to go. "Would you send word to Aelvan? He's watching on the west."

"We sent word last night." Dollon smiled. "He should be here soon." He glanced at Boy. "Dunwadi will be coming down for the harvest drumming, but perhaps you won't want to wait that long. Aelvan knows the way."

True to the old man's word, a few minutes later they heard footsteps running across the ledge. The vine curtain swayed back and a young man of about twenty years burst into the room, breathing hard, as though he had run a distance. His eyes swept across them and instantly fixed on Boy. The resemblance between the two was impossible to miss.

Mirna introduced him. "My *younger* son, Aelvan." Alana's eyes met Mirna's and they smiled at each other. "Aelvan," Mirna said. "This young man has lost his memory. Will you guide us to Dunwadi?"

He nodded, speechless, his eyes still fixed on Boy.

Mirna turned to Murdoch. "I leave you in your daughter's care. You will find everything you need in the other room," she told Sophie. She looked at Boy and motioned toward the door. "Come," she said. "We have a long way to go." The vine leaves rustled against each other, and they were gone.

* * *

Alana considered the events of the last few days. *I have lost everything: my kingdom, my dowry, even my hairbrush. Murdoch is wounded, but his hoyden of a daughter has proved herself better than expected. Boy, although valiant, has found his people and seems hardly likely to have any further interest in my concerns. This prince, my supposed rescuer, is an eager wolfhound pup of a man. He will be of little use unless we can get to Amytans, where his friendship might prove of some influence. My greatest strength is Murdoch. He is the deadliest swordsman alive and knows the defenses of every castle in Gwalhafed. He is the key to Rolf's undoing.*

All her life, she had been cosseted and treated gently, even by Rolf as he maneuvered tirelessly to supplant her. She thought back to the stopping place on the road, where Murdoch's refusal to fetch water had seemed such a grievous offense. Then she thought of the hideous night at that squalid and stinking tavern, and finally the attack by those she had assumed had come to escort her. *Rolf,* she thought. *How I hate him. He must be stopped before he destroys Gwalhafed, and unwittingly he has set me free to do so. Rolf wants a war. I have Murdoch. I have the support of the prince of Amytans. Oh, yes, I can grant my uncle his fondest wish, can I not, and let him rue the day he ever wished it!* Her emotions took hold and she found herself in a stew of rage and grief. She mourned for her father and Richard, for her kingdom, and her stupidity. *But to wage war? Papa spent his life seeking alternatives to that path, reminding me, again and again, of the cost in lives, in destruction. But what else can I do? And*

162

what would bring greater satisfaction than to meet Rolf on his own ground and best him?

Prince Roderik strode in from the ledge. He knelt on one knee before Alana and presented a nosegay of flowers he had picked. "A poor gift for the fairest blossom of all," he said, smiling at her.

She looked at the flowers in astonishment. *Hopeless*, she thought. *I lose my kingdom and he wastes his time picking flowers. Still, I cannot offend my ally.* She took them. "Thank you, Your Highness."

"Your Highness? Come, we are of equal rank. You must call me Roddie. All the ladies do."

"Roddie, then. Would Amytans be willing to send force against my uncle? He has left no weak point in his stratagems against me. All the nobility of Gwalhafed support him."

"If you command, my lady. I will lead the charge myself. I was just knighted, you know. The festivities lasted a month. It was glorious. . . ."

Still, Alana thought, *his connections will prove useful.* She looked up to see Sophie, seated on the edge of her father's bed, watching Roderik, shaking her head slowly. Murdoch had gone back to sleep.

* * *

Boy followed the others for an hour or more, out of the village and the open lands and northeast toward the steeper verges of the *faer* domain. The ground was more broken here, with ravines opening on either side as they passed. They ascended the largest of these. These gullies were different from those near the witch's house, he noticed. Instead of cracked, dry earth, they were lush with life, with ferns clinging to their sides, wildflowers going to seed in their beds, and huge trees forcing the path to twist and turn about their massive trunks. Aelvan stopped periodically, checking his count of the tributary ravines they passed and looking about, as if for some sign. Finally, he found it. They turned to the right, passed two gullies, and took the third, toward the left.

This one sloped steeply and required their hands as well as their feet to climb it. Aelvan climbed with no apparent effort. Mirna, too, flowed up the ravine, which would be a waterfall during the rains, and Boy, following behind, was struck with wonder that a middle-aged woman could climb such a slope with such ease.

The ravine diminished to a narrow trail. They followed its meanderings through pine groves and across upland meadows. To the west, pine forests blocked their view. To the east, they could see the rich patchwork plain of Gwalhafed. At last, the trail dipped down the outer cliff and arrived at the entrance to a cave, its mouth facing southeast.

A figure sat before it, facing them, wrapped in an unadorned tan robe. Her hair was white and her eyes, nearly black, stood in bold contrast. She looked directly at Boy.

"So, you have come back to us," Dunwadi said in a voice as soft as rustling grasses.

Boy was seized with fear. He glanced at the others. Both regarded the speaker with respect, but with no trace of nervousness. They stood relaxed on either side of him. *I could turn and run*, he thought. *It would be a downhill race. They couldn't catch me.*

As these thoughts passed through his mind, Dunwadi addressed him again. "It is not you who fear me. The spell you are under, the *ksh*, knows that I will break it."

The words soothed and terrified him at the same time and he did not know what was his own mind and what had been imposed by the witch.

"Sit," Dunwadi said, patting the ground beside her.

Mirna took his hand reassuringly and they walked to the aged figure. Boy sat, the muscles of his stomach trembling. Mirna and Aelvan sat facing them.

"Now, my child," Dunwadi began, patting him on the knee. "We must find out who you are." She looked into Boy's eyes and continued patting his knee in a soothing, rhythmic fashion. "Let the images come," she directed him. "The remembering may bring pain, but it will pass. Remember, we are here with you. What do you see?"

Boy was ten years old. He was thin, dressed in rags, and struggling with a bundle of firewood much too large for him. The frayed rope binding it burst as he lifted it into the wood box by the door.

The witch stuck her head out of the door in an instant. "Clumsy oaf!" she shouted. "I gave up my best goat for you." She brought her hideous face down to his, grabbed his jaw, and tilted his head up to meet her gaze. "Don't make me regret my bargain."

"What do you see?" Dunwadi asked.

Then, Boy was four. He lay in a straw bed in the witch's barn as she tenderly tucked a cloak around him. "Nona is good to you. Nona takes care of you," she sang in a droning singsong. "Your father hates you. You killed your mother. Never leave Nona. Nona is good to you. Nona takes care of you."

"What do you see?" Dunwadi asked.

He saw the butterfly. It was blood-red and fluttered softly on a blackberry just out of his reach. His hands and face were sticky and purple with berry juice. His mother stood nearby, on the other side of the basket that they had been filling. From down the hillside, he could hear the sound of his father's stone ax as he cut a fallen tree into firewood. He reached his hand toward the beautiful insect and it fluttered off lazily and came to rest on a branch a few feet away. He followed and reached out his hand again. It waited until he almost touched it, then took flight again. He wanted to touch it, to take it home and make it his friend. He followed it down the hill, always nearly catching it, always certain that, next time, he would. His mother, tiny baby in a sling on her hip, was engrossed in her gathering. He could see his father now, sweating as he struck the log again and again with the sharp blade of his ax. The butterfly lit on a flower. He reached out his hand again and touched the wing with his finger. Instantly, he found himself held and pressed hard against a soft, stinking collection of rags. He screamed and struggled. He heard his parents' cries as they ran to his aid. He watched his father run up and swing the heavy ax at the witch. She held up her hand in a gesture of warding, and the handle became as soft as a snake's body. It swung round, missed the witch entirely, and the keen edge bit deeply into his father's neck. Blood spurted wildly and his father, his strong, loving father, who could pick him up and toss him and catch him in play, fell dead at the witch's feet. He heard his mother's cries, growing fainter as a mist encroached on his sight. "Mother!" he screamed.

"I am here, Tovan."

He opened his eyes and saw Mirna, his mother, and Aelvan, his brother, tears streaking their faces, looking at him. She opened her arms and he fell into them, shaking with sobs. As she embraced him, and his brother swarmed over his back, laughing and sobbing, he had the sensation that he was melting into them and his soul was soaking far into the ground, like the roots of a great oak tree.

The feeling overwhelmed him, so strong that his joy at reuniting with his family faded into the background. He sat stunned.

"This is the *vaira* that you feel," Dunwadi told him. "Your birthright, stolen from you by the witch's spell."

Chapter 20
Like as Like

The shadows slanted from the west in Mirna 's cave. "My lady," said Roderik. "We must leave for Amytans as quickly as possible. The sooner we reach my father's castle, the sooner I can act against this uncle of yours."

Alana shuddered at the thought of the sort of strategy Roderik would employ. Still, she gave him a gracious smile. "Thank you, Your Highness, but I cannot leave until Murdoch is well enough to travel. He is my personal champion and my only remaining vassal."

Roderik looked at the grizzled warrior, sleeping soundly, blood seeping through his bandage. "My lady, I am here now. I will be your champion. Murdoch is old. His day is past. Look at him. He's wounded."

Sophie, coming in from the other room with a basin of water, looked at him with disdain. "And if fifteen men ambushed you, I suppose you'd do better?"

"For the sake of my lady, of course I would," said the prince.

"Then why didn't you give it a try when you passed us on the road? I saw you. You read the signs aright. You knew where we were and you rode on."

"Well, strategic considerations—"

"Your horse gave you strategic considerations?"

"Dreyfala?"

"You asked your horse for advice, you idiot. I heard you!"

"I did not!"

"And it's a good thing you took it, my fine warrior, because I would have had you the moment you turned from the path."

"Had me! I'd like to see you try."

Murdoch moaned.

"Now look what you've done. You've waked my father."

"Roddie," said the princess, "perhaps some fresh air would do you good while Sophie and I change Murdoch's bandage."

With a smile and bow for Alana and a scowl for Sophie, Roderik went out to sit on the ledge overlooking the village. He watched, contemptuous at first, but with increasing fascination, as the people came and went, greeting one another, carrying food-stuffs from the gardens, sitting in sun or shade as their preference dictated, and working on a variety of crafts. On the terrace below him, a grandmother's skillful fingers wove a basket of intricate design. A man, streaks of gray in his hair, sat in the shade of the pines and showed two children the rudiments of clay work as he nimbly formed long gray coils and built them into a round-bellied storage jar. It was so unlike his expectations of sullen, brutish, bloodthirsty savages. He watched in wonder the ease and respect with which they treated each other, from the tiniest toddler to the grayest of the elders, and contrasted it to his upbringing by ser-vants and the formality of the court. Two men came back, a long string of fish draped over a sturdy pole resting on their shoulders. They were greeted with praise and sat in the shade to gut their catch. Small children toddled about investigating and the larger ones ran errands, collecting firewood to cook the fish, hauling wa-ter, taking the scraps off toward the gardens.

A small child burst into the clearing. "The bee man! The bee man!" she called, dancing with excitement. There was a bustle throughout the village and they all followed her down the path toward the meadow.

Roderik went with them. When he reached the edge of the trees, he could see a tall figure, still some distance away, pushing a barrow cart containing four large pottery jars. As the others ran to join the man and take charge of pushing the cart up the slope, Roderik could see that the silver-haired man, although bent with years, was taller than the rest. He wore the same simple peasant leggings and shirt as the others, and a broadbrimmed, round-crowned straw hat, secured under his chin with a cord. As Roderik walked down the slope toward the group, the bee man looked at him with some interest, and addressed him as soon as he was within hearing.

"You are not from these parts, young warrior." There was a gentleness in the man's manner. Several bees escorted him, some-times flying around his head, sometimes walking on his hat or bumping affectionately into his face.

"No, sir, I'm from Amytans."

168

"Ah!" the other replied. "And what might be your name?"

"I am Roderik, of the house of Arn," he replied with some pride. "And who are you? You are not by birth of the *faer*."

"My name is Anselm, and I too hail from Amytans."

Roderik started in shock. "Grandmother's brother Anselm?"

"Grandmother?" The old man seemed stunned by the thought. "Little Dwynna a grandmother? Oh, my, my, my."

"What happened to the others who followed you?" Roderik asked.

"They met their fates as the Lady disposed."

"The Lady? Grandmother spoke of a woman who would not let her pass the Gate of Death."

"She is the same. This land is under the protection of the Lady. Each one who enters must encounter her and be put to her test. Some choose to stay, some choose to die. I was the first to come and am the last remaining."

"Why didn't you return to Amytans?"

Anselm looked about him, at the children playing and the sunset filtering through the fine branches of the firs. "Who would want to?" he replied.

"But you were a prince in Amytans! Here you are a beekeeper."

"There are worse occupations than keeping bees. Being a prince may be one of them."

"But they make you work here. In Amytans, your servants would care for your bees, or anything else you cared to own."

"A mixed blessing. Look around you, Grandnephew. Have you ever seen such beautiful, healthy children? Do you see any beggars? Any men crippled in war, fighting for that which they will never enjoy?"

"But what about glory, Uncle? Or honor? These things are important, aren't they?"

"What of happiness, Nephew? Must the happiness of the many be slaughtered to feed the honor of the few?"

* * *

Sophie found and lit a thick beeswax candle, the better to see Murdoch's wound. The blood had soaked the bandage through, and she decided not to wait for Mirna 's return to change it. Alana knelt beside her, content to play assistant, relieved not to have to touch Murdoch's wounded arm. He gritted his teeth and stared fixedly ahead as Sophie untied the bandage and began to gently unwrap it. His tight, controlled breathing was the only sound.

"It looks much better," Sophie said, holding the candle up and inspecting it closely. She rinsed the blood from the bandages in the basin and wrung them out. "These bandages are still good." She rinsed the flecks of herb from her father's arm. Alana, a bit ashen-faced, took the linen strips to the little room with the hearth for drying.

"Whatever else these *faer* may be, they know their leechcraft," Sophie said. Murdoch nodded, his jaw still clenched. "You're in pain."

He nodded. "Hurts like hell. There was a drink she gave me that took the pain away and made me sleep."

Sophie went to the other room and rummaged through the pots beside the fire. The bandage had dried quickly, and she brought it back as well. "Smell this, father. Is this it?"

"Yes."

She held it for him and he drank deeply.

"Here, can you hold your arm up? I want to put the bandage back. She put a handful of fresh herbs into the poultice cloth and folded it carefully into a packet. She pressed it onto her father's wound and began to wrap the stained linen strip around his arm. Murdoch's eyelids began to droop. "Highness! Please hold my father's arm while I bandage it."

Alana knelt beside her and grasped Murdoch's elbow. Behind them they heard the rustle of the vines.

"My name is Tovan."

They turned. Boy stood before them, his eyes fixed on Alana. He seemed larger, and radiant. She noticed his hands, held relaxed at his sides, square-palmed, with strong, straight fingers. Mirna and Aelvan followed.

"My mother, my brother," he said, grinning.

"Oh, no!" Mirna cried out, her smile dissolving into dismay. "Never put a dirty bandage on a wound!" She bustled past them and brought fresh linen from the other room.

"I washed it out," Sophie protested as Mirna pushed past her and began to strip the stained bandage from Murdoch's arm with deft fingers.

"Always new. *Always* new. The spirit of the sickness goes into the cloth. Never, never use it again. Burn it. Fetch clean water." She stripped off the bandage and poultice, which she gave to Sophie in exchange for the basin she brought. "Here. Burn this. Never, ever use a dirty bandage."

"Sounds like heathen superstition to me," muttered Sophie.

"No," said Alana. "Tell me more, Mirna. How do you know this?"

Mirna 's hands wrapped Murdoch's arm in clean linen. "We have known this since the days of the grandmothers. When a wound festers, the evil spirit in it grows, feeding on the life of the person and weakening him. It becomes too large for the body and spreads to that person's belongings, so that anyone who touches them may become ill as well. We have seen that the bandage from a wound will put the sickness back into the wound, or sickness into a wound on another who was healing well."

"But what if there is no wound?" Alana said. "What if the sickness is, say, a fever?"

"Like as like," Mirna replied. "The spirit of the sickness grows too large for the body and seeks a new body, or many bodies. That is why, when a person dies, all her possessions must be buried with her."

Alana said nothing, but gazed thoughtfully at the sleeping warrior. *Father. . .* she thought, remembering the cloak, as blue as the twilight sky.

Chapter 21
The Watchers

In the morning, as they ate their porridge with the others in the village center, Roderik turned to Aelvan and asked, in an aggrieved tone, "Is it always so quiet here?" Aelvan looked up, surprised. "I mean, don't you ever *do* anything except work in the garden and take care of children?"

Mirna, amusement glittering through her voice, answered: "Aelvan, I think our guests should go with you to the Watchers. Village life is fine for the families and the elders, but I think our young friends need the company of people their own age. What say you?"

Aelvan, his mouth full of breakfast, nodded eagerly.

"Murdoch no longer requires close watching," Mirna continued. "So I think you can all go."

She regarded Alana for a moment. "We'll have to do something about your clothes, dear."

Unlike the others, who all wore leggings, boots, and tunics or shirts of some description, Alana still wore the dress she had set off in as a bride. Even though her finery stood out strangely among the *faer*, she had thought nothing of it. It was the way she had always dressed.

"Those shoes!" Mirna said, regarding Alana's delicate slippers, which had never recovered from their mud bath outside the tavern. She beckoned a passing child and whispered instructions to her. The girl smiled, nodded, and ran off. By the time the others had finished eating, the child was back, carrying a pile of clothing for the princess. Alana and Mirna left the others and Mirna came back a few minutes later with a person recognizable only by the amazing color of her hair. Alana's new clothes were a shirt the color of the breakfast porridge, tan leggings, and sturdy brown boots. Her hair was pulled back into a simple braid so long she had tucked it into her belt. Her companions stared and she looked self-consciously at them.

They walked for most of the day, stopping to eat lunch with a cousin of Mirna's in a village on the western side of the valley. The garden lands crossed, they began to climb through rolling hills toward the row of peaks that hemmed the *faer*'s domain to the south and west. They climbed through orchards of apple and wild cherry, and on paths that threaded through bramble thickets that still bore a late crop of berries, which Tovan picked and ate as he passed. The brilliant sky was a deeper blue here than in the lowlands and the autumn foliage shone like a king's treasure. On their way, they met other *faer* going about their harvest-time tasks. All the *faer* seemed to know one another, and were glad to stop their work for a moment and meet the newcomers.

The group stopped on one of the orchard slopes for a moment's breathing space. Tovan immediately climbed a tree and began to toss apples down to the others—those, that is, that he did not immediately eat in great chomping bites.

"I don't understand," Sophie said, between bites of tart apple. "Down below, we are taught to fear these hills. But everyone seems so friendly here."

"The Lady protects us," Aelvan replied. "If you are here, it is because she has allowed it, so there is nothing to fear from you."

"Where are you taking us?" Alana asked.

"Up to my camp," Aelvan replied. "I'm a still a Watcher on the west, in Bartrym's group, although perhaps not for much longer." He said this with an emphasis whose import his guests all missed.

"A Watcher?" Sophie asked. "What's that?"

"Well," he explained, "when your childhood is past, and you are not yet ready to have children of your own, you go to the borders to watch."

"To watch?" Roderik asked.

"Yes."

"You mean watch for enemies?"

Aelvan thought for a moment. "What is *enemies*?"

Roderik snorted at the young man's ignorance. Sophie gave him a scathing look and turned to Aelvan. "You know, people who would hurt you and take the land from you."

"The Lady protects us. Besides, who'd want to do that?"

"My uncle," Alana told him. "But surely you have some word that means the same as *enemy*. For example, the wolf is the enemy of the rabbit."

Aelvan looked puzzled again. "Wolf?"

"Any large predator," Roderik shouted impatiently. "Wolves, bears, lions, dragons . . ."

Aelvan shook his head again. "We don't have any of those things here."

"Hawks!" Roderik shouted, watching one dive into the valley below them. "The hawk is the enemy of the mouse!"

Aelvan pondered that for a moment, then brightened. "Ah! I am the enemy of the apple." He took a huge bite of the one in his hand.

"No," said Sophie. "That's not it, either."

"But if you have no enemies," Roderik argued, "then what do you watch?"

"Everything," Aelvan replied, with his mouth full. "You'll see."

* * *

The sun danced on the tops of the mountains before them as they entered the belt of pines near the edge of the plateau. Tovan had finished the last of the apples he had carried with him and was looking about for whatever food might present itself next.

"We're almost there," Aelvan told them and he whistled like a yellow warbler. There was no reply. "That's odd," he said and led them on through the pines. They had not gone more than five steps when the answering whistle sounded, from behind them. They spun to face it, and another sounded to their right, then to their left, then ahead, then back, again and again, one after another.

A moment later, a smiling, dark-haired young woman dressed all in green came up the path they had just walked. She ran to Aelvan and hugged him.

"I thought you were a thunderstorm, making all that noise. Didn't you see me in the tree?" He shook his head. "Two days in the center and you've gone soft already." She sighed in mock despair. "Who are your friends?"

"This," Aelvan said with some pride, "is my brother Tovan." Her eyes grew as round as little moons. "And these are visitors from below—Sophie, Alana, and Roderik." He turned to his companions and said, "This is Ranell."

174

The other whistlers had silently come up to the group. Roderik, taking a step backward, bumped into one and let out a bellow as if he had been stung. He spun round and shouted, "Don't sneak up on me like that!"

"They're used to people making lots of noise," Aelvan explained.

"So I see," the offending *faer* grumbled, flexing his trodden toes.

"It's time to eat," Ranell told them. "Let's go." She and Aelvan accompanied their guests, but the others scattered into the forest and quickly disappeared.

"How did they do that?" Tovan asked, awestruck.

Aelvan smiled at him. "You'll learn."

There were no caves in this part of the mountains. The Watchers' camp was hidden in a canyon, behind a giant pine tree with low sweeping branches that concealed the approach from the valley. There were two large lodges made of lashed poles and covered with a thick layer of pine boughs, and a space between the two with a fire pit in the center of it. Several young men tended the great clay cooking bowl, as big as a bushel basket, that sat on a bed of glowing coals in the pit.

"The men do the cooking here?" Roderik whispered to Aelvan.

Ranell laughed. "It's their turn tonight, I'm afraid. You'll have to wait until tomorrow to get a decent meal."

* * *

Dinner, despite Ranell's warning, turned out to be quite tasty: a thick stew of rabbit with wild onions and the roots of the Lady's Star, and more of the flat bread that seemed to accompany every *faer* meal. There were thirty young folk in the group, ranging in age from Boronil, fourteen, to Aelvan, Ranell, and a few others who appeared to be about twenty years of age. After the meal, many of the women went to their lodge and returned with lap-sized looms. They sat by the fire, weaving narrow, brightly colored sashes. Others spun, setting their spindles dancing in the firelight. Some of the men whittled as they sat, and others mended tools. In addition to the Watchers, there were two elders: Bartrym, a short, barrel-chested man with salt-and-pepper hair and a swarthy complexion that spoke of a life outdoors, and Dworning—older, grayer, thinner, and taller.

Aelvan presented his guests to the elders and Bartrym looked them over. He seemed already to know exactly their capabilities, faults, and how to remedy them. Dworning was reserved and unreadable, and seemed to assess the visitors on an entirely different level.

"Well," said Bartrym, as they ate. "I've never had to start so late as with you four, but I suppose you'll learn eventually. In the morning we've a stack of work to do, so you'd best cut the talk short and get some rest if you want to keep up with the others. Aelvan and Ranell will act as your hosts, so ask them if you have any questions." That said, he left them and spent the rest of the evening helping one of the young men attach the head to a wooden drum.

Sophie spent the evening in a state of bliss. For the first time in her life, she was dressed in the same fashion as every other woman in sight. It was clear, as well, that these women had been schooled in the same skills as the men. She sat with Ranell in a group of the older Watchers and listened as they recounted the events of their day. Two women, Netumna and Lorin, had snared the rabbits for the evening meal. Adela had foraged the remaining ingredients with Boronil. Belnor and Adara, a couple who sat by the fire with their arms around each other, had brought the bread from one of the villages. The remainder—women and men alike— had spent the day repairing a ravine. Sophie listened and said little, until Roderik escorted Alana to Ranell's side.

Despite Bartrym's words, which made them all eager to stay up as late as possible, they found that their long walk in the thin mountain air had taken its toll and one by one they asked their hosts where they might sleep. Alana was the first. Ranell led her to a soft bed of sacking stuffed with leaves in the women's lodge.

The Watchers still sat by the fire, discussing the events of the day and planning those of the morrow. Roderik sat and pulled out his knife, a slender, polished blade with rubies set in the hilt. He began to idly whittle a stick.

"What's that?" asked Lorin, her eyes wide.

"A knife."

"But what's it made of?" She pulled her own from the sheath, its wooden hilt and stone blade neatly fastened with sinew. It was well-made, but crude next to the prince's elegant weapon.

"Steel. With gold on the hilt." He handed it to her and she handled it carefully, running her thumb cautiously across the blade to test it.

"How do you make one of these?"

"Well, I've never made one, but to the best of my knowledge, you heat the metal until it softens and then beat it into shape with a hammer."

"What is *met-tul*?" There, she had him. Other than to say it was something that could be shaped when hot, he hardly knew how to answer her.

"Here, hold it by its tip. Careful now."

She held it as he asked, and he placed his thumb and forefinger on either side of and about half an inch distant from the blade, near the hilt. "Drop it."

She did, and he caught it before half the blade had passed. "Let's try it again," he said, and this time he held his fingers halfway up the length of the blade. The group stopped their talk and watched. "Whenever you're ready."

She dropped it again and he caught it, again with inches to spare. "Again," he said, placing his fingers barely an inch below hers. She dropped the knife and he grasped it by its tip. "It's a little game we amuse ourselves with in Amytans."

Sophie squirmed in her seat. "Your Highness." Roderik turned toward her. "Have you ever used your abilities for aught but the amusement of your friends?"

"My lady," he replied. "Have you ever used your lips to do aught but spew vinegar?"

Sophie blushed crimson. She had never given any more thought to her lips than to her boots, but now she felt them as keenly as if she had kissed a coal.

"I knew you had it in you, Prince," she said coldly, "but I had hoped it would stay there." For a moment they stared at each other, and then Sophie stood and walked into the women's lodge with as much dignity as she could display.

Chapter 22
Work

When the sky blazed blue but the sun had not yet risen over the eastern mountains, they were waked and fed. It was porridge again, with jewellike berries picked that morning in the thickets, and they ate with an enthusiasm born of hunger, exertion, and fresh air. The air was biting cold and Alana and Roderik drew their cloaks around them and sat near the fire. Sophie cast off her cloak as soon as she saw that the *faer* wore none, but stayed near the fire as well. Tovan, accustomed to life in the witch's barn, seemed to notice the chill as little as the other watchers.

"Isn't it awfully cold here in the winter?" Sophie asked Ranell.

"Oh, yes," she replied between spoonfuls of porridge and fruit. "There's snow as tall as Bartrym up here in the canyon."

"How do you endure it?"

Ranell laughed. "I keep forgetting that you don't know our ways. We go to the winter caves, of course. After the harvest drumming, everyone begins to move to the great caves before the snows come." Her voice dropped to a confiding whisper. "This year, Aelvan and I will be the last to go. We'll stay here by ourselves until the snows begin. Exciting, don't you think?"

As the Watchers finished eating and the cleaning up progressed, Bartrym and several of his charges emerged from the men's house with armload after armload of tools and materials. There were wooden shovels, flint-bladed axes, adzes, and knives with blades as sharp as razors, and what appeared to be several miles of rope. These, and food for their lunch, were parceled out and the whole party set off down the canyon mouth. Two Watchers, however, carried empty baskets and heads full of messages for friends and relations down below. They would bring back that day's bread.

They entered the belt of pines and fanned out, and in only a moment it seemed that Bartrym, Boronil, and the four guests were the only ones in the entire valley.

"They did it again!" Sophie gasped. She turned to Bartrym and demanded, "How do they do that?"

He answered her with an amused look. "There are three rabbits watching us. Who can see them without frightening them?"

The five youngsters all stood stock still, only their eyes roving as they tried to find what Bartrym had seen so effortlessly.

"Two are over here, by the fallen log," Boronil whispered.

"Good. And the third?"

Sophie answered him. "At the edge of the thicket."

Bartrym nodded. "When we arrive at our destination, I will expect each of you to tell me all the animals we have passed on our way."

Boronil looked about eagerly and the others merely looked stunned. Bartrym set off, the others following, looking about them in something close to despair. He stopped suddenly and Tovan, busy looking for animals, bumped into his back.

Bartrym eyed him sternly, and then smiled. "I expect better from you, of all people," he said in a tone that made it a joke, rather than a reproach. "We won't see any animals at all with the noise you're all making. Here, watch me."

He turned and set off at a swift pace, walking with such care that they could not hear a single leaf rustle or twig snap. He turned and explained as he walked back toward them. "Put the side of your foot down first. That way you have more control. Walk with care. Listen for your own sounds. Look for the place with the best footing. Feel what you are stepping on. Pay attention." They set off again, their attention centered on their feet. "And don't forget about the animals."

The Watchers had been working for hours when Bartrym and his little flock caught up with them. They walked down out of the pine belt and up a slight rise to a dome-shaped knoll protruding from the steep hillside.

"Your brother scouted this, Tovan," Bartrym said. "Look at the top of the knoll. What do you see?"

"Grass, weeds . . ."

"Anything else?"

"Rocks . . ."

"That's important," said Bartrym, "Why?"

There was silence until Boronil spoke. "It means the soil is washing away."

"And that means?"

"That there will be flooding lower down during the Rains."

"Exactly. And that is what we are here to prevent." He led them to the top of the knoll and they looked down its side. "See here," he said, stepping to where the rim of the hill dropped off. He squatted and touched a shallow depression in the earth. "This is the beginning of a gully. Look below." They crowded around him and could see that twenty feet lower, a scar had opened in the soil. Further down, it grew to a dry stream bed and crews of Watchers were busy building a series of small dams of brush lashed to logs set into the gully's sides. "After lunch we will continue the work up higher. This slope will need wattles dug in and brush mats up here where the rill begins. Come along now and we'll get you your tools."

"Tools?" chorused Roderik and Alana.

"You expect *me* to do manual labor?" the princess said.

"You expect to eat?" Bartrym replied politely, but firmly.

Roderik leapt to her defense. "She is a lady, a princess. You can hardly expect. . ." Bartrym eyed him curiously. "I shall do the work of two," Roderik announced.

"I doubt it," the elder replied.

Roderik and Tovan were sent to work with those hauling and shaping fallen logs for the check dams. Sophie received an adze and worked with Ranell and several others digging slots in the ravine walls to hold the logs in place. Boronil showed Alana how to weave the mats that would stabilize the soil in the shallow rill at the top of the slope. They sat surrounded by piles of twigs and long grass, their dexterous fingers busy.

The bread bringers' arrival signaled lunch. With a whoop the others greeted them and bounded down the ravine to where they stood with their burdened packs. The four lowlanders watched astonished as the others leapt from foothold to foothold with no apparent concern for their lives.

Aelvan turned and looked back at his brother. "Come on, To-van, don't be a baby. The food won't wait all day for you."

Tovan shook his head and made his way slowly down the steep slope. Sophie followed. She had already decided she would master this trick, but not just yet. At length, slowly, Alana and Roderik followed. He held her hand and escorted her as gracefully as if they were dancing at a palace fête. He placed his cloak on a log for her. He brought her bread.

"Why is he treating her like she's his grandmother?" Aelvan whispered to Tovan.

Tovan thought for a moment. How could he explain it all? "It's a custom we have down below," he said finally and sighed. There she was, the kindest, most beautiful woman in the whole world, with the prettiest hair, the loveliest eyes, and the most adorable freckles on her nose, and between them, with his back to Tovan, his face never more than a handspan from Alana's, it seemed, was a handsome, stupid prince.

Sophie sat with Ranell and watched the tableau. Roderik served Alana. Tovan watched Alana. Alana ignored Tovan and played up to Roderik. And they all ignored Sophie. Sophie had worked hard at denying the fact of her womanhood, and had never regretted it. But now things were different. The very air of the hills was scented with freedom. But along with her joy she felt irritation deep in her soul. She did not understand its reason, but she knew precisely where its source lay.

Roderik brought Alana more bread and served it to her with a courtly bow. She took it and thanked him with a maidenly smile.

"She's not crippled, you know," said Sophie. He turned and glared at her.

"What would you know of Courtly Love?"

"I know we're not at court," she said and stormed off.

Roderik fumed. *What a quest this is turning out to be! I've offered her my service, just as the forms dictate, even though she's hardly what I imagined. All she ever talks about is politics. And those freckles! But I've set out on a quest, and that is that. I'll not have it said that I failed.*

"Roddie," said Alana, "tell me more of this Whisted's strategy. Is unending conquest his only goal, or is there a further purpose behind it?"

My quest! Where are the dragons? Bring me villains and I'll topple them into bloody heaps with my sword! Why am I surrounded by peasants, with my chief adversary that ridiculous tomboy?

"Roddie?"

He watched Sophie's slender form retreating and pulled his eyes from it with difficulty. He turned his gaze to his beloved and smiled. "Yes, princess of my heart, what was that?"

Utterly lacking in attentiveness, she thought.

* * *

That evening, after the meal, Sophie worked at a stick with her dagger, peeling the bark from the smooth white wood.

"What are you doing?" asked Tovan. He seated himself next to her on the log by the fire.

"Making a practice sword," she replied.

He dunked the last of his bread in his bowl and chewed it thoughtfully. "Why?"

"Because I've gone three days without practicing and that's much too long."

"But there's no one to fight here. Do you want the rest of that bread?"

"What? No, go ahead, you can have it." She stripped the last of the bark from the stick and set about whittling a handle from the thicker end. "I don't know that I'll stay here forever, and anyhow, I miss it."

"How can you miss fighting? I'd be happy if I never had to do it again."

"Well, it's not the fighting, really." She stopped whittling as she sought for words. "My father calls it the Dance. That's what swordplay is to him. And it's true. It's. . . it's like a dance, in a way, where you must be aware of yourself and of your opponent in a way that—well, there's nothing like it. Do you know what I mean?" Tovan shook his head. "Well, you can't look away. Your attention is absolute. And the penalty for any lapse is instant pain, or death."

Tovan nodded, chewing the last of the bread. Then he sighed. "Yes. I know. That's the way I feel about Alana."

"What? Why? She may be a princess, but she's really very ordinary, you know."

182

"She rescued me. And you, too."

"How?"

"All my life, I was ruled by the witch. She starved me, beat me, and told me it was the best that I could ever expect, that she was showing me great kindness. Put yourself in my place. I don't know if you can. Your life is so different from mine. Imagine yourself in that life, living half-starved in a barn, and then, one day, the most beautiful princess in the world—in your case, I guess it would have to be a handsome prince—comes to you and says, 'You deserve better.' Do you think you were the first traveler to sleep in that bed?"

"I really hadn't thought about it."

"Before that night I never disobeyed. I stayed in the barn and never so much as peeked through the shutters. But that night I did. And I saw you and I knew the witch would kill you unless I acted. And since then my life has been like a dream. I have a family, and food. People like me here. And it's all because of Alana."

"You love her."

"Yes. I would do anything she asked, even throw myself off a cliff. Every part of my life, every person I meet is special because she brought me to them. How could I even look at another woman?" He turned and looked to where Alana sat, listening politely to Prince Roderik.

"What are you going to do?" Sophie asked.

"What can I do? She wants to regain her kingdom. He's the prince of a powerful realm. She needs him." He looked at his feet. "The best thing I can do for her is to stay out of the way."

* * *

Sophie awoke in the dull light of early morning. She threw back her cloak and left the women's lodge as the pair assigned to cook breakfast set out to rekindle the fire from the evening's coals. Wooden sword in hand, she set off toward a level place she had found some way behind the men's lodge. As she passed the entrance, Roderik came out. He looked scornfully at the crudely carved sword.

"Going to play soldier?"

"Going to practice. Want to join me?"

"I think not. I only spar with those on my level."

"Well, then, perhaps Alana will oblige you. Or Boronil." She turned on her heel and stormed off.

Roderik controlled his curiosity long enough to splash water on his face. Alana had not risen, and so he left the group, thinking it time that he revenged himself on Sophie for the continual onslaught of scorn she had shown him.

He climbed the slope and stood behind a thick-trunked pine. Her back was to him as she practiced lunging. With each lunge, she extended her reach fully and then snapped swiftly back to a standing position. Then she spun, her sword arcing to block an attack from behind, ending with a swift thrust. Then, with a two-handed grip, she moved her sword in a horizontal figure eight, advancing step by step with each upward cut.

He watched, entranced. He had trained at sword, of course. His rank demanded it. But this was a level of practice he had neither experienced nor even imagined. She moved with a fluid, deadly grace, her concentration as focused as that of a hunting lioness. A master had seen to her training, it was clear, but more than that. She had been a pupil worthy of a master's time. She used her weapon in ways new to him, which, he could see, were designed to take advantage of her speed and neutralize the attack of a stronger opponent. For all his advantage in size, he realized, she could best him with her skill and quickness of movement. The longer he watched, the more certain he became of it. Silently, he returned to the fireside.

* * *

That day the Watchers bore axes and ropes and searched for widowmakers: dead branches, sometimes whole trees, that had gotten caught by their living brethren and hung suspended, waiting for the first storms of winter to send them crashing to the forest floor. Not just a hazard, they were a useful source of firewood, and so a few days of each month were devoted to seeking them out and bringing them to good use. After lunch, the group went to work on a thicket of trees and grapevine dense with dead wood.

Alana worked halfheartedly, daintily stacking cut branches on one of the rude sledges they would use to haul the fuel back to the camp. Roderik worked with her, talking incessantly and handing each piece to her as if it were a valuable gift.

Boronil, working beside Sophie, stopped to watch them and sighed. "Look at their hair, all red and gold like the leaves. They look so pretty together."

"Pretty?" Sophie fumed. "They look ridiculous. She doesn't even come up to his armpit."

Alana broke a fingernail. Roddie kissed her hand. The absurdity of the scene irritated Sophie beyond measure. The other women all seemed to have no problem picking up wood by themselves while the men swarmed through the trees releasing dead branches, or worked on the ground with axes, cutting them to manageable size. She could see that Roderik's behavior was worse than useless. It allowed Alana to drift along in a preoccupied state of helplessness, and that was the last thing she needed.

A warrior does what must be done, she thought and walked over to the pair. "Are you sure you're not straining yourself, Prince Roderik?" He turned and glared at her. "Perhaps I could help Her Highness while you did a little *men's* work." She faced him, arms crossed, smiling sarcastically. "That's if you're up to it, of course, Your Highness."

His anger robbed him of the power of speech. This woman was absolutely insufferable. He picked up his ax and stuck the handle through the back of his belt. He glared at her again, took two long strides, leapt and swung, with an easy grace, up into the nearest tree. It was the last thing she had expected. She watched him, amazed, glimpsing once again the man she had at first thought him to be. There was so much more to him than anyone would guess from watching his normal behavior.

"What on earth do you think you're doing?" Sophie started, and turned to face Alana. "My regaining the throne depends upon Roderik. Do you wish to see Rolf rule Gwalhafed?"

Alana's vehemence took Sophie off-guard. "I . . . didn't . . ."

"Don't meddle in affairs beyond your understanding. I'll not stand for it, you jealous wench."

"Jealous!"

"Do you think I don't see you looking at Roddie every chance you get?"

"That's ridiculous!" Sophie shouted, but her throat felt tight and she knew she was blushing again.

"What was it like, living with the witch?" Sophie asked Tovan that evening as they ate.

"Not nearly as nice as living here."

"I could guess that, but what was it like?"

"Well, there wasn't much food, or at least she didn't give me much—hand me another piece of that bread, will you?—and I could never seem to do anything to her satisfaction."

"Did she hit you?"

"All the time, and she lied to me. This is good soup."

They ate in silence, savoring the broth, thick with greens.

"But, Tovan, you don't seem angry. If I were treated that way, I'd be furious. I'm angry just thinking about how she treated you."

"It's over, Sophie. That's the important part. If I saw her again, I might well be angry. But there's no point wasting my time on it. She took enough of my life without me letting her memory blight what I've found here. And it wasn't all bad."

"Not all bad?"

"No. There were moments when the world was so beautiful. I remember one time she sent me to the forest to fetch wood. It was cold, right after the first storm of winter, and the branches were so black, the snow so white. There were no footprints and not even the sound of a bird. And then in the summer, there were the dragonflies . They would hover near the well, as bright as jewels. And the sun shining on the spiders' webs in the barn, especially at dawn, when the dew still hung on them, and one day in the fall there was a leaf, just one, perfect leaf, as red as blood, that blew into the barn and landed exactly in a sunbeam."

"But those things are everywhere."

"Yes." Tovan smiled, showing strong, white teeth. "Isn't it a wonderful world we live in?"

* * *

The group spent the morning digging wattles into an eroding slope. First, Bartrym constructed a cross from two staves his own height, lashed together with cord. He left a length of the cord free and tied a rock to the end of it, making a pendulum. Then he lashed a shorter stick between two arms of the cross, set it with those two ends resting on level ground, and cut a notch at the place where the rope tied to the rock intersected the crosspiece.

"What's that?" Alana asked.

"This will help us make a level line across the slope. We'll make a line with it, then dig a small trench and plant it with brush and saplings."

"And what will that do?"

"For now, it will stop the soil from washing off this hillside. In two years' time, we'll be picking berries. In five years' time, I'll send you a basket of pears."

They climbed halfway up the slope, the others following him with their burdens of tools and seedlings. He placed one leg of the contraption on the ground and moved the other until the dangling cord touched the notch in the crossbar. One of the men hammered pegs next to the places where the legs rested. Then he pivoted the tool on one leg and rested the second leg on the ground, again carefully lining up the string and the notch. Another peg marked the new spot.

"You see," he explained to Alana, "this way, the trench will be level. If it slants, it would just channel water and make a new ravine. This way, the brush will slow the runoff and the soil will be trapped." He handed the level to Lorin. "After this line is marked, go five strides uphill and do another. I think we'll need four wattles in all. Let me know if brush mats are needed above."

Alana stood stunned by this display of simple genius. She thought of Gwalhafed, of the barren uplands of the Eisen, whose banks overflowed with brutal regularity. *Father would have loved this man. There is so much here to learn, to bring home to my people.* That day, for the first time, she wielded a shovel and worked with a will.

* * *

"Ha!" shouted Aelvan. "The bread bringers! Let's eat!" With that, he stepped into the ravine and bounded down it.

Tovan watched him. He stood for a moment and then began to follow, not so slowly as he had when he first reached the Hills, but cautiously, for all that. Ten feet down, he stopped for an instant, took a deep breath, and let go of his caution. He ran the rest of the way down, letting his weight carry him. To his surprise, it was effortless. His fear abandoned, he felt at home on the slope, not out of control as he had expected.

Sophie watched him leap from rock to rock, more goat than man, and decided that it was time for her to learn this trick as well. When he reached the bottom, she leapt. She bounded, whooping, down to where the others gathered, embracing Tovan and cheering, and was swallowed up by the throng. Alana watched from the top of the ravine and envied Sophie for the first time in her life.

As she hesitated, Roderik came up beside her. "So unladylike," he said, shaking his head. "Allow me to assist you, my lady." He extended his hand to escort her. She accepted it with a faint smile, for the good of her kingdom.

Chapter 23
Waking Up

Tovan sat up on his pallet. The others in the men's lodge were still sleeping, some stirring in the gray light, but none yet awake. Tovan could no longer sleep. He rose and left the lodge. The morning air, keen and dry, made the edges of his nostrils tingle. An owl—a larger, congealed piece of the grayness of that hour—flew across the space between the two lodges, toward its nest for the long day's sleep, the tip of its wing brushing the top of Tovan's head.

He was not startled. Who could be startled when one's life is already a dream, when energies, vast and unsuspected, course through one's veins and every breath brings unexpected pleasure? This he recognized as the unintended legacy of the witch. Her cruelty, the starvation to which she had subjected him had only served to make its absence a continuing ecstasy.

Against all probability, he was alive, more than alive, and *she* had done it. *She*, of course, could only refer to one person: to the kind, wise princess whose sorcery had undone the witch's spells with three small words: "You deserve better."

Tovan ran to the great pine that stood at the foot of the clearing, leaped for the bottommost branch and began to climb. He reached the swaying top, felt the sharp breeze on his face, and delighted in his perch as the tree, caught by the wind and his weight, danced with him upon it. The climb was easier for him than it had been the day before.

Below him, the others began to wake. He saw the day's cooks emerge from the women's lodge and begin to build a fire from the coals. His brother and Ranell came out of their lodges at nearly the same moment and went to each other. Even from the treetop, he could feel the warmth of their passion as, hand in hand, they left the clearing together.

The space between the lodges began to fill, but still *she* had not emerged. Roderik came out next and stood in the doorway of the men's lodge, yawning and stretching his long limbs. When he turned to go to the fireside, Sophie came out from the women's lodge, carrying her wooden sword. She turned to her right and took the long way around the back of the men's lodge to go to her practice rather than cross Roderik's path, but Tovan could feel the fingers of their souls reaching for each other and wondered how long they could continue to deny the truth. Their passion loomed, as bright and sharp as the swords they were accustomed to wearing, far more intense than the fire that burned between Aelvan and Ranell. *Perhaps they are afraid of it,* Tovan reasoned. *Why else would they hesitate to own it?*

As his strength grew, nourished day by day by the ample food and active life of the Watchers, his feelings grew apace. His love for Alana sharpened his newfound pleasures to the point of torment. He found that, by giving his utmost attention to whatever came to his hand to be done—to the least task, to the words of Bartrym or Dworning as they gave the group instructions, to the needs of his friends and kinsmen as they went about their day's work—he could bear his love, but still, he could never lose awareness of it for an instant. It sang through his soul in an endless measure. Again and again, his eye was drawn to where she sat talking with Roderik, and even when he looked elsewhere, he saw her face before him.

At last, Alana came from the women's lodge, her braided hair like the bright streak of a comet, tiny and distant. Roderik went to her immediately, bowed gracefully, helped her to a seat on the log by the fire, brought her a bowl of gruel, and busied himself in a thousand tasks she could do just as well for herself. Tovan sighed and climbed down. She had not noticed him, and still bent all her attention to the prince, to learning the politics of Amytans and whether help for her cause might be found there.

"Your Highness," she was saying as Tovan came within hearing.

190

"Roddie, please, my lady. We should not let such formality stand between us."

"Roddie. This Whisted. How many knights can he put into the field?"

"Oh," sighed Roderik, and he ran his hand through his curls in an attempt to pull the information from his memory. "There are the three dukes below him, and their sons, and, let's see, Arhand has, oh, thirty vassals, Begnam sixteen, and—what's his name—Pollart eight or nine . . . no, ten, I think . And then, of course, each of their vassals has his own retainers. Can I get you more gruel?"

"Thank you, Roddie, no. And could this Whisted be persuaded that it would be advantageous to have myself on the throne of Gwalhafed, rather than my uncle?"

"Well, his interest lies in the empire, to the south and the west."

"Then the means to persuade him would lie in my reminding him of my uncle's ties to Velendruch. If Velendruch were to have a foothold on your eastern border, troops would have to be withdrawn from the south to guard it."

"Yes, quite. What a mind you have, princess of my heart!"

She stirred the gruel in her wooden bowl and thoughtfully ate a bite. "Now Tolsturm . . . how many vassals has he?"

Tovan helped himself to a bowl of gruel and sat, choosing his place carefully, near the edge of the group so that his looking at Alana would not be too obvious.

"She is a foolish young woman."

Tovan started, and looked behind him, toward the voice. Dworning stood there.

"The lowlands are different," Tovan replied. "She is a princess and he a prince."

"He is a boy," Dworning replied. "She deserves better." He walked away, leaving Tovan's head spinning.

* * *

They had been in the Hills for nearly a week. The waxing moon rose high and fat and shone down into the women's lodge through the smoke hole.

Sophie lay on the pallet next to Alana's, and dreamed. She sparred with swords, and her opponent matched her perfectly. She felt exhilarated. She had never fought so well, and yet, try as she might, she could not get the advantage. And try as she might, she could not see his face.

Tovan dreamed of Dreyfala. He rode at a frantic pace through forests, across green rolling hills, his mind filled with urgency and Alana.

Alana sighed and dreamed. A dark-eyed woman smiled and placed her hand on Alana's belly. The dream shimmered and shifted. She felt his lips, gentle, forceful, passionate. She moaned in her sleep and returned the kiss wholeheartedly. She felt his face, his strong arms around her, his warm breath on her neck, her fingers entwining in his hair. Still in her dream, she opened her eyes and looked into his, as dark as coal, his hair straight, and black. He was not the prince, this man of her dreams. He was Tovan.

She felt the lean hardness of him stretched against her and, for the first time in her life, a whirlpool of deep, soft, inexorable energy flooding from her center, where the woman had touched her, to the outermost edges of her being.

She bolted awake and lay there, eyes wide, the moonlight full on her face. She thought of Tovan, her heart still pounding from the intensity of the dream, and that slow, swirling vortex still in motion. She remembered how he had looked at her at the cottage, of his words when he had decided to go with them to the Hills, of the change in him after his visit to Dunwadi. And how, when Roderik appeared, he had made himself invisible.

* * *

Alone of all the camp, Roderik did not sleep. He lay on his pallet, tossing, restless, irritated because it was too short for him. At last, he rose and walked out into the moonlight. He had spurned the tasks that occupied the Watchers as beneath him and the one task remaining, that of squiring Alana, did not come close to using up his fund of vitality. Were he home, the problem would be easy to solve. If the day's activities—hunting, riding, wenching, entertainments far into the night—did not tire them, he and his friends would send a servant to the wine cellar. He would match them, drink for drink, and wager on anything that came into his head: catching the knife blade, throwing their daggers at a target chosen in the elaborate paneling of his antechamber, walking the edge of

192

a parapet. If the *faer* had discovered fermentation, there was no evidence of it in the Watcher camp.

He paced the length of the clearing, turned, and strode back. He leapt for a branch of the pine, grabbed it, and pulled his chin to touch it. He did this again and again, not bothering to count, and found that he grew bored before he grew tired. He dropped to the ground and resumed his pacing. *More exciting than hunting boar*, he thought in disgust. *Tolsturm was right. Who could trust the word of a minstrel? What would such a mouse of a man know of hunting?* He flung himself onto one of the logs that served as a seat by the now-dead fire. *I am wasting my time here. She refuses to leave the Hills until Murdoch recovers.* Roderik scowled. *The man is old. He must be nearly forty. He has gray in his hair! It will take months for such an old man to heal. I'll have crawled out of my skin by then.*

He paced again and then threw himself at length on the ground and raised himself with his arms. This time, he kept his mind firmly on the count, until somewhere past twenty, where the repetitiveness of it became hypnotic. He lost count and shortly afterward could think of nothing but Sophie's face, smiling up at his in the most profound pleasure. He leapt to his feet, paced the length of the clearing in a panic, and sat again on the log.

How could he possibly desire Sophie? Her shoulders were too broad, her chest too flat. *Her hands.* He looked at his own. *They look like mine: square and long-fingered, not the soft white hands of a maiden.*

Everything is wrong. I've even lost my sword. Do the faer *have it? Do they even realize what it is? If I only had my sword, at least I would be able to. . . . be able to what? To practice? With that hoyden waiting to laugh at me and, no doubt, offer her advice?* The thought made him cringe.

She's like Sword Master Varnik, the only person in Amytans who finds me lacking. She would look at me like Varnik does, critical, impossible to please. Envy. The man is small, dark-haired, and from a family of no renown. I can best them all—Tolsturm, Brent, even Perwicke, yet he kept after me. There was no reason to continue training. I am the prince, after all. No one can make me do anything. His bravado dissolved in a shuddering sigh. *She could best them all, and me, to boot.* As he sat by

the ashes of the fire, high in the Hills, at last he began to understand something of the thought of Sword Master Varnik.

He picked up a stick and prodded the ashes. Its end caught
fire from the coals beneath. *I came seeking the Princess of Fire. I found
Sophie. Oh God, what am I to do?*

All his life he had been everyone's darling: the long-awaited
son and heir, the golden child, the young man to whom every
maiden turned her longing gaze. Now, he had met a woman who
found him lacking, whose standards he could not reach. She criti-
cized his every move, it seemed. She made him feel petty, idle, a
bumbling jackass. His position in society counted for nothing. It
was she who was far above him.

What a botched job I have made of it. He thought of Alana, with
scarce less comfort than the thought of Sophie brought him. The
princess spoke no word of discouragement or criticism, but there
were volumes behind those gray-blue eyes that he could not read.
He wondered if she saw anything in him beside his connections.
Still, he could not turn aside now. He had pledged himself to her
service. She needed his help. Having a villain like her uncle on
Amytans's border could hardly come to a good end. *The man has to
be stopped.* He blew out the flame on the end of the stick. *Whatever
might be said about me, I'll not have it said that I failed my quest.*

He dropped the stick and returned to his bed. As he drifted off
to sleep, he thought he heard Dworning's voice: "When one is in
such a state, young man, it is wise to pay attention to one's breathing."

It made no sense to him.

* * *

The following morning, when they loaded up with gear and
set off to restore another gully, Alana was, for the first time since
the ambush, fully aware of her surroundings. The porridge tasted
rich and sweet and the berries made tart, bleeding stains as she
stirred them in with her wooden spoon. She noticed the way the
berry juice soaked into the spoon, accentuating the grain of the
wood; the feel of sun and wind; the heat of the fire on her skin and
the crackling of it in her ears. The glittering of the golden leaves
against the blue of the sky astounded her.

She began to see the *faer* as individuals, instead of a blur of dark faces, and to perceive the network of friendships, kinships, and antagonisms that connected them. She noticed that Sophie's eyes were constantly drawn to the oblivious Roderik, and she became keenly aware that Tovan, for all his reticence, all his refusal to assert himself, rarely took his eyes off her. She was aware of her breath and felt alive in a way she had never before experienced. The whirlpool continued to swirl slowly in the depths of her being. Roderik's chatter seemed of no more substance than the wind in the trees compared to Tovan's focused intensity.

Tovan. How much he has changed, and so quickly. Unlike Roderik, whose attentions to her seemed always to interfere with his ability to learn new tasks, Tovan had thrown himself into his new life and was already as skilled in those tasks he had been taught as any of the other *faer*. He soaked up his surroundings like a piece of bread dipped in milk. He was eager to take on the hardest tasks. But most of all, he ate.

As she watched him that morning, he quickly finished three helpings of porridge. Then he wandered through the campsite, watching for those whose eating slowed before their bowls were scraped clean. He no longer had to ask for leavings. Feeding him had become a custom with the others, and, she noted with some surprise, the Watchers treated it as an honor to share their food with him. Most of them simply handed him their bowls, but when he reached the youngest women, Lorin and her friends, they fed him with their spoons, as one would a baby. He smiled and did not take this as an insult. It was clear that none was meant. Each girl vied with the others for his attention. He thanked them and then ambled over to those who had prepared the meal and began to eat the stuck food from the bottom of the cooking bowl, relieving them of the most onerous part of the cleaning up. He had never asked Alana or Roderik for food, though, and she sensed that he would not take her leavings, even if she offered them.

Bartrym came out with the tools and gave directions for the day, and they left the encampment. While they walked through the forest, Tovan foraged leaves, nuts, and fruit. Alana remembered how frantically he had done this when they first reached the Hills, but now, as he began to make up for twenty years of short rations from the witch, his activity became relaxed, but no less constant. He conversed with the others between mouthfuls. The capacity of his stomach, at first an object of amusement to his companions, had become one of awe.

He never stopped eating and he never stopped moving. Although he was still hungry almost all the time, the influx of nourishment stimulated him to nonstop activity. After the evening meal, in part to avoid having to watch Roderik court Alana, he would leave the camp and practice gliding silently through the wood. He would find a tall tree and climb it, trying to do as much of the work as possible with his arms for the challenge of it and the feeling of strength it gave him.

This was a new sensation to him, after so many years of hunger and subservience, and he could not get enough of it. His body, fueled properly at last, compelled him to endlessly set and surmount challenge after physical challenge. All this time, waking, sleeping, eating, climbing, he was acutely aware of the *vaira*, the roots that had sprouted that day with Dunwadi, growing, sinking, entwining themselves in the earth, growing thick, gnarled and powerful, so that what one saw of him became, in time, only the small, protruding tip of his being, like the bones of granite that one could see on the surface of the hills below the mountain path.

It did not occur to him that anyone else would notice, but notice they did. While the youngest women among the Watchers gravitated toward Roderik, fascinated with his blond otherness, the older Watchers, women and men both, were drawn irresistibly to Tovan. His careful attention enabled him to learn their skills effortlessly. He said little, other than to ask if anyone else were interested in a given piece of food, but he always seemed to know exactly where he was needed and to be there, ready to lend a hand, or a shoulder, or to give a person exactly the tool they were just about to ask for. He seemed not to notice that his abilities were in the least out of the ordinary.

Dunwadi had broken the witch's spell, but habits of mind are far harder to change. In the past week, Tovan had gone through more transformation than most men are privileged to experience in a lifetime. He had regained his name and his heritage. He had left dismal surroundings and shown valor. Everything about him

196

was changing. It was now possible to see, after only a week, the outlines of a body within Murdoch's shirt, which had flapped like a handkerchief on a clothesline when he first put it on.

Alana, sitting by the breakfast fire, noticed this change, as she had noticed his arms when he hauled water for her at the cottage. But her father's words came back to her: *Alana, your life is not your own to live. You will be queen, and you must always consider the kingdom's welfare before your own desires.*

* * *

That day, when they stopped to eat at noon, she chose a seat on the partially constructed check dam near Tovan. Roderik, of course, sat beside her. A group of the younger Watchers clustered about them, listening to Roderik's discourse.

"Of course, the finest hunting of all is the boar. Do you have them here?" As he expected, they all shook their heads. "Vicious creatures, with teeth like this." He held his forefingers curled next to his jaw in imitation. "They can rip a man wide open. Good eating, though."

"Have you hunted boars?" ask Boronil.

"*Boar*, not *boars*. Of course. Many times. I remember once, on the estate of my friend Tolsturm . . ."

Alana sat, listening politely, all the time feeling Tovan's presence. She found that she did not need to look to tell where he was. She could feel his presence on her skin just as easily as she could feel the direction of the sun.

The rest of Roderik's audience had to make do with the small scraps of attention he threw their way. For the most part, he spoke to Alana.

"The hounds raised a scent and we followed at the gallop. When we caught up to them, they were gathered round a thicket, nearly frantic."

She put her half-filled wooden bowl down on a fallen log before her and then, deliberately, but seemingly by accident, crossed her legs and knocked it from the branch with her foot. Tovan caught it and handed it back to her, scarcely daring to meet her eyes. It seemed to them that the universe compressed itself into their fingertips as he handed her the bowl.

Roderik stopped in midsentence. "How did you do that?"

Tovan seemed embarrassed by the attention. "I was watching," he explained.

Dworning, coming down the ravine, passed them at that moment and patted Tovan's shoulder approvingly. Dworing stopped in surprise and patted both shoulders this time. "Mercy, young man, so that's where all that food has gone. You'll be as big as your father soon, at this rate."

"Did you know my father?"

"Oh, everybody did. He was one of the finest. But Bartrym knew him best. Talk to him tonight."

* * *

That night, as they sat by the fire, Tovan carried the cooking bowl over next to Bartrym. It was a cauldron of thick, hand-built stoneware, as big as a bushel, and usually moved by two people working in concert. Tovan seemed to notice nothing out of the ordinary in his lifting it alone, but Bartrym noted the ease with which he did so with astonishment. Tovan put it down and set to work scraping the brown crust of that evening's stew from its bottom and into his mouth.

"You knew my father," he said between bites.

"Rennor was my best friend. It was an honor."

"What was he like?"

Bartrym sighed, and a smile flitted across his face. "He was perfect." He thought for a while before elaborating. "We grew up in the same village, and came here, to this camp, to be Watchers the same year. I have never seen his like for good temper or presence of mind. . . or strength. Do you remember how he would pick you up and toss you?"

Tovan nodded, remembering the utterly trusting way he had flown through the air, the world spinning and his father's face advancing and retreating.

"I can understand why your mother never sought another all these years," Bartrym said. He watched Tovan scrape the last of the scorched gravy from the pot and eat it. He waited until the young man met his eyes. "Tovan, you are so like him."

Tovan took this in. The full life force of those massive, gnarled roots, the *vaira*, flooded his spirit. The picture of himself built by the witch in his mind—that of a thin, weak boy—cracked and

198

crumbled into dust and from its wreckage that of a man, strong, loving, and kind, emerged. Over Bartrym's shoulder, he could see the others sitting by the fire. Roderik was courting Alana. But Alana was looking directly at Tovan.

As she watched, he seemed to her to bloom like a deep red rose. His shoulders, which he had held tensed and pulled inward, relaxed and broadened. His chest came up and made contact with the front of his shirt. Some new being, or quality of being, came to live in his eyes. Their look drew them together, like great cables draw a ship to the dock, like tree roots seek water. Twenty feet from her side, he could feel her on his skin.

Falling into his look, she felt an aching hollowness open up at the center of the whirlpool. *But I am a princess, not a farmgirl. How can I follow my desires when the good of the kingdom rests upon an alliance with Amytans?* In her confusion, she looked away, at the ground. He tore his eyes from her and bolted into the forest.

Roderik was in the middle of another story. "Dragons?" It had begun, in response to a question by one of the youngsters. "Of course I've dealt with dragons. There was a rather nasty one a couple of years back in Beldania that tried to eat the Princess Carinna. Of course, I set out as soon as I heard about it. I was about halfway there when I heard someone crying. It was louder than a bull at the butchers." The *faer* looked at him blankly. "Well, louder than anything *you* can imagine. I came round a bend in the road and there, would you believe it, sat a giant under a tree, bawling like a baby. He must have been twenty feet tall."

"Twenty feet tall? Weren't you afraid of him?" asked Timna, a tall, thin girl seated next to Boronil.

"Of such a big baby? Hardly. I rode up to him. He was crying so loudly that I had to put my hands over my ears. I shouted 'What's the matter?'

"He said, 'I hit my head.'

"'Well, come out from under the tree,' I said. So, the fool stood up and bashed his head on the tree branch again.

"'Ow,' he shouted and began crying even louder.

"'Stop that noise!' I said. 'You're frightening my horse. Look. Don't stand up under the tree. Crawl out on your hands and knees.' So he did, and he was pathetically grateful. I decided he might prove useful on my quest and invited him to come along. We got to Beldania the next morning and, sure enough, there was Carinna, chained to a mountaintop, and climbing right up the side of it was the biggest, meanest, fire-belching dragon you could ever imagine. I climbed up a tree to get a better look. Stump—for that was the giant's name—crouched behind the tree.

"'Roorgahroorgharoorgh!' bellowed the dragon. He shot flames thirty feet and burned up a pine tree."

Sophie came out of the women's lodge and sat next to Ranell.

Roderik continued. "'This is not going to be easy,' I thought, and then I had an idea.

"I turned to Stump. 'I marvel at your calm,' I said, 'after what he just said about your mother.'"

"What?" whispered Sophie to Ranell.

"Shh," she replied. "Roddie's telling us how he rescued a princess from a dragon."

"'Roorgharoorgharoorgharowlll!' howled the dragon.

"'Well, I certainly wouldn't let anyone say things like that about my mother.'"

Roderik looked to Alana, but she was paying no mind to his story. Her eyes were locked on Tovan. Roderik faltered in his telling. Suddenly, Tovan leapt to his feet and raced from the clearing.

"That liar!" Sophie whispered to Ranell. "I know for a fact that it was a farmboy named Clever Hans who rescued the princess." She leaned forward to announce it to the entire group, but before she could speak, Ranell took her arm and led her to the far edge of the firelight.

Ranell had been watching the tension build between Sophie and Roderik as the days progressed. It was a matter of concern to all the *faer*. In such a small, closed society, conflicts were not allowed to fester to the point of anger. Since childhood, they had all been taught to speak their concerns to one another. But these two with the empty sword belts refused to do so. In fact, neither seemed to understand what their conflict was about.

"Looks aren't everything," Ranell said with her usual good humor, glancing back at Roderik, who sat on a log watching Alana. "Although, in his case, that might not be true."

Sophie gaped at her and then, as the comment sank in, began to giggle. Ranell joined her and they burst out laughing, hugging each other, and the atmosphere of the whole camp lightened. Roderik, keenly aware that he was the only one who didn't get the joke, stormed off into the men's lodge.

"I have been told of the *ksh*, that in the lands below there is a blindness, a sickness that keeps you from seeing and speaking your truth," Ranell mourned to Sophie. "Why can you not see how it harms you?" She looked at Alana, alone by the fire, close to tears. "What do you do to each other down there?" She walked across the circle, sat down next to Alana, and took her hand. Sophie slowly turned and went into the women's lodge, to be alone with her thoughts.

* * *

Tovan ran through the forest, seeking a tree tall enough to bear him away from his dilemma. He found a huge twisted oak, ran at it, and pulled himself upward, determined to scale it with the force of his arms alone. He reached the top, among swaying branches, and clung to them, breath ragged, his arms and chest burning like fire. He could see the camp, and Alana sitting with Ranell. His mind held him trapped, suspended like the needle of a compass, unable to either turn away or to leave its moorings and follow the object of its desire.

* * *

The next morning was devoted to gathering beechnuts in a grove not far from the Watchers' camp. By noon, they had finished and, much to the surprise of the lowland visitors, Bartrym had no further tasks for them. The women left en masse for the bathing pool, where they stripped off their grimy clothing and threw themselves squealing into the icy water. Shining and wet, they put on clean clothing and went back to their lodge, where the rest of the afternoon was given over to the swapping of sashes and clay beads and braiding of hair into intricate patterns. As they continued their grooming, they could hear the shouts of the men as they took their turn at the pool. The moon would be full that night, and the Lady's cave would thrum to the rhythm of the harvest drumming.

Chapter 24
The Healing

Mirna watched Murdoch, looking for signs of the infection's reappearance. More than that, she saw the wound in his soul. His eyes awakened in her not fear, but compassion. She knew the desert within them intimately, having dwelt there after the theft of Tovan and the murder of Rennor. She wondered what old grief could afflict him so, and considered in her mind how to reach him. For the moment, he had more pressing needs. His only shirt was torn and stiff with blood from the ambush.

The afternoon was warm and golden. Murdoch slept and her cave was filled with restful silence, now that the youngsters had gone to the Watchers. Mirna knelt and removed the lid from the storage basket where Alana had sat. She emptied it of neatly folded clothing, linen strips torn and rolled, ready to bandage wounds not yet inflicted; a blanket or two; and finally, at the very bottom, a homespun shirt, yellowed and soft with age—all she had left of her husband, Rennor. She lifted it carefully from the bottom of the basket, the astringent odor of cedar bark clinging to it, and remembered how, when her hurt was still new, she would wear it for days at a time and weep as she suckled her infant son. She did not wake Murdoch, but left the shirt on the bed for him to use.

The next day, Mirna permitted Murdoch to walk to the doorway of the cave and sit in the sun. He soaked up the warmth gratefully, and felt rested but frail as a scrap of paper. By the following evening, he was strong enough to join the others at the evening fire and take his meal with them.

Each day, she would massage his wounded arm with red oil infused with the herb the *faer* call Yellow Star and the lowland people call St. John's Wort. Each day, he regained more of his strength and she let him walk farther. His admiration for her and her skill had begun the moment he had awakened in her home, and as his strength returned, he found himself noticing more and more the serenity of her manner, the curve of her neck, and the sway of her full hips as she walked.

As his strength returned, she, too noticed the change in him. She noted the way his eyes lingered on her, the solidity of his arm as she massaged his wound, and the way the shirt fit him, tight across the shoulders, the way they had fit Rennor. She was amazed by the speed with which he recovered.

Once the infection had been cured, the wound healed rapidly. When a week had passed, she determined that he was healed. To celebrate, they walked up the slope above the village to a vantage point that overlooked the *faer*'s domain. They sat in the sunshine on that knoll in silence, acknowledging that a bond had grown between them, the dimensions of which they had yet to explore.

"You have a gift," he said.

She nodded. "When Tovan was stolen and Rennor killed, I felt so angry, so helpless. It was then that my calling came to me, to heal. It was the Lady's gift of consolation."

"The Lady. I would like to meet her again. Who is she? Does she live in the village?"

She smiled. "Not in the village, but in this whole valley. Perhaps she is this valley. She has protected us since the beginning of time. Now that the prophecy has been fulfilled, and Tovan returned to us, her protection will end. Perhaps that is why she sent you. The ways of the world below are different."

"Perhaps," he said. He sat silent beside her, wrestling with thoughts he did not know how to express. At length, he turned to her again. "There may be another reason." He halted, unsure how to proceed. "My daughter, Sophie, is not like other women. I had begun to despair of ever finding a suitable husband for her. Your son Tovan, though. . . I think he shows great promise."

Mirna looked at him, surprised. "His heart is given to another," she answered, "as is your daughter's. Had you not noticed?"

"Well, I. . . no, but. . ." He stopped in confusion. *Sophie? In love? With whom? With. . . great heavens, not. . .*

Mirna watched his confusion with amusement. "I think there is another reason for your being here." She waited, eyes shining. "And I think you know it as well as I. Shall we speak of it?"

"I am not a man of words," he confessed. She took his hand, and it trembled at her touch. "I am not a man of words," he said again, and slowly, hesitantly, he leaned forward and kissed her.

Chapter 25
Power

Gwalhafed roared with anger at Amytans's treachery, as Valan had predicted. Recruitment for the search party exceeded all expectations. On a brilliant autumn morning, one week to the day after the attack, the army set out from Gwalhafed Castle.

First came twenty knights, vassals of Drent's, each bringing fifteen soldiers bearing freshly forged swords and wearing glittering chainmail. Rolf followed, flanked by Valan and Drent, busy exulting in his new role as military commander. Behind them rode the fifteen knights sworn to Valan's service, each with his own following, bearing new weapons and armor. Behind them walked the castle guard, mingled with the new recruits, with helmets of leather, battered blades and hauberks dark with age. This group was flanked by Rolf's personal guard, mounted warriors who glittered in the sunlight. The remaining nobles each rode at the head of his own troops following the guard.

As they rode, the three leaders discussed strategy. "And then, once we have the Hills, we will need to punish Amytans for this hideous crime," Valan explained to Drent.

"Of course," Drent agreed. "Has a declaration of war been sent?"

"Good heavens, no!" Rolf exclaimed. "We'd lose the element of surprise that way!"

"But, sire! You can't just march in and attack. The forms, sire!"

Rolf snorted in disgust. Valan cut in: "But, Drent, with a surprise attack we can end the war quickly. Otherwise, it might prove impossible. You wouldn't want to see unnecessary loss of life, would you?"

"Why, no, my lord. I take your point. Your plan certainly seems the most humane way to proceed."

"And then, once we occupy Arnhem Castle, we will be in an excellent position to put down any resistance."

"But, sire, there would be no resistance."

"I beg your pardon?"

"The rules of war forbid an uprising in an occupied country. A *levée en masse* is permissible to resist an invasion, but once an army occupies a country, it is unthinkable to continue hostilities. And your plan, sire, a brilliant one, if I may say so, would preclude any resistance being offered in a timely fashion."

Rolf and Valan exchanged satisfied smiles. "Of course, the citizenry might not be as conversant in the rules of war as you, Lord Drent," Rolf suggested. "In that case, however, I suppose a little poison down their wells would teach them some manners."

"Good lord!" exclaimed Drent. "You can't poison the enemy's wells!"

"Why not?" Rolf argued. "It seems like a singularly efficient tactic to me."

"It is against the conventions of war, Highness."

"Marvelous," Rolf sighed sarcastically. "With access to water, they could hold out for months."

"Access to water? Why, that's another matter entirely."

"What do you mean?"

"The rules say nothing about destroying their wells, or capturing them and denying their access to water. It's poison that is unthinkable."

"Well, what's the difference?" grumbled Rolf.

"We are a civilized people," Drent replied with great dignity.

* * *

When they reached the witch's well, Rolf was glad to call a halt and seek the shade of the great oak beside it. He had only placed his hand on the gate when the witch bustled out of the house with her customary greeting.

"Oooooh, your lordship," she squealed, with the subtlety of an ungreased wheel. "This is such an honor. Here, sit and rest. I will serve you."

"Water, my good woman," he said, sitting on the end of the bench furthest from her. His servant handed her a jeweled silver goblet.

She hauled the bucket up and set it on the rim of the well. She filled the goblet and then picked up a pebble from beside the bucket and dropped it into the cup before she turned and handed it back to him with a toothless smile.

"I thank you," he said and drank deeply. As he drank, the sounds of the horses and calls of the sergeants receded and he sat in a place of echoing silence.

"What do you want?" the witch whispered, her voice entirely changed.

He looked, with a start, and saw another woman there, surrounded by a shadowy shape the dimensions of the witch. She was proud and beautiful, with a stern, cold, face. He wanted to ask who she was, but could not.

"What do you want?" she asked again.

"Power," he replied, entranced. "Power such that no man can stand against me."

She smiled. "You shall have it," she hissed. "But you must bring me payment in return."

"What do you wish?"

"The heart of a beautiful young woman."

"Will that of the princess Alana do?"

"Admirably," she replied, with her cold smile. She took the cup from him. "Come," she said.

He followed her into her hovel. She pointed to a chair for him to sit. She bustled about the room, collecting oddments and grinding them in a mortar, muttering all the while. When foul wisps of dark green smoke rose from her brew, she scraped it into his cup. It hissed as it met the remaining water there. She held it out to him.

"Drink," she commanded.

He took the cup, unseeing, and drank it to its dregs. He let it fall onto the table and doubled over retching. His limbs twitched and he slid from his seat, convulsing as the lightning magic ran through his veins. He tried to stand, but stumbled, falling across the table and rolling to the floor as the spell swept through him and over him. He felt himself falling, falling endlessly, and felt relieved, that perhaps he could fall away from the pain that ripped through his every muscle. He plummeted through a twisting maze of vile dreams and then landed softly. His head felt clear. He was himself. He was more than himself.

He stood and felt the strength race through his veins. The witch picked up the pebble from where it had rolled from the cup.

"Try your sword," she told him.

He drew it and brought it crashing down on the solid oak table. The table shattered and Rolf began to laugh. His laughter rang through the house and out to the road, as ominous as a roll of thunder. Horses shied and whickered nervously and the men looked at one another, filled with a sudden dread.

When Rolf's black mirth had subsided, the witch addressed him again. "For now, you hold your power at my whim. When I receive payment, it will be yours forever."

He left the house, still chuckling, and returned to his waiting army. No longer would he have to sneak, to charm, to act the part of the loving uncle. Gwalhafed was his, and after that Amytans and its far-flung possessions. Then he could turn his eye to Velendruch and take for himself the wealth of its mines and its trade. And then, with such power at his command, the rest of the world would know him for its master. And there was nothing to stop him. No man could stand against him.

The difference in his appearance was subtle, but every one of his men felt the power of the spell. The hairs of their necks rose as he passed and they feared to look upon his face. Even the obtuse Drent rode in silence.

The witch sat in her chair, rocking. She gazed at the pebble in her hand and laughed.

Chapter 26
The Harvest Drumming

Ranell and Aelvan led their guests downward through the twilight. The Watchers followed, laughing and singing. As they walked, they could see others thronging the spiderweb of paths of the *faer*'s inner domain, the torches they carried bobbing and flickering like fireflies. Finally, they reached the entrance to the largest cave the lowlanders had yet seen. From the narrow entrance, the ceiling arched high over their heads, receding in darkness from the light of the torches illuminating the floor. Like all the other caves, its floor was swept clean and the curving walls decorated, not with tapestries like the homes, but boldly painted in the rich russets and ochers the *faer* loved. Most of the decorations were geometric, but there were pictures, too: animals and hunters, sheaves of grain, and towering above all at the end opposite the entrance, the figure of a woman.

Below this figure, on a low shelf of rock, several musicians had set their drums and were beginning to tap out exploratory rhythms. The villagers mingled as they entered, greeting friends and kin and exchanging news. Dunwadi, leaning on her staff, limped into the cave and made her slow way across it, graciously greeting all who approached and laying hands of blessing on the infants they held up for her touch. When she reached the drummers, they made room for her at their center and she sat and looked about her at the *faer* she so loved. The crowd fell silent as Gorned, whom Bartrym had helped make his first drum, came forward and handed it to Dunwadi. It was small and narrow, polished smoothly, and stained a dull red. She held it, blessing it, and then turned and gave it to the gray-haired man sitting beside her.

"That's Ernan, the chief drummer," whispered Aelvan to Tovan. "When Gorned went to the caves last year, he learned that he was called to drum. Ernan must approve his drum for him to be accepted. He's spent every free moment on it this season."

The Watchers, particularly those from Bartrym's camp, waited, scarcely seeming to breathe. The elder handled the drum reverently, caressing its taut head and smoothly polished sides. He checked the cords attaching the head for tightness. Then he struck it. The tone was high, and it rang out boldly and resonated from the cave walls. Satisfied, Ernan smiled at Gorned and made room for the young man beside him. Gorned took his place with a look of determined seriousness.

Dunwadi stood. Ernan handed a drum to her, then picked up his own. Silence grew in the great chamber as all, at last even the smallest, playful child and fretting baby, stilled. She raised her hand and brought it swiftly down. The drum boomed, a deep tone that was felt as much by the heart as heard by the ear.

"We give thanks," she called.

"We give thanks," they chanted.

"We give thanks to She who feeds us all. Who holds us safe in her arms. Who bears us upon her body . . . ."

At each line, she struck her drum and the throng responded.

"Who gives us light." *Boom.*

"Who gives us air." *Boom.*

The crowd began to sway.

"Who is our Self." *Boom.*

"Who is our strength." *Boom.*

A tension began to build among the assembly. Alana looked around her. Sophie and Roderik looked as uneasy as she felt. Murdoch, she saw as she looked behind her, stood guard warily. She could see Tovan, tears running down his face. *He is born to this,* she thought. The *faer* stood transfixed, eyes shining, chanting their responses. And then Ernan began to play.

The rhythm changed, becoming deeper, more insistent, richer, more complex as, one by one, the other drummers joined. The crowd began to sway and dance. There was no structure to the dance that the lowland visitors could perceive. Individuals shook and stepped, small groups and families held hands, packs of children ran among them, spinning in circles and snapping in long chains. The rhythm grew, holding them all firmly in its grasp.

* * *

There was no way to tell how long they danced. At last, the beat abated and left the dancers gently, like bits of driftwood deposited on a beach by the tides. The dancers moved toward the sides of the cave, where they had left their cloaks and the jugs of drink they had brought with them. Conversations resumed, or started, as people found each other. Children sought their parents and snuggled close as they sat on cloaks, refreshing themselves. Babies suckled.

Then, all around Alana, eyes sparkled with anticipation as the *faer* gathered, men in knots, women in clusters, conversing excitedly, heads poking up occasionally to eye the other groups.

"What's going on?" Alana asked Mirna.

Mirna's eyes, too, were shining. "The women will choose their partners in the next dance." She left Alana's side and moved toward Murdoch, who stood talking with Bartrym in a group of elders.

Alana looked about her. Sophie stood with a group of women watchers and Alana could tell that she had already been told the purpose of the dance. She followed Sophie's gaze and saw Tovan and Roderik together in a group of young men, their eyes also roaming the crowd, seeking. At the same moment they both found Alana. She moved toward them, and the drums began again. They stood, watching her come closer, until she stood before them, in the fidgeting ring of the youngest women from Bartrym's camp. Tovan watched her approach, then glanced at Roderik and despondently dropped his gaze.

She could not do it. Wise policy dictated that she continue the charade of preferring Roderik, but she found she lacked the strength. Murdoch had recovered. They would leave the Hills in the morning. Her future lay with the prince. Events would take her from Tovan and she would never see him again. *Just this dance,* thought Alana. *Here, I am not a princess. I am nobody. Just this one night, I will dance with my beloved, and then I will return to my duties.*

Sophie reached them and stood behind Alana. *I will dance with Tovan,* she told herself, finding great relief in the thought. She avoided looking at Roderik.

Alana went directly to Tovan, took his hand, and led him into the dance.

She chose him? Roderik thought, watching the two disappear into the crowd. Then he saw Sophie standing before him, her hair in a swarm of braids like the others, a brightly patterned, borrowed sash decorating her plain garb. The muscles of his jaw tightened. Watchers mingled all around them, leaving in pairs. *Reach out your hand*, he thought. *Reach out your hand to me and then —no, not you. I have given my word.* But below both thoughts lay the fear that she would reject him, find him unworthy.

Sophie stood silent, looking at him, then through him, seeing the nameless fear that had ruled and shaped her life. She could no longer remember the sight of her mother, dead in childbirth. She only knew with certainty that the woman's path, the path that drew her to Roderik with a painful intensity, was one that would destroy the being that she had worked so hard to become, would crush her, squeeze the life's blood from her as it had from her mother. She turned and ran into the crowd. Roderik spun round and walked away, heading toward the cave mouth.

* * *

Murdoch stood with Bartrym, Dworning, and several of the grandfathers.

"Your daughter learns fast," Bartrym told him. "It's always a joy to teach a young one who's been properly brought up."

Murdoch looked at him in surprise, his eyebrow raising slightly. No one had ever complimented him on his daughter's upbringing.

"She and Tovan have exceeded all expectations. Those other two, though. . ." He sighed. "The girl's beginning to come round, but that young man you brought with you—why ever did you choose him as a companion?"

As they spoke, Bartrym's eyes watched the crowd. Before Murdoch could reply, Bartrym smiled. Murdoch turned and followed his gaze. A short, graying, strongly built woman came to Bartrym and led him into the dance. As Murdoch watched, all around him the scene repeated itself. From the Watcher women to the grandmothers, women chose men for the dance.

And then he saw Mirna, coming for him. Just for an instant, he was in another time and place. Flutes and viols sounded in his ears and he smelled the spicy scent of mulled wine. Joy—young, beautiful, copper-haired—came smiling toward him, wearing a plain dress dyed with blue woad, to take his hand and lead him into the dance. And then his vision shimmered and it was Mirna

212

who stood before him, eyes alight, reaching her hands to his. For the second time in his life, a woman had chosen to lead him into the dance of life. He took her hand in his, aware only of how soft her small hand felt against his rough palm, and of her dark eyes shining. But he did not dance, not at first. His heart's long drought was broken. He embraced her and wept.

* * *

All too soon, it seemed to Alana, the drums subsided and she and Tovan came to a standstill.

"Thank you," he said, and leaned forward to kiss her.

She pulled away. "No, Tovan, I can't."

"Why?"

"I told myself I would dance just this one dance with you and then I would return to my duties as princess. I must stop here. I can't go any further and then leave you. I couldn't bear it."

"Yes. You are a princess and I am a slave. I keep forgetting."

"No, Tovan. That's not it." His hands rested lightly on her shoulders. "I am not free to follow my own desires. I must do what is for my kingdom's good. If it were only a matter of who had a better claim to rule, myself or my uncle, I wouldn't care, I would give up my throne for you, but there's more involved. My uncle is treacherous. He wants only power for himself and does not care how the kingdom and its people will suffer to gain his ends. If he is not stopped, there will be a pointless war and thousands of men will die. There will be orphans, Tovan, and widows and famine because men who should be tilling the fields are dead or far away. I must stop him."

"And for that you need a prince."

"I need powerful allies."

"And I am not."

She looked at him, at his broad shoulders and forceful eyes. "You are powerful, Tovan, more powerful than you realize. But yours is not the kind of power that I need."

"Please, just this night."

"Tovan, no. Don't you see? If I am ruled by my desires, what is the difference between me and Rolf?"

Tovan stood motionless, staring at her. His hands tensed, and she felt the strength of his desire for her. She could not breathe.

And then, gently, he released her and walked into the moonlight. She turned and slowly walked back into the Lady's cave, her tears glistening in the torchlight.

* * *

Roderik wandered for miles on moonlit paths, trying to make sense of the shambles of his quest. He started at a rustling behind him and turned to see a ghostly figure that greeted him with a soft whicker.

"Dreyfala!" he whispered. "Aren't you a marvel."

The great horse came to the sound of his voice and nosed his pocket for a treat.

"No, boy, nothing in there for you now." But Roderik was wrong: Dreyfala's insistent nose nudged a forgotten lump, deep in his pocket. Roderik pulled it out and held the witch's tiny packet in the hollow of his hand. It seemed to him to radiate an unseen power. Perhaps his quest could be salvaged after all.

Chapter 27
The Love Potion

The dancing had ended hours before, and only a short time remained until dawn. Those from the nearest villages had returned to their homes and most of the Watchers to their camps, but many from Mirna's and the other more distant villages remained and slept, wrapped in their cloaks on the floor.

Light from the setting full moon slanted though the cave's mouth, silhouetting the tall man who stood at the entrance and glimmering as it reflected from the gold of his hair. Roderik waited for his eyes to accustom themselves to the darkness of the cave, now illuminated only by the moon. Slowly, he walked among the sleepers, seeking his quarry, with the witch's pouch in his hand.

He found Alana and Sophie sleeping beside the platform where the drummers had sat, the moonlight shining on them like a beacon, Sophie nearest him and the princess facing the wall. Roderik crept up to them. He knelt on one knee and reached across Sophie, parcel in hand, to sprinkle the powder on Alana's face.

Sophie felt his presence and was instantly awake. She brought her knees up sharply into his ribs and pushed him away with all her strength. He fell backward and landed on the floor with a grunt. She leapt to her feet and watched as the tiny parcel arced through the air, trailing bright red sparks like the trail of a comet. It hit him on the bridge of his nose, its contents exploding softly in his face. She watched, puzzled, as the glowing sparks crawled like live things across his face and soaked into his skin like rain into soil.

"Oh. You," she said, and began to turn away.

He opened his eyes and saw her, jumped ardently to his feet. and trapped her in his arms. "I want you," he said.

For a moment, Sophie stood frozen. She could feel the strength of his arms surrounding her, holding her motionless with no seeming effort. His left arm circled her back, pinning her right arm to her side and he gripped her left wrist painfully. She could not reach her dagger. She squirmed in his grasp and tried to kick him. He laughed and swept his free arm under her knees. All the veneer was gone now. The civilized, housebroken courtier had vanished. He began to carry her toward the cave mouth. Quickly, she jabbed her knee toward his head. He dropped her legs and his arm snaked around them again, trapping her knees between his side and his arm. He slid his hand up along her thigh.

"The maiden of fire," he said, his fingers reaching beneath her jerkin. "You want me. Admit it."

"You conceited pig!" she said, glaring into his glassy eyes, with the sparks swimming beneath their surface. "If I ever saw anything in you, it just vanished!" She struggled harder, and to less effect. "Father!" she shouted, at the top of her lungs.

All around them sleepers stirred as Roderik tore at her clothing. Suddenly, Murdoch's strong right hand yanked his head back by the hair and the face of his beloved was replaced by that of her father, one inch away, jaw clenched.

* * *

The witch sat dozing in an armchair as her darlings played around her. She awoke with a start.

"The love potion!" she whispered. She chuckled as she stood. "Time to go to work."

She began to turn counterclockwise, muttering and mumbling as she spun, slowly at first, then faster and faster, like a leaf spinning in a storm. As she sped, her voice rose to a moan, to a shriek, to a keening cry, and she dissolved into nothingness.

In a moonlit dell near Mirna 's village, a patch of mist began to grow.

Chapter 28
Counsel

Roderik left the Lady's Cave escorted by ten young men, whose unfriendly looks made it clear that he would soon be on the lowland road. Halfway there, however, they were met by two others, breathless with haste, coming from the east. The two spoke to Roderik's escort, who suddenly seemed to forget about him. Roddie somehow couldn't understand what they were saying. He had more important things to concern him, although he would have been hard-pressed to say just what they were.

Roderik strode purposefully down the hillside toward the mist. Just as he reached the swirling edge of it, a voice spoke behind him.

"Young man," Dunwadi said, as softly as the wind moving through dried grass. "Why do you go into the mist?"

Roderik stopped and turned to face the speaker. He had no answer.

"You are not a warrior." There was no scorn in Dunwadi's voice. It was a simple statement of fact.

Roderik flushed with anger. His hand crept toward his scabbard, empty since the night by the meadow.

She watched him impassively. "Your weapon will not help you. Only the quality of your mind and heart will be useful in the mist."

Dunwadi's dark eyes met his own and he felt the hollowness in his chest and realized the old woman's words were true. His shoulders slumped and he looked at her in anguish. "Help me," Roderik whispered.

"Two gifts I can give you," Dunwadi answered. She held out a plain, empty, leather pouch, dark and soft with age, about the size of Roderik's hand. "Remember this when all else fails." Roderik took it and looked at it doubtfully before tucking it into his belt. "The second will require more effort." She reached up and grasped the young man's head firmly, pressing her thumbs into the space between his eyebrows. Roderik's eyes opened wide in surprise and fear and then his expression cleared. Dunwadi removed her hands. "The witch's spell is broken. Do you still choose to enter the mist?"

"Is there a task for me in there?"

"Yes."

"Then I will go." The mist swirled around him, and Dunwadi disappeared from his sight.

* * *

Murdoch sat, gazing across the valley, watching the dawn turn the world to roses, an unaccustomed feeling of peace deep in his soul. He watched Tovan lead Dreyfala up the steep slope to where he sat.

"He gave me his horse," the astonished Tovan told Murdoch, as he stroked the animal's snowy nose. "When the Watchers came to lead him away, he handed me his horse's reins and said, 'Take good care of him. He won't be much use to me in the mist.' Just like that."

"Roderik's gone, then?"

Tovan nodded. "He has been made outcast."

"About time." Tovan sat down by his side. They said nothing for a while, allowing the beauty to soak into their souls.

Then Murdoch turned his head toward Tovan. "What did he mean, 'the mist'?"

"I don't know. They were taking him down the path toward our village, though."

Murdoch shrugged and turned back to the view. "Our village," he whispered, smiling.

Far below, they could see Mirna climbing the rocky hillside. She hurried toward them, concern clouding her brow. "Murdoch, Tovan, come quickly! The Watchers have seen something."

Startled, they ran down the hillside toward her.

* * *

Ranell stayed with Sophie, deep in the darkness of the Lady's Cave, watching her with the care a mother would lavish on a sick infant. Sophie sat silent, her mind spinning in circles.

"Are you all right?" Ranell asked, when the silence had become intolerable.

"Yes, I'm fine."

Ranell hesitated, and bit her lower lip. "No, you're not," she said at last.

"It would seem not. I suppose Alana's ladies were right all along." Sophie looked up at Ranell. "They used to laugh at me, you know. Behind my back."

"Why?"

"Because I could fight. Because I wore men's clothes and could come and go as I pleased."

"They laughed at you for that?"

"I ignored them. A more useless bunch you couldn't imagine, but every one of them, every one, will marry well, some noble or other. It's all they think about. I suppose I should have watched them more closely and learned their tricks. Maybe things would have worked out better."

"With Roderik?"

Sophie nodded.

"Oh, Sophie," Ranell said, "there are much better men than him about. You haven't met the Watchers in the other camps."

She shook her head. "He drives me insane, Ranell. I have been trained by a master. I have seen my father train others, take men with much less promise and turn them into polished warriors. I see his faults—oh, do I see his faults—but I also see the man he could be, and that man takes my breath away.

"The moment I first saw him, I . . . even though I thought he was an enemy. I . . . I see him in my dreams, Ranell, but . . . oh God, Ranell! With every other woman, it's 'Yes, my lady. At your service.' All bowing and scraping and sweet little smiles. For me, there's nothing but spite. The pig!

"I called for help! *Me*! I never realized how strong he is. I called for my father. My father! I wanted him and I couldn't . . . I resisted . . . I . . . maybe that's why he could never see me as a woman.

Maybe the ladies were right. Maybe I'm not a woman. Oh, God, Ranell, what am I?"

Ranell moved to sit beside her. She took Sophie's hand. "We've watched you and Roderik all this week, deeply enmired in the *ksh:* how you both denied your true feelings, how you failed to treat each other with honesty and respect. We were all afraid of something like this, but we do not know your customs and you are not of our people so we did not interfere. But he treated you horribly. His behavior is his responsibility, not yours."

* * *

Dunwadi, Alana, and a group of men and women elders sat in the sunlight at the mouth of the Lady's Cave, conversing quietly as Mirna, Murdoch, and Tovan joined them. Dunwadi held up her hand for silence and waited for them to sit before she began. "An army from the east is camped at the top of the eastward path. What shall we do?"

"How many are there?" Murdoch asked.

"Three thousand have been counted," said one of the men.

"Are they heavily armed?"

"They are a fearsome sight."

"How many have we?"

The man thought for a moment. "The two hundred Watchers, a thousand parents, perhaps a hundred elders, and the rest children."

"How many that bear weapons?"

"We have knives and axes and the tools the Watchers use in their work, but we have never fought. The Lady has always protected us."

"Tovan has returned to us," Dunwadi said softly. "We will no longer be a people apart."

"Rolf knows that I am here, and he covets these mountains," Alana said.

"The army of Gwalhafed is well-trained. By me," Murdoch added apologetically. "If we try to meet him directly, we will lose."

One of the women spoke: "We must protect the villages."

Murdoch smoothed the sand in front of him. "Draw me a map of your realm."

A bee landed on his hand. As he shook it off, a shadow fell across the sand. They looked up to see a tall, armored figure. A faint bloom of rust covered the mail coat and marred the fine engraved tracery that decorated the helm.

"Anselm?" Murdoch said.

The old knight lifted his visor. "Perhaps I can be of help. I have given much thought to the defense of this land, particularly since Tovan was taken from us."

The others moved aside to give him room to sit. As he eased himself down among them, it was evident how much effort it cost him to wear the heavy armor.

"You don't intend to fight?" Murdoch asked with some concern.

"This is my home," the gray-haired warrior replied, with his gentle smile. "Today is as good a to die as any other."

* * *

In Queen Mother Edwynna's chamber in Arnhem Castle, King Ulrik was aghast at what he saw.

"I thought you should see this, dear," Edwynna said.

Her tapestry showed Roderik on his knee before Alana, and next to it, another image of him, with a swirling, glittering mist about his head, embracing a copper-haired woman.

"Upon my honor!" Ulrik bellowed. "He has been enchanted! We are an honorable house! What will they all think of us? What a fool I was to let him go." He strode to the window and shouted to the ostler below in the courtyard. "Call the guard! Saddle my horse!"

* * *

The council lasted for hours. By the end of it, they had a plan, but Murdoch was not satisfied.

"If our plan works perfectly," he said, "we may hold our own, but we cannot count on it. If Rolf cannot be lured into our trap, we are not enough to stand against him."

Anselm spoke. "We could appeal to Amytans."

There was muttered conference around the circle. "But how," Murdoch asked, "with an army coming up the path?"

"There is a path to the west, as well," one of the elders replied.

"These old bones lack the strength for such a journey," Anslem apologized. "But I will send this with the messenger." He reached into a pouch tucked into his belt and took out a heavy gold ring, with the crest of Amytans engraved on it.

He addressed the group. "What say you?"

The group conferred and at last Dunwadi spoke. "There is danger at every turning on this day. We need help, but those who come to our aid today may covet these hills tomorrow. This is not a decision to be made in haste, but if we wait, there may not be time to send for help if we so choose. What say you?"

Her pitch-dark eyes fixed on those of the man to her left. The man nodded. The next in the circle, a woman, nodded as well. Around the circle they went, some nodding, some shaking their heads. When all had responded, she said, "Most favor the plan. But some do not. What are your concerns?"

The first who had shaken his head said, "There is not enough time. It is a day's walk from here to the bottom of the path and who knows how far beyond?"

Several others nodded in agreement.

Anselm said, "Our lowland guests have horses. When I came here, it took me a day to climb the western path on horseback. Going downhill will be faster. From the base of the path, Arnhem Castle can be reached in a day's hard riding."

A woman asked, "Can we trust these people of Amytans?"

Murdoch looked to Anselm. "My people are warlike, it is true," Anselm confessed. "But Amytans is threatened by Rolf as well. There would be grounds for alliance."

"They have always respected their treaties with us," Murdoch added.

Dunwadi looked at each of those who had voiced objections. One by one, they nodded, giving assent to the plan. "Who will go?" she asked.

"Your grandnephew would be the logical person to send," Murdoch muttered to Anselm. "Wherever he might be." He raised his voice to say, "Perhaps I or Sophie. . . ."

Tovan stood. "I will go. Murdoch and Sophie are warriors and are needed here. I cannot wield a sword, but I can ride a horse."

* * *

Tovan saddled Dreyfala and tightened his girth while Alana and several of the village children watched. The preparations finished, Tovan turned to Alana and walked to where she stood.

"Since I met you, my life has been like a beautiful dream," he said. "I . . ." He reached out his hand to take hers, but as his fingertips brushed her knuckles, he drew back and dropped his hand again to his side, and he spoke to her shoulder. "I wanted you to know that."

"Tovan, no matter what happens—no matter what I am forced to do—remember. You are the man I love." She hesitated. "And I thank you for doing this. It is more than I deserve."

"I am doing this for my people," he said. He turned and mounted Dreyfala, and with one last look at Alana, rode away. The children drifted away to more interesting pastimes, but Alana stood, touching the place his hand had brushed hers, long after he had gone.

* * *

Dreyfala threaded his way nimbly down the western path from the Hills. When he reached the base, he proved to Tovan and everyone they passed that his reputation as the fastest horse in three kingdoms was well-deserved.

While Arnhem Castle was still a shining point on the horizon, Tovan saw a body of two hundred mounted warriors cantering toward him, led by a red-faced man in such opulent clothing that Tovan naturally assumed him to be the king. Ulrik had not thought it would take such an army to retrieve his son. He simply had firm ideas about what constituted a proper bodyguard for one of his rank. Dreyfala raced toward them, stopped short, and reared, whinnying loudly.

"Dreyfala!" shouted the king. "And who are you, bold warrior, to ride my son's horse?"

Tovan looked around himself for an instant to see who the bold warrior might be. To his surprise, he was alone. "I am Tovan, sire, of the *faer*. Roderik gave the horse to me. I was sent to seek your aid."

"I'm not surprised," Ulrik snorted. "What's the boy got himself into this time?"

"He's gone into the mist."

"The mist?"

"But that's not why I was sent. Here." He rode Dreyfala close beside Ulrik's horse and handed him the ring. "This is from Anselm."

"My uncle Anselm?"

"He awaits you in the Hills."

The captain of the guard leaned toward Ulrik. "This is some faerie trick, sire."

"Please listen," Tovan said. "Princess Alana of Gwalhafed has taken refuge from her uncle in the Hills. He and his army are attacking at this very moment. When he has taken the Hills, he plans to attack Amytans."

"For what reason?"

"He deceived the princess that a marriage had been arranged between herself and your son. When she was on her way to Amytans, he sent men wearing Amytans livery to attack her party." Dreyfala danced, feeling the impatience of his rider. "I must go now. She needs me."

Tovan put his heels to Dreyfala's side and the great horse burst into a furious gallop. The captain and his men sat openmouthed as their king weighed his decision. Finally, Ulrik put his spurs to his horse and they followed the white stallion and its dark rider.

All the long way back up the narrow path, Ulrik's twin statements—naming him, Tovan, the witch's boy, a bold warrior, and calling the king's own son, the magnificent golden prince, a boy—worked at the last illusion remaining in Tovan's mind like two burly woodcutters hewing an oak. By the time he reached the top and began his descent into the valley, nothing could stand between Tovan and his love.

Chapter 29
Invasion

Rolf and his troops threaded their way up the path Alana and the others had followed. With their many hands and horses, they were able to clear the ledge of the boulders that had stopped their quarry. They made no attempt at secrecy. They camped in the meadow beside the pines, cutting a great many trees to make bonfires every twenty feet around the edge of the encampment.

The next morning, they formed into broad ranks and marched down into the valley, singing songs of battle and conquest. A group of *faer* had been sent to the meadow to lay down a convincing trail for the army to follow, and so Rolf and his followers were led around the verges of the *faer*'s domain and kept carefully away from the villages.

Hundreds of eyes watched them pass: Watchers concealed behind the trunks of trees or in their branches; men and women, armed with axes, hidden in forest glades; grandmothers and the mothers of the very young, infants at their breasts and youngsters clinging in silence, all watching from the caves of the two villages nearest the route created for the army.

After walking for most of the day, the army emerged from thick forest into another meadow, in a valley shaped like a deep bowl several acres in size and surrounded by slopes ringed with thickets of bramble. Trees stood on the hillside facing them, their leaves now brown and thinning, and great gray boulders showed among the trunks of the trees.

Rolf smiled. He saw what he sought at the far end of the vale, standing on a flat outcropping of rock a little way up the opposite slope. Three figures greeted his sight: Murdoch and an armored knight, and between them the princess Alana, the gold on her green dress glittering in the sunshine, hood thrown back, her red hair like a burning beacon.

He set the spurs to his horse and raced into the valley, Valan close behind. As they rode, another helmeted warrior, small and lithe, ran down the opposing slope and stood beside Murdoch.

Rolf and Valan reached the base of the rock and halted. Those following filed into the valley.

* * *

Grimbold glanced nervously at the terrain. As he expected, the new recruits, with himself and the other guards commanding them, were stationed in the center, surrounded by the glint of new weaponry borne by the vassals of Rolf's supporters. The valley suited Rolf's purpose perfectly.

* * *

Alana watched them file into the valley, her heart in her throat. She willed her hands to relax and her breath to come deep and slow. It took all her strength. Her rage at her uncle was nearly drowned in the fear she felt washing over her, and Rolf, she knew, was the moon that drove that tide. Murdoch looked at her, and she seemed to him as wan and frozen as a lake at midwinter.

"Do you wish me to speak for you, my lady?"

"No," she replied. "I must learn to speak for myself."

"Remember to breathe," he said, "and remember that you are not alone."

She reached for his hand and clasped it and it seemed to her that warmth and strength flowed from him into her.

The army filled the valley, and halted.

"Men of Gwalhafed," Alana called, looking at Rolf, but speaking so that all could hear. "My uncle has sent me here, into exile. Those who assailed me on the road were in his pay. If you love me, and honor the memory of my father, I bid you stand aside."

She swept her right hand outward. There was a murmuring and rustling within the ranks. Rolf raised his hand. At his signal, captains shouted to their men and those surrounding Alana's supporters turned inward. Alana's men were trapped.

"Check," said Rolf.

She looked at him closely. He seemed larger, somehow, and fear clung to him like an ominous, shifting cloud. Once again, she felt her tongue immobilized. *No*, she thought. *He is only my uncle. I will not let him cow me.*

"Mate," she replied. "Look about you."

She raised her arms and the *faer* rose from their hiding places behind the hedges. Soon, the entire valley was ringed with their

226

dark heads. A murmur of dismay swept through the soldiers. Rolf, since his encounter with the witch, was frightening, but to be confronted by the *faer*, whose terrors they had heard of since their cradles, was beyond bearing.

If Rolf was surprised by this turn of events, he did not let it show. "It is customary," he replied confidently, "to settle such matters by single combat between the two parties." He dismounted and said, in a voice of menace, "Name your champion."

"My lady?" Murdoch inquired. Alana nodded. He slid off the edge of the rock and faced his adversary. He could feel the difference in Rolf. In the pit of his stomach and the tingling down his spine he could feel the force of the witch's spell. He took a deep breath and drew his sword. He had his duty, the guarding of the princess, and more to fight for. The matter of Joy, his wife, still lay between them. Sixteen years had passed since Rolf had had her beaten and sent her to the dungeon, years during which Rolf had hidden himself in exile, and then been protected by his role as regent and his facade of repentance.

Rolf now felt a twinge of doubt. This man was not cowering like the others, and seemed to actually relish the thought of combat with him.

Murdoch walked away from the rock, toward the level ground in front of the massed troops. Rolf, seeing his chance, attacked from behind, only to find the old warrior's reflexes undimmed by time. Murdoch spun and caught the edge of his sword on his own and deflected the blow. A growl passed through the assembled men, Rolf's as well as Alana's, at this breach of fairness. The two now circled each other cautiously, each waiting to see the other's strategy. Murdoch stepped toward Rolf and feinted toward his right. Rolf's sword moved to block the blow and Murdoch swung his blade around and cut upward from beneath. Rolf leapt backward, fell, and rolled nimbly to his feet again, sword ready to block the blow that Murdoch aimed at him.

All eyes were on the swordsmen and their masterful display as they cut and parried, spun, and dodged in their deadly dance. After a time, it became evident that neither would be able to best the other with skill and that the outcome would be decided by endurance alone.

As the others watched, entranced, Valan saw his chance to turn the battle by treachery. Alana and the two warriors stood on the rock watching the fight. Cautiously, he moved around to the side of the rock and climbed it, sword drawn, advancing toward the princess.

"I think not, friend," said a soft voice, close over his shoulder.

Valan turned swiftly, hoping to strike the other down, but his stroke was parried. It was Anselm, his years concealed by the armor and helmet he wore.

"Put up your sword, sir," the ancient knight courteously requested.

Valan looked nervously about him. The troops stood as if rooted, part in fear and part in fascination with the expert swordplay being enacted before them. Valan saw he had no help in this fight. The second warrior now stood guard before Alana, sword drawn. Valan turned his attention to his adversary, who stood ready, but showed no desire to attack him. He looked carefully, assessing the man's size, the slow deliberation of his movements, the bend of his back and the antique fashion of his armor. He decided to fight.

He roared and leapt at Anselm, aiming a wicked blow at his head. Anselm ducked and swung at Valan's body, but Valan stepped back, and then forward again, thrusting his sword deep under Anselm's mail coat and into his groin. Anselm toppled and fell. Valan pulled his sword free and stepped across the body to where Sophie waited to face him. She noted that he fought left-handed and knew what she would do. He brought his sword up backhand and she blocked it, twisting her sword so that his was flung upward and back, into the perfect position for a forehand cut. When he brought the sword whistling down, she stepped back and pivoted, as her father had taught her. Her back to him, she heard the clang of his blade hitting the rock they stood on. She spun faster, shifted her weight to her right foot, and swung with all her force. Her blade sliced into his neck. He crumpled into a heap and lay there, lifeless.

She dropped her sword and turned to Anselm. Alana had already run to him and was carefully removing his helmet. Sophie supported his shoulders and both women wept. His eyes fluttered open, a radiant look on his pale face.

"I have seen the Lady," he whispered, awestruck. "There is a garden, even more beautiful, beyond the gate." With that, his life left him. Alana closed his eyes and they laid him down again.

The clash of steel brought them back to the dangers of this world. Below them, Rolf and Murdoch still fought. Sophie watched closely. Murdoch had slowed, and she could tell that the weakness from his wounding was beginning to show itself. She replaced her helmet, picked up her sword, and waited. Still the two men circled, leapt forward, and retreated, like two snakes.

Murdoch attacked and the two stood for a moment, their faces inches apart across their blades.

"Give it up, blacksmith," Rolf hissed. "You cannot win. I have the witch's promise."

"I have my wife to avenge."

"Why?" Rolf sneered. "I'm not the one who killed her."

The words cut deeper than any sword could penetrate. In that instant, Rolf struck. Lightning fast, the point of his sword struck Murdoch just under the arm and he fell with a groan. Rolf stepped forward and raised his sword over his head to finish his adversary.

Alana screamed. Sophie roared, "*No!*", and Rolf found himself tumbling backward as Sophie leapt from the rock and threw herself headlong into his chest. She tumbled across him and her helmet flew off, rattling as it rolled across the stony field.

He regained his feet and faced her. "Fool! No man can stand against me."

"Perhaps," she said grimly, as she stood and turned toward him. "But I am a woman."

* * *

Grimbold, standing in the center of the troops, could not see what had happened, but he knew the voice. Deep within his heart a spark ignited, born of love for this girl who dared to face Rolf's terror alone.

"Sophie!" he whispered, and then, his voice growing as his confidence returned, he said, "Shall we stand here and let a woman do our fighting for us? Men of Gwalhafed!"Are we to be outdone by a girl? Fight now! Fight for the princess Alana!"

The outnumbered recruits drew their swords and began the hopeless task of fighting through the ring of better-armed men surrounding them. The *faer*, perched on the slopes above, threw stones at the backs of Rolf's troops, and the valley filled with the racket of rocks striking chainmail and the cries of the men when the stones found their mark.

* * *

Rolf advanced, but his confidence had been shaken. Sophie saw that in his eyes, as she gazed steadily into them. She knew that she had never faced such an adversary, and she tried to think of a strategy that would deny him the advantage of his superior size and strength. As she parried his first blow, and felt the shock of its impact tearing at the muscles of her arm and shoulder, she knew she was completely outmatched. There was only one thing she could do. She would draw Rolf away from Alana, and hope that help would arrive from Amytans.

Rolf advanced again, and she dodged his blow. Step by step, she retreated down the space left between Rolf's army and the first row of hedge. Step by step, she backed, weaving from side to side, thrusting with her sword just often enough to disguise her true intent.

With each step, Rolf's anger grew. Fighting Sophie was like fighting smoke. He came at her faster, each blow harder than the last, attempting to drive her to his left, into the mob of his own troops, to block her retreat and finish her. She realized his aim and redoubled her efforts to stay in the clear space, moving away from the troops and toward the valley's mouth.

"Seize her!" Rolf shouted, and the two soldiers nearest leapt to obey. She spun, sword flashing, and they fell, but as she completed her pivot and turned to face Rolf again, she saw his sword slice toward her face. She could not jump back, out of reach of the blade—her momentum would not allow it—so she leapt forward. Her sword clattered uselessly against his armor and he struck her on the head, not with his blade, as he had hoped, but with the pommel. The force of his blow sent her flying across the gap and she landed, unconscious, amid a thicket of wild rose.

Alana had not moved. She still crouched on top of the rock. Rolf turned. Holding his shield above his head to protect himself

230

from the shower of rocks that rained down on him, he strode down the hillside toward her. Alana had no one left to turn to. Murdoch, Sophie, and Anselm had all fallen. Roderik, her would-be champion, had disappeared entirely. Her troops still fought in the center of their trap. The *faer*, blocked by the impenetrable brambles, could do no more than they were already doing.

She watched his cold blue eyes and realized that Rolf intended to kill her. In the heat and chaos of battle, no one would see his action and he would be free to blame her death on whomever he wished. She undid the clasp of her cloak and wrapped the fabric around her forearm. Each of his steps seemed to take a century and boom like thunder in her ears. She stood, the spell's power robbing her of movement, of speech, as a snake robs its victim of its will.

The neighing of a horse sounded faintly. Alana looked toward the sound. A white horse with a dark rider appeared at the top of the valley. It checked and reared as the *faer* blocking the path scrambled out of its way. Dreyfala had once again outdistanced the other horses of Amytans.

Rolf reached the base of the rock and walked, unhurried, around to the side to climb up it. She swept her cloak up over her arm, wrapping it securely. He reached the top and she could see his dagger in his right hand, concealed from the troops.

"My lady," he said, his voice as courteous as ever. "Do you really think you can resist me?"

"Your Highness the Prince Uncle Rolf," she answered, pushing each word from her lips, fighting the fear that made her feel as though she were at the bottom of a lake. Rolf came toward her, as slowly as if he were swimming. "Surely *you* would know that a cloak can be used as a weapon."

He stopped, and smiled. "Well, well, I give you full marks, Alana. But if you knew how I killed your father, why did you not act sooner?"

"I learned from the *faer*. I have learned much here."

"A pity you will find no use for it."

Tovan sat on Dreyfala. He, like the others, felt the force of the spell as it radiated from Rolf, but another force in him rose up and pushed the iron coldness back from his heart. Alana was there, and from her no witch's spell, nor death itself, could hold him back. He set his heels to Dreyfala's side and the great horse flew down the slope like a lightning bolt.

Alana heard the hoofbeats. In answer, she leapt lightly off the rock and began to run. Rolf laughed grimly. Burdened by his heavy chainmail, he could not leap, but went down the way he had come and followed her. Closer came Tovan to the fleeing princess, and closer came Rolf to her. She struggled against the weight of the cloak and the bulk of her skirts. Rolf grabbed her arm. She dug in her heels and pulled against him and they swung around, as his momentum carried him past her.

On came Dreyfala, bearing Tovan. Rolf raised his knife and struck. Alana blocked the blow with her arm and he caught only the many layers of the cloak padding it.

"Stop!" roared Tovan as the great horse checked and reared.

"Fool!" shouted Rolf. "No man—"

Dreyfala's iron hooves crashed down upon Rolf, striking him to the ground.

* * *

Rolf saw a blaze of light, and then nothing. When he awoke, he lay on a bench in a strange garden, surrounded by high stone walls. He sat upright, startled, and looked about him. He was alone. He saw the gate at the end of the path and ran for it, desperate to go back to the prize he had come so close to winning. He reached the gate and laid his hand on the latch. He felt a woman's hand atop his and shook it away with a savage motion. He pushed the gate open and with a scream of terror found himself falling, falling, falling into a dark and stinking void, the sound *ksh* echoing endlessly through it.

* * *

Rolf's death broke the spell holding his troops in thrall. They grasped their weapons and looked around in despair, at Alana's soldiers facing them, at the *faer* ringing them, and at King Ulrik and his men, who had appeared at the entrance to the valley. The *faer* stopped their barrage and began to chant Tovan's name. Sophie sat up, rubbing her head. Mirna was already tending Murdoch. She had removed his mail shirt and begun to staunch his wound.

232

In all this sea of motion, Alana and Tovan remained an island. He dismounted and stepped across Rolf's inert form to her side. Lost in the rhythm of their own dance, he took her hand, then touched her cheek and kissed her. She returned his kiss gladly and his arms encircled her and lifted her and he carried her, still kissing her, down to where Mirna was caring for Murdoch.

Drent sat on his horse, in the front rank, feeling uncomfortably warm, his attention focused on the enormous lump that had suddenly appeared in his throat. Tovan set Alana lightly on the ground in front of him. They needed to do no more than look at him for him to unbuckle his sword belt and hand his weapon to Tovan. Tovan refused it. He stood to one side with his arms folded.

"You will surrender to me, Lord Drent," said Alana, "and swear fealty to me as your liege."

Pale and sweating, Drent dismounted, knelt, and handed her his sword. Tovan looked to the top of the valley and beckoned to Ulrik to bring his men down. Considering that no one had given the monarch an order since he had left the nursery, the king took it well. He ordered his men to begin disarming Rolf's followers.

Hand in hand, Alana and Tovan went to where Mirna tended Murdoch's wound.

"It will take stitching," Mirna said, in response to Alana's concerned look, "but he heals quickly."

Alana knelt at the warrior's side. "Again, you have saved Gwalhafed. Ask any boon you wish."

Murdoch smiled, teeth gritted against the pain. "Release me from my oath, Highness, so that I may stay here, in the Hills."

"Gladly," she said, smiling, "but I will command your presence at my wedding."

She stood, and called out, "Grimbold!"

He ran to her and took a knee.

"Your sword, Murdoch."

Mirna handed it to her. Alana tapped Grimbold's shoulders, left, right, left. "I dub thee Sir Grimbold, True Man, captain of my guard."

Sophie joined them, rubbing the bruise on her cheek. "Father?"

"I'll mend," he said. "That's a wicked bruise he gave you."

"I'll mend," she said.

King Ulrik approached the group. "Where's Roderik?" he demanded. "Does my son live? Is he wounded?"

Dunwadi approached them. "He went into the mist this morning." With a slight motion of her head, she indicated the direction.

"Into the mist?" he snapped.

"This is the witch's doing," she replied.

Sophie felt fear grip her heart. *That idiot!* She stood, dizzy, balanced on the edge of a sword. On one side, her anger at Roderik, her wish to see him suffer for his treatment of her, on the other, cold fear for his life. She wavered, ignored by the others. *A warrior does what must be done,* she concluded, at last.

"That idiot! He'll get himself killed." Without another word, she mounted Dreyfala and was gone, leaving her companions speechless.

Chapter 30
Into the Mist

Dreyfala, carrying Sophie, raced to the edge of the mist, then shied and refused to go further. She leapt from his back and ran in, heedless of the danger signaled by the animal's behavior. Once into the impenetrable fog, she slowed her pace. Advancing cautiously, sword drawn, she called Roderik's name softly. The voice that answered grated on her ears and turned her spine to ice. It was the voice of the witch.

"Not who I was expecting," she wheedled, "but you'll do."

Sophie turned and saw the lumpy, shadowy shape come toward her. She grasped her sword in a two-handed grip and held it out before her, threatening. The witch laughed and kept advancing slowly, but with no hesitation. A long knife glinted in her hand. She drew closer, within range of the sword. Sophie stepped back and then swung, lunging forward as she did so. The witch held out her hand in a warding motion and the sword began to curve, as flexible as a snake, striking for Sophie. Sophie felt the change in its balance and let go of it.

It flew toward the witch but missed her and fell clanging to the ground behind her back. The witch advanced, knife held low. Sophie stood poised, waiting for her to strike. When the witch stabbed at her, she kicked the knife from her hand. The blade flew glittering through the thick air and landed with a clatter on the stony ground. While Sophie's weight was still on one foot, the witch leapt for her throat. They fell heavily backward, with the witch's weight full on top of Sophie, trapping her. The witch's stubby fingers grappled at her throat. Frantically, Sophie tried to pry them loose but could not. Clutching Sophie's neck, the witch lifted her head and slammed it onto the stony ground. When Sophie shouted in pain, the witch redoubled the pressure on her windpipe. Still Sophie struggled.

Again, the witch lifted Sophie's head, but before she could bring it crashing down again, she was sent sprawling by a powerful blow to her temple.

Breathing hard, the witch struggled to her feet. Roderik stood between her and the prostrate Sophie.

The witch struck out at him with her hand and, although she was too far away to reach him, he flew backward and landed heavily on the ground, next to the knife. He grabbed it, leapt to his feet, and again ran between her and Sophie. Again, her hand flew out at him, but this time there was powder in it.

The dust went into his nose and he began to sneeze. When he left off sneezing, he could see neither Sophie nor the witch, only a huge, mountainous presence towering over him in the fog. He was the size of a mouse.

The witch walked toward him, laughing. She reached out her foot to step on him. He stood, too panicked to run as the foot descended and then, like a cold, bracing wind, the thought of Sophie entered his mind. *What can I do to help her, even if I die?*

He dropped to one knee and thrust upward with the knife in both hands against the immense, crushing weight. It bore down on him, the thick leather of her shoe resisting, but finally, slowly, as the pain in his arms became unbearable, he felt the blade slip through.

The witch screamed in pain. She wrenched her foot away and the blade broke from the handle. Her concentration broken, the spell dissolved, and he again stood towering over her. Screaming curses at him, she reached into her ragged bodice for yet another potion.

He was weaponless. He reached for his sword and found his scabbard empty. The witch limped closer, chuckling. His fingers found Dunwadi's pouch and he drew it from his belt, not knowing what he would do with it. It seemed larger than he remembered. As the witch drew back her arm to cast her magic over him, he thought, *If I can put it over her head, I can strangle her, or at least blind her so I can carry Sophie away.* He leapt at her and pulled the bag over her head.

The potion in her hand flew wide. He pulled the sack downward with all his strength, hoping to force it beneath her chin, but

236

to his surprise, it gave no resistance. As he pulled, the sack kept swallowing her, stretching over her shoulders and the enormous bulk of her belly, but seeming, somehow, to never grow any larger. When he had finished, it was no bigger than his hand, with a small, soft, wriggling lump inside. He pulled the strings taut, tied them securely, and tucked the pouch back in his belt.

Triumphant, he turned to Sophie. She was sitting up, right hand on her sword, the left rubbing her throat where the witch had bruised it. Her skin was soft, her hair gleamed, and her great, dark eyes looked at him. The chasm that had opened in him when he first set his eyes on her began to fill with a buoyant energy. He went to claim his prize.

"Nice trick," she said. "You really might amount to something after all." He stopped short, as if she had slapped him. She raised her left hand and grinned. "Help me up?"

He stopped, stunned. He had just saved her life, and she would say such a thing to him, Roderik, heir to Amytans? A blinding rage swept over him. Her fingers tapped the hilt of her sword as she watched him, alert.

"No," he snapped. He turned on his heel and stormed off.

"Pig," she muttered to his retreating back.

The mist began to fade, revealing Roderik's father seated on his horse, watching, a stern expression on his face. Ulrik said nothing, but turned and rode back to the scene of the battle, leaving Roderik to follow on foot.

At last, he came to the valley. Rolf's followers stood in ranks, guarded by Alana's troops and Ulrik's. Their weapons lay in a great heap, but the *faer* gathered around the rocky platform, silent. Roderik, coming down the slope above, watched as two of the elders gently arranged the body of a silver-haired man on a bier. Roderik began to run and pushed through the crowd of Watchers. As he feared, the man was Anselm. The strength left his knees and he wept. He felt a hand on his shoulder, then many, like the gentle fluttering of birds' wings. It was Aelvan, and Ranell, and then the rest of the Watchers on the west came to touch him, working their way toward him through the crowd.

"It should have been me," he whispered. "Not this old man."

Dunwadi stood before him. "You have something for me." She held out her hand. He looked at her blankly, then remembered the pouch in his belt. He gave it to her. "Well done," she said. "You show promise after all."

Some of his anger returned. "*She* said that. I saved her life, and that was all she could say."

"Murdoch was wounded today," Dunwadi said, her voice soft as the wind. "He was nearly killed. Sophie threw herself upon her father's opponent and fought him. He far outmatched her in strength, but not in skill or presence of mind. She drew him away from Alana and kept him there long enough for help to arrive. Although she was hurt, she went into the mist after you, because she feared for your life." Roderik hung his head, overwhelmed with shame. "There is more." Dunwadi commanded, "Look at me." He raised his frozen face to hers. "This is *ksh*, the blindness of your kind. It has no place here. It is a danger to us all. Your foolish self-indulgence brought the witch here. By capturing her, you were doing no more than is expected of anyone." She handed him his sword. "Go. Never return."

Epilogue

Corwin drank deeply from the goblet and looked about. Most of the children slept on the ground or in their mother's laps. Tears glistened in the eyes of the lady, and her daughters, mending forgotten, looked soft and almost pretty in the firelight. The lord and his sons seemed to see something far away, just beyond the edge of sight, and the spell of the story held all in the courtyard. They knew it was not yet finished. Corwin spoke.

"So it was that peace was restored to that part of the world. Alana, doubting herself no longer, returned to Gwalhafed to continue the peaceful policies of her father and begin the healing of the land.

"Her love, called King Tovan of the *faer* by the lowland folk, never touched a sword, but maintained his uncanny ability to be at the right place and take the right action at any point of crisis. That, combined with the mysterious powers granted him by the lowland beliefs about the *faer*, earned him the respect of even the most recalcitrant nobles. The people of Gwalhafed loved him for his saving their princess and bringing her back to rule as queen, and, as the long years progressed, for the love he showed her, his gentle good nature, and the skills he brought to the mending of their realm.

"Roderik returned with his father to Amytans, riding a borrowed horse. He was a changed man, although his transformation required time to complete. Sophie, having found a place where she could be both herself and a woman, remained with the Watchers, until her restless spirit sent her back into the world to meet her true love."

Corwin's voice was hoarse. He sipped at the goblet again. "As for Murdoch, he took up the keeping of bees. He lived a long and happy life in the Hills with his beloved Mirna. Many years after his death, the tales of his valor mingled with the legends of the Lady and he became known as her consort and protector."

Corwin stopped and pointed overhead. "Look above! You can see him, three stars shining in his belt, watching over Her even now."

Corwin's Chronicle continues:
ᚷhe ᚷale of Roderik and Sophie
Book 3 of Corwin's Chronicle

"One may lose a horse, a sword, a lady love, a battle, a kingdom, or life itself, but the most painful loss of all is the loss of one's illusions." — Queen Mother Edwynna

Sophie remains in the Hills with her father and the *faer*, a place that Roderik is forbidden to enter. There, she deals with the aftermath of their encounter. Roderik returns to Amytans, having utterly failed his quest and determined, against all odds, to redeem himself in Sophie's eyes. He finds that as arduous as that path might be, it is nothing compared to the changes his transformation will wreak on the kingdom of Amytans and the firestorm that those changes will ignite.

How did Corwin come to write his tales of Murdoch and the royals of Gwalhafed? Find out in

Murdoch's ᚷale
Book 1 of Corwin's Chronicle

Young Corwin is saved from the massacre of his village by Tovan, A *faer*, or "Faerie" as we call them, launching him into a life of uncertainty, creativity and adventure.